D0505174

The Journey
with
Two Eagles

For Merriet,
Please keep reading
E J Lyle.

E.J. Lyle

Grosvenor House
Publishing Limited

The right of E.J. Lyle to be identified as the author of this
work has been asserted in accordance with Section 78
of the Copyright, Designs and Patents Act 1988

The book cover is copyright to jgraphika

This book is published by
Grosvenor House Publishing Ltd
Link House
140 The Broadway, Tolworth, Surrey, KT6 7HT.
www.grosvenorhousepublishing.co.uk

This book is a work of fiction. Any resemblance to
people or events, past or present, is purely coincidental.

A CIP record for this book
is available from the British Library

ISBN 978-1-78623-351-6

Acknowledgements

I would like to apologize to all the scholars of the Battle of Shiloh. I have done my best to express the noise, confusion and slaughter. My thanks to the serving soldiers I spoke to who agree that most of the time they didn't know why they stood where they were. Also, my gratitude to members of the Tain Rifle Range who let me fire a Sharps rifle, so I could smell the cordite and choke on the fumes. To my friends and family who have lived with this war over the last three years, I owe you more than I can ever repay, especially Jim.

E.J. Lyle

Chapter 1

Buck followed along quietly through the snow banks as he had been doing for nearly three days. His foot crunched into the high crisp snow and once he got into the way of swinging his crutch in time with his maimed leg, he didn't think he was slowing them down on the journey back to their campground. Winter had been late arriving but was making up for its tardiness. He'd never been so far west in Kansas so maybe his home town of Validation had different weather.

The native peoples tended to keep to themselves while walking for a purpose, so he was pleased that he was able to follow in a straight line and in rhythm with them. The moon was trying to make itself plain every once and a while by glowing red through the patches of tall forest – some pine but most bare leaved. No wind made a nuisance of itself, so the cold was, as the cold was – there and no more, sitting in wait on the forest floor. The loss of part of his foot gave him no pain, so he crunched his way on top of the snow, saying nothing and asking no quarter from his guiding Cheyenne. Moonfeather, his Spirit Guide and his horse in spirit, Piddlin, kept pace beside him.

Mark, in the lead of eight, gave a high trill, cutting into the air like the scream of an eagle. Smoke from the other side of the icy river welcomed home the wanderers. Buck saw tents and tipis which became more obvious when people in fur wraps were seen running outside and toward their kinsman. Buck wondered if he would be as welcome as Moonfeather and her father said he would. He moved more closely to his friend in front.

Mark told him his time in the cave and encounter with frostbite would most likely count as a vision quest. It would be interesting to Standing White Raven, the tribe's newly discovered young medicine man.

"As men, you will find each other interesting and helpful," Mark told him. "He studies life and lives, present and past. He will be curious about what you do without learning."

"I don't do anything."

"That proves what I say. The Raven will want to know why you don't understand your gift from the Great Spirit."

Buck shook his head, looking down at his bloody foot.

"That looks bad." Mark said something in Cheyenne to the man behind him who quickly turned back the way they had come. He nodded and pointed to the ground. Mark made a sweeping gesture to him and others joined him to fuss the snow.

"How long have you been bleeding?"

"I don't know because it's too cold for me to care and I just want to sit down for a bit to wrap it up again."

"A healer must take care of himself first. That way the tribe will be safe. You may have left a trail," Mark sounded as angry as he could ever sound. "There are times when you can be so white."

"I can't help being this color."

"No, but you can be brought away from thinking it." Mark laid a fur on a snowbank and got another member of the tribe to help Buck collapse onto it as he snatched the crutch away. The people in the village were scurrying around their campfires and occasionally looking toward their relatives, obviously wondering what was causing the delay. A tall dark-haired young man, two eagle feathers tied into his hair and wearing a long wolfskin jacket, came closer to the river edge to stare across.

"Where is your healing bag?"

Buck took it from his shoulder.

Mark dumped its contents on the snow and selected one of the bandages that Poppy had rolled. He handed it to the boy. "You do it." So, Buck wrapped his toe again while Mark stuffed the bag, making sure he left nothing behind. He did pause at the wrap of steel needles that had been a gift from Validation's doctor. Buck was not happy that his foot felt no pain. According to Doctor Fraser it wasn't a good sign. Maybe the local medicine man or healer would think differently. In this clear air, he thought he could smell gangrene. His stomach turned.

The others returned from sweeping Buck's blood away; all of them anxious to get home now. One of the men, Oswaka, spoke to Mark in their own language and both just shook their heads as they looked disparagingly at the naïve child sitting helplessly on the ground.

"Oswaka wants to know how a person who has seen his family murdered can remain so innocent of the ways of man. I told him it's because you are a healer, not a killer and will most likely never understand." Mark lifted him up by the arm and handed the crutch and healing bag to Oswaka. Mark would assist Buck down the short slope leading to the narrow river.

The tall man was seen to be aiding with a short canoe, sliding it onto the water on top of the ice. He pushed it toward Mark who manhandled Buck into it. Giving it a hard shove, Buck was easily retrieved by the waiting natives. Women were standing back a bit until their men began to slide down the embankment and find the stepping stones that had always been just under the water since the Great Spirit had created them. The wives whooped and fussed, especially when they discovered the fresh turkeys that were hanging headless and bloodless from the belts of their men. None paid attention to Buck. Oswaka helped him out of the craft as Mark rejoined his wife. He returned the hard-worn crutch and healing bag before adjourning to the small village. The tall dark-haired man manifested in front of him.

"You are Buck." The deep voice reverberated and made him sound a foot taller than he was. "I am Standing White Raven. The people have named me medicine man. Come, we will sit, and I will look at your wound."

Buck limped after him using both hands on his crutch. The Raven threw back the deer hide acting as part of the door to a tipi and held it for him as he waved the lad inside. A fire burned in the middle of the room, tended by a young woman. Moonfeather was hovering over her.

"This is my sister. She is called Sand Owl. She is still young." The Raven looked Buck in the eye. He looked back. "You really are pure of heart." The Raven folded himself into the fur coverings on the floor. "Sit please, young Buck."

Buck knew he would have trouble returning to his feet, so looked around for something with height, even a bedroll.

"We will assist when needed, but for now you will rest. Many works are required of you and many workers will help. We are the first." Sand Owl had a whisper of a voice – a voice that required a keen ear, nonetheless.

Buck threw himself into the nearest fur pile away from the fire and nearly got bitten.

"That's Firedog." The Raven had teeth as white as the fangs of his pet wolf and was laughing as he hugged his animal. "He's a coward since he was ripped away from his mother and just lurks at every fire. Who got the bigger scare, then. Buck?"

Buck's mind hadn't been fully in the room since Sand Owl had spoken. It reminded him of his mother's voice, but then, he'd never really heard her voice. Maybe it was a memory from in her womb. Buck sat perfectly still, looking at Moonfeather who told him to respond to The Raven because he was already envious of his natural ability and once again he needed to conceal as much of it as he could. Sand Owl was looking back and forth between them. "Who got the bigger scare, then Buck?" She brought him back to reality by repeating Raven's question.

"I would think the dog. May I call you Raven?"

"Yes, Buck. You may call me Raven. Why do you think my dog was more scared than you?"

"Perhaps because I should have sensed he was there." The wolf moved to the other side of the fire, flopped down and stared at Buck who hoped it was regularly allowed to hunt or maybe fed plenty of scraps, because the last encounter he had with wolves cost him his toe; he didn't want to lose any more of himself to one of his four footed brethren.

The Raven stretched his leg out in front of him. Sand Owl removed the top layer of boots.

"You will have much to learn while you're with us for the next moon." The Raven spoke in definites. "Stretch your legs toward me. I will look at your foot now."

Sand Owl repeated the process with his leggings. The mess the removal of his right toe had made was now much worse looking and there was an odor coming from a black spot just below the ankle.

"More must be discarded. Tonight."

"Do you have a surgeon? A doctor?" Buck was feeling faint. Hunger didn't help the situation.

"Did you have a doctor to remove that toe?"

"Yes."

"No, you didn't. He should have taken more off then. If he had, you wouldn't have to go through this again, but you do and just after you have two meals. You must have a good meal now and another before I cut you at dawn."

"I don't want to be cut again," Buck shouted.

"I wouldn't want to be cut again, but I wouldn't want to die either, not if I could stop it." The Raven stood over him. He wasn't glaring or shouting. He was stating an obvious fact; one Buck would take with him until he died: a statement of fact can never be argued with.

Sand Owl scurried back into the tipi carrying a hot bowl of red meat stew. Buck didn't care what it was. He was ravenous, thanked the girl and used the wooden spoon provided to finish all of it. He became sleepy and content. He stopped caring about his situation. He was warm for the first time in many days. He had a full belly. He slept. He woke up later, hungry again, and this time had a bowl of maize of some kind – unless he was dreaming of course. He even dreamed he'd been washed and dressed, shaved and all ablutions performed for him. Then for just a minute he had the most god-awful nightmare that Doc was cutting off his toe again, but it didn't last long, so knowing it was only a dream he curled up on his soft bed behind the fire at Aunt Jenny's and went back to sleep.

Chapter 2

"You have done well." The Raven hovered above him and for the first time he noticed the dark eyebrows, strong beardless jaw and narrow pointed nose. "Today you will sit in the air and breathe deeply. Then before the evening meal we will assist you to stand. It is not good to lie so long."

Buck glanced down at his foot. It was no longer there. Standing White Raven had done his job well. Buck panicked into an angry tirade of all the injustices he faced since the day of his birth. He was helpless in this moment. His soul and gut were screaming a why me? The Raven sat beside him, Moonfeather and Sand Owl joined in silence as the young man screamed and cried himself into oblivion again.

When Sand Owl woke him later she aided him into a sitting position and helped him sip a thin soup of some description.

"Turkey," she told him.

He nodded. She spooned in more and then handed him the bowl. "You do."

Buck wasn't sure if he was strong enough to lift the spoon to his mouth.

"Is there anything in this that will make me sleep again?"

"No," Mark appeared in the tipi. "You'll feel no pain though." He was smiling a bit.

"What's gonna happen?"

"White Raven will care for you and teach you about a few herbs and prayers. I will carve a new half leg for you and Oswaka would like to create a softer stick, a taller stick, and he says, a stick that will fold." Mark laughed at the thought of this. "He's a bit on the loony side but some of the things he comes up with have come in useful to the women." Mark squatted beside him as the wolf crept toward him on its belly, thumping its tail on the ground like a normal dog. Mark tugged its' ears. "Yea, Oswaka looked at them grinding the corn and then made them a large tub with a stirring spoon so they could wash the babe's clothes faster. It's started some trouble though. The grandmothers won't share." Mark helped Sand Owl sit him up a bit more. "Take your soup."

Sand Owl sprinkled some sweet-smelling herb on the fire that hadn't been allowed to die but the aroma wasn't overwhelming. The smoke rose gently to find its way through the top opening.

"It must be very cold out there. Look at the blue sky." Buck was aware he no longer cared about how he felt, that he might as well be floating away back home or even to the land Froika and Rebecca were aiming for on the West Coast. Oregon, was it? California? He wasn't bothered about anything anymore and was getting sleepy again.

Sand Owl insisted he finish his soup and then wouldn't let him rest again. White Raven wanted him to be standing on one leg and outside the tipi by the time the sun was in the middle of the sky. Oswaka entered, carrying a long piece of hickory stick.

"This will fit you." He stood beside Buck, eyeing it up and down for length. Buck was just a few inches shorter than the stick.

"How am I going to ride a horse?"

Oswaka placed the wood beside him and grasped his arm just as Mark did the same on the other side and Sand Owl caught the empty bowl and spoon. Buck's head swam like the eddy at the end of the river running through the farm as he struggled to place his feet on the ground.

"Don't try to walk." Mark commanded. "Let us lift you outside into the air."

Buck felt the soup rise to the back of his tongue but trusting the two men, especially Mark who had seen so much with him, he relaxed as much as possible. Strong arms held him in a cradle position as Sand Owl opened the flap of deer skin on the tipi. The Raven was facing him and came forward with a light wolf fur for his lower body and a fox fur to be placed around his neck and chest. Then, a sage stick was lit to smoke away bad spirits and encourage the good, with much attention paid to what was left of Buck's right leg. Buck wondered if he was really looking down on all of them or it was yet again an herb imagination.

Other tribe members, especially the children, all warmly dressed in various shared furs, stopped to stare as Buck was lifted to the center of the campsite where a tall stool made from various woods and bone was placed.

"Sit here."

Mark and Oswaka placed him gently on the waist high stool.

Sand Owl began to tap a medicine drum in time to her slow heartbeat. Women and some men came to participate in a soft chant.

Buck wanted to know what was happening and started to ask but was silenced by an answer from Mark who spoke softly in his ear: "White Raven will go into a short trance and when he comes back he will have a name for you."

Buck wasn't sure if he needed another name or even wanted one, but his anger was settling with his lack of pain. He began to feel grateful to these people who owed him nothing – absolutely nothing.

The sun was rising quickly in the flashing diamond bright blue sky. The Raven's feet began to move in time to Sand Owl's heartbeat, Moonfeather came to stand beside her charge, gifting him a stroke of his cheeks which brought him up short. Piddlin, just off in the distance, had her nose in a bag of oats or something equally delicious. Aunt Jenny stood beside her, dressed and smiling.

Standing White Raven stopped, looked up, raised his arms, and declared that Man Who Stands in Shadow was welcome at his camp.

There were shouts, yelps, whistles and jeers. Food came from nowhere, as did an ale of some description. The children were sent for firewood and Buck was still perched on his special chair feeling very lost in the middle of it all.

"You will stand now."

Mark and Oswaka helped him slide away from the stool. He wasn't happy about it, but he had the feeling this ceremony had been done before and he must go through with it if he was going to live. By the time the sun was screaming noon, Buck was standing on his left leg and Oswaka was supporting his right side. There was no shadow. Buck was standing in it. The sun was directly above him.

"Man Who Stands in Shadow, we have much work to do. Tomorrow. Today, I will let you make a friend of your new leg. Have you even looked at it yet, the wound that will prevent you from ever being a fighter as the white man expects? The wound that will allow you to be a healer as the Great Spirit expects? All healers pay a price. You have paid most of yours but there is more to come before you can be so good as to be considered as Shaman."

Buck was starting to waver on his one good leg.

"Take him to the outside fire so he can absorb the good of his new people and even take meat."

"What price did you pay?"

"Tomorrow we will talk. Today we will take the measure of each other. I feel we will fit well together." He gestured to his helpers to let Buck go to join in.

There wasn't much snow on the ground once the people walked on it, but patches of ice were starting to form and the children were making longer and longer slides from it, falling and crying as they bashed into each other, then laughing as one would wind up head first in a snow pile. Mothers began to show concern when they weren't paying any attention to the call for food. They were rounded up like the puppies they were and corralled close to the fire. Hands were examined before a piece of rabbit was blown cool or a small bit of turkey was given to a baby to suck. Buck was aware he was being observed from all sections of the group.

A grandmother moved to look at his leg, forcing Buck to finally do the same. He no longer had an ankle. He was shocked and tried to jump away from it as if the wreck belonged to someone else. Grandmother tutted and wagged her finger at him.

"She's just saying she didn't mean to startle you. She wasn't going to touch it," Mark translated.

"Tell her I'm sorry, please."

Mark did so and Grandmother went back to her group of cronies closer to the tents.

"Why don't I have any pain, Mark?"

"Should you?"

"Hurt like hell when they took my toe off last year."

"There's some stuff we do better than white doctors I think."

Mark stood to get some food. "You want some turkey, good fired up turkey?"

Buck nodded. "What's a fired-up turkey?"

"Meat tastes different when it's cooked different. This turkey was proper cooked when I put a fire up its ass and turned it on a spit. Tastes better than when a white woman shoves it in an oven for hours that much I can tell you for sure. Want a bit?"

Buck laughed for the first time in days and oddly, his foot began to hurt when he told Mark yes, he would like to learn the difference between a corn-fed turkey and a well fired one.

Chapter 3

//////////////////////////////

It was snowing. The fire in the tipi hissed at the flurries that tried to invade through the chimney hole and the winds battered the complete structure trying to find a weakness.

"What time is it?" In his head, Buck's voice sounded like an echo.

"It's time for food again." Sand Owl slid toward him with another bowl of soup.

"The sun is trying to rise." Raven extended his long legs toward the fire, now struggling against the gathering elements. "Do you feel pain, Buck?"

"Yes, and it's rising with the wind." He scratched his head.

Raven laughed at him. "You've been granted a name, so you don't have to pretend you're anything but who or what you are. I'll try again: do you feel pain in your leg?"

"It's throbbing like a row of hot boils on my arse." He was using both hands to scratch his whole head.

"Something's wrong."

"No, you just need to stand again. The pain in your leg is good. It means we've cut off all the bad. So, it's a pain I can understand and work with."

"When I get an itch like this it means there's something bad, something real bad gonna happen."

The medicine man bent toward him now. "Take a bit of that soup and then I'll have a look. It's been a couple of days now."

The door-covering was flung back. Oswaka's hand, knuckles covered in blood, arrived in the shelter before he did and Mark pushed in behind him. Gunfire was very distant.

"The war has come. Hurry out. Must leave." Oswaka glared at Buck. "You stay."

The Raven shoved past his angry men to be confronted by a young man with fair new whiskers riding on a bay horse, wearing a somewhat grey uniform and flashing a long sword. The snow packed around the feet of the horse and then the lust-for-killing men followed on behind. There weren't many – only about twenty or so but they had a rifle each along with knives and other war-like paraphernalia.

The women and children had the sense and experience of these things to stay in hiding, but this small troupe were out for sport and pickings of whatever was deemed by them to be of value. The man on the horse took time to circle before he cut one of the ropes on the tipi containing Sand Owl and Buck.

Whoops and neighing joined in with shots fired. Firedog howled. More dogs arrived from the trees, some of which may have been owned by the band of stragglers.

Standing White Raven stood his ground. Firedog found him and sat, licking his lips.

"Where's your chief, then? Hiding?" The young man had a high-pitched voice that sounded as if it needed to find a home.

"He is not with us at this camp. This is only set for hunting, officer," Mark said.

There was a pause before the young man, not releasing his weapon, slid from his horse and handed the reins to another, but, unkempt older man.

"Y'all talk good English."

"Raised as a Christian in an Orphan school. You?" Mark meant to imply the officer wasn't much of a Christian and the officer caught the insult as it flew by.

"You got a name, boy?"

"I'm Mark." He gestured to The Raven. "This is Isaiah. You got a name, kid? Just so I know who killed my dog and a few of our chickens."

Buck was listening to all this and even though the snow was getting heavier and the wind brisker, he could sense the temperature outside rising. He motioned to Sand Owl to help him stand. She shook her head no. He began to roll on to his good side, forcing her to either co-operate or let him fail. He still had his old walking stick and between the two of them he stood. Buck hugged on to her, holding onto the tiny young woman for a short spell while he tried to balance.

"What's all that noise in your little tipi, then?" The officer wrenched open the door to see an unshaven Buck standing in fox and wolf fur, supported by Sand Owl and his trusty old stick, missing a foot and glaring through him with eyes so brown they looked black.

"I am Man Who Stands in Shadow. You will come in from the storm and you will leave directly after. You are army, so you will have supplies for yourself."

"You're a white boy."

"So are you. One of us is content with that," Buck rejoined.

"We remain un-introduced, sir. May I have your name?"

"Lieutenant Johnston, Missouri Volunteers." He sheathed his fancy sword and gave Buck a quick nod of recognition completely ignoring the natives.

"Dismiss your men to their bivouacs as they may find and then join us for some heat and a bowl of Sand Owls' soup." He looked down on her affectionately and squeezed her shoulder, implying more to the Lieutenant than was meant.

Once back inside, Mark, Raven and Sand Owl spoke quietly in their own language. Buck got a translation from Moonfeather, or at least bits of it because he hadn't practiced listening to her for a very long time and it was difficult to hear her.

"We will still have to move from here, Buck."

"Yes, I know. Moonfeather told me and I had already figured it out. We will still have a month before the war gets too close for us."

"I forgot about your Moonfeather. I didn't remember either about the abilities granted to you. You glowed with power while you spoke to the Army man." The Raven was looking at him with a respect Buck felt he hadn't fully earned.

Oswaka crawled in under the collapsed part of the tipi. "They have moved under the trees and closer to the river. The children cry for the dog and the women are cooking the chickens." He held his hands against the fire.

"Did you tell them where to find us, Oswaka?" Buck asked.

Oswaka started up, small knife in his hand. Mark kicked his wrist and Sand Owl used Buck's empty soup bowl to deflect it into the ground before it did any damage to anyone.

"Why? Why would any of us tell an Army where we were hunting?" Raven felt no animosity, just curiosity.

"I don't want to live like this anymore – my wife dead, no child left, no tipi. I am nothing. I have age but no wisdom so no respect. They paid me with a wooden house and a soft bed. It is warm in winter and cool in summer. I can grow corn and tobacco. I can have a good life." Oswaka was squatting by the fire again. Sand Owl returned his knife.

"No, Oswaka," Buck stated. "You will always be a native, and a red man living as a white man will never be left in peace long enough to see the harvest of his crops."

The others nodded and for the first time since Buck arrived he was offered a smoke from The Raven's pipe. There was silence and in that quiet, the acceptance of what had transpired. When there was a polite knock on the wood support of the door Buck and Mark exchanged amused glances and Buck shouted a "come in" and the pipe was put away as the Lieutenant ducked inside. He stumbled over Oswaka's foot and toward the small central fire.

"Sit, Sir." The Raven ordered, and Sand Owl tried not to giggle, so covered her chubby mouth with her hand. She added her dried sage to the soup and stirred it with a brush of other ingredients, dried during the autumn months. That night a stew of dog was served. Two rib bones had been reserved for The Raven's medicinal use but had to be cooked first.

"You are probably the coldest and most hungry. Please accept this small rib as a token of peace." Sand Owl was capable of being feminine, almost flirtatious, when required

"It's fine, Sir. We won't poison you."

"Can't bury bodies in frozen ground y'know," said Buck, and grinning, slapped the Confederate Volunteer on his shoulder while he nodded his thanks to Sand Owl for his special bowl of stew. Moonfeather told him that it was Sand Owl who'd been feeding him pain-killing medicine. She was a quiet healer and medicine woman of course, but always seen to act under The Raven's instructions; when she felt she should and he allowed it.

The Lieutenant sniffed the stew as most reasonable men would do, and picking up the bone between his forefinger and thumb queried the source of the meat.

"This is a hunting party. We kill what we eat. Now you do the same." Mark enjoyed the obvious discomfort he caused. "We eat deer when we can and turkey most of the time."

The Lieutenant wasn't sure what understanding he should take from this information, but was sure, in his very soul, that if a white man was eating it as Buck was, then it was most likely good enough.

"Well, I'm sure hungry enough and would say a grace of thanks to our Lord."

Mark, The Raven and Buck stopped their meal and thinking they were waiting for him to take the lead in this the young officer began with: "For what…"

"We said that. This morning. Every morning. We always show our thanks." Oswaka kept eating. He was ravenous and didn't even look up to notice a reaction.

"True. True. Why do you only give thanks before you eat and on Sundays?" Mark shrugged and took another spoonful. Sand Owl was fascinated by the silver bits on the soldier's uniform and reached to touch them. Lieutenant Johnston flinched away from her. "Back off, whore," he snarled, holding his spoon in the air as if to use it as a weapon.

Raven raised his hand in the air and slapped the empty space above the soldier as he would have slapped his face. The Lieutenant reacted as if he'd been injured, falling face first toward the fire and holding the back of his head when Raven again slapped at the air.

Sand Owl didn't move one little bit away from her seat. She did catch the bone the soldier had nibbled on and offered it to the medicine man. He took it and bowed his head to her briefly.

Moonfeather told Buck that Johnston was now a marked man.

"You have never had a true woman, if you had, you would know there is no difference in temperament, only in circumstances. My sister, yes, sister, will never have to scrounge for food in that way. Your people let it happen to your women. You have so little respect for those who give you birth. Give my sister a pretty badge and finish your meal." The Raven spoke forcefully.

"My uniform is the property of..."

"Bull. Now, give her two of your pretty badges before I take your tin belt buckle to hold up my pants." Mark said.

Sand Owl was disappointed in the weight of the epaulettes but still, she put them on the hem of her long skirts and enjoyed their clinking noise.

Chapter 4

Buck found himself getting sleepy again and in front of even Lieutenant Johnston, Raven removed his bandage from his wounded foot. He heard a thud.

"Leave him, sister. He's never been in a real battle," Raven said, as Sand Owl moved to assess the situation.

The soldier had fainted.

"Your leg is good, Shadow."

Buck wondered why a man in uniform had passed out at the sight of it. He might pass out himself once he properly looked at it. He left his body long enough to glance. Raven was right. His leg was good; very tidy; well-sealed. He dropped back to sleep.

"I have less to teach you than I thought," Raven's voice was so low and close to his ear it rumbled like thunder in the distance.

"I must make it a part of me."

"Yes, accept, not argue. It is easier and more healing."

A grunt arrived from the floor near the fire. The Lieutenant was reaching for his bravado again and by way of grasping, missed the target. He sat up, looked at the scene before him and vomited his stew. This angered Sand Owl who threw a cloth at him and made the motions of scrubbing.

"She's telling you to clean up after yourself." Mark spoke from the collapsed wall of the tipi. "That'll teach you to kill a dog. It has come back to bite you."

"Oh, God." Johnston covered his mouth, to clamber out of the hunting tent where he was heard to be violently sick once more. Other people outside, some of them his own troupe made noises of disgust, laughter or even sympathy, but essentially Johnston was on his own experiencing the revenge of just one dog.

"Soup didn't agree with me, boys," he explained to his compatriots.

Sand Owl came out with the cloth and made a hand movement for him to return inside. On unsteady legs he saluted her and began to wander to the riverside. She shouted something to the inside of the tipi. Oswaka threw back the deer-skin and repeated the motion. Once again, Johnston saluted and began to weave away. Two of his men, not understanding the situation as Sand Owl did, got between him and the two natives. She continued to scream at their retreating backs and then spoke to Oswaka.

Oswaka walked carefully toward the small group of white men. The Lieutenant continued his departure, his volunteer two-man bodyguard covering his back.

"Your officer saw ripped up leg. He fell. When woke up, puked up. Now he must clean up."

The officer froze in his tracks. The men in his command, some of them trying to get clean in the icy river even while the snow was still coming down and the day was shortening, tried not to laugh or to get more information from a buddy they thought may have heard the news better.

"How many of you ate the stew tonight?" Johnston didn't move, just asked the question in a full parade ground voice. No hands went up. "Just chicken, sir. Not in a pot. Just over an open fire in a pit." A very young private tried to be helpful.

"You kill chicken?" Oswaka asked.

"No, Mr. Indian, Sir." The private was trying to be polite. It amused Oswaka but he nodded his head in appreciation of the gesture of youth.

"Then you not get sick."

Some of the men looked at each other, obviously feeling chastened about the events of the last few hours.

"If you're so smart, Private, go clean up the sick in the tipi," Johnston adjusted his scabbard and began to march to the river, his legs now back in military condition.

"Yes, Sir." The skinny young Confederate Volunteer was proud to serve.

"No, Sir." Mark caught the whole conversation. "A leader leads from the front and is responsible for the welfare of his men." He placed his forearm against the Private's chest, preventing him from following his orders.

"Are you a leader or not, Lieutenant Johnston, Sir?"

Lieutenant Johnston was tired of tolerating these natives.

"Stand down, Private. You too Chief." The officer continued his march to the river. "Follow me, boys. We're going to continue south in the morning."

Raven came to stand beside Oswaka. "We have enough enemies without adding the white army. Let the snake go. He'll bite someone else soon and get bitten himself once again. It is the way of his life. The mess is cleared. Return to the warmth while you can, old friend." He rested his hand on Oswaka's shoulder and pushed gently at him, guiding him back to the snowy campsite.

Sand Owl was in very bad temper.

"There is much to forgive, Sister. I ask it of you."

All five feet of her stood at him. She had snow attached to her leg wrappings and feet, bare hands, white with cold, dark hair hiding behind a fur hood also covered in weather, dripping wet as it melted in the warmer temperature of the temporary lodge, and eyes that always made her older, bigger brother, the great Medicine Man, Standing White Raven, have nightmares of being murdered in his sleep. Sand Owl, the name she demanded he gave her when the tribe asked him to take over the job of Medicine Man when their own father, Resting Bird, had gone to Spirit. He did what he was told because he also knew that she was as good a healer, if not better, than he was, but she would need to find her own way in this world.

"I had to clean that sick by myself. There was much unwellness in it. He will die young but not from wounds. His family will mourn."

Oswaka and Mark sat by the fire again and Raven lit the pipe. Buck was silent and staring at the native woman. He took a long draw of the pipe and held the smoke in his chest perhaps a little longer than he should have because his head began to spin. He felt the wind move him from the tipi, lift him, take him to a place he had never been. It had cliffs, high waters that roared louder than a river and in time to the beat of Mother Earth's heart. There was green land as he never known, hills he didn't imagine could be so tall and he floated above and beyond until the river was so wide he couldn't see the other shore. He flew, he danced in the air like the white bird that followed him, he breathed deep in clean fresh air and then he floated down, gently back to the tipi.

Nothing changed. The men were still smoking and wrapped in their own thoughts. Sand Owl joined them. Her work was done for the day.

A clatter was heard outside.

"Just the wind." Mark took another draw and then repacked the pipe.

"Oswaka, you will create that walking stick for Shadow?" Raven queried.

"Before I leave."

"You do not need to go."

There was a quiet pause before Oswaka said: "If I go now, I can come back."

The Raven acquiesced. "After the soldiers and west, not south. Agreed?"

"Agreed."

"You will return at this twelve moon and at this place. If you are not here we will think you found a white man's life a better one."

Buck was fully present. It was obvious that Oswaka was being banished for one year and that he had been given the dignity of choosing his banishment as an atonement for what could have been considered a treachery. The pipe was nearly out. He cleared his throat, quietly, and waited for the pipe to come to him again before he asked if Raven's Christian name was really Isaiah.

There was a gentle laughter at that from all the fireside participants.

"I didn't go to the special school. Mark said it would be safer if the whites could put me in a box and gave me the name of Isaiah. He's a prophet, I've been told." His eyes twinkled.

"How'd you get so good at English, then?"

"That's another thing that makes us safer."

"He's got a musical ear, Buck," explained Mark. "He even speaks a bit of Navaho, which language I personally think has come directly from the Gods. Standing White Raven got his name because a White Raven is a kind of vulture – as you would say in your language – and he is a vulture for knowledge. All he must do is stand still and listen. It's then stuck in him forever."

Raven drew his knees together and used them to help him stand. He shook himself down and announced he would sleep now. Buck saw him embarrassed but didn't say a word, smiling to himself he started to adjust his furs for the night.

The jangling noise came from Sand Owl's skirts as she made to leave for the women's tipi across the circle.

A bullet ripped through the roof of the tipi. She ducked, and rolled out of the deerskin. The Lieutenant fell in to their lodge.

"It's not us. Please, it's not us."

Buck knew who it was – most likely, anyway – Ryan O'Grady from Validation, come to fetch him back because Joss the kid he'd taken in out of a kindness to the lad's mother, had done it: taken off for the army. He stayed where he was to let the others figure things out and because Raven oversaw his own tribe and he wasn't officially a member yet, so it was none of his business. For all he knew there could be another hunting party come to call and that meant it really wasn't a thing to do with him and perhaps even showing his face would bring down trouble. He listened. He was right and worse, Ryan wasn't alone nor even sober. The MacLaren wouldn't be there but maybe Pete just to keep an eye on things. He sat up when he heard Ian's voice. Was Mary involved? He smiled at himself when he thought Mary may have given Joss some money for the trip. No, she would have blabbed to all who would have listened, embarrassed the kid and left him to slink away back to the livery where he knew he was safe. No, Mary wasn't the reason for Ian's appearance. He'd better get up.

Chapter 5

"I don't think it's Yankees, either." The Lieutenant was breathless as he fell toward The Raven.

A young Private rolled in behind him followed by an older man with an extra stripe on his jacket.

"We're all that's left. They came at us like a bunch of Indians, slicing and cutting."

Sand Owl rolled back into the tipi. "You showed them the way." She stood to point at Buck's chest, brown eyes flashing in the remains of the hearth fire. "Your blood left a long trail."

Movement was heard, a Bowie knife ripped down behind the small cluster of humanity. Ryan O'Grady, timber merchant, late of Validation, Kansas, lurched into the dwelling, knife first and waving it as a shield. Covered in old snow, red eyes searing into each of the party he wanted to know only one thing:

"Which of you bastards kidnapped my kid?"

He was hooched up on drink and most likely tobacco of a different sort and then he saw Buck lying on the ground.

"They worshipping you yet, scumbag? You and your light little ways?"

"What's happened to Joss, Ryan?" Buck stayed calm, trying to buy some time. Ryan wasn't a leader. There must be others outside. The Lieutenant said only three of his troupe were left in one piece.

Mark took a station near the exit, Raven held his sister protectively in front of him and crouched down near Buck. Oswaka was gone. Vanished somehow, but to show up again on whose side was anyone's guess.

Tribal whoops and clashes of steel were heard outside. A guide rope was sliced. The tipi began to collapse. Now, Raven stood with Mark to hold it up before it caught fire from the center stove and so the inhabitants could escape. Ryan remained inside. People outside watched a knife slashing at the fabric of the tent before the bottom of it began to smoulder.

"Get Ryan out." Buck screamed, his view of the world limited by his inability to stand. "Mark, you know him."

Mark fell flat beside him in the snow, face up, blood pouring from his throat. He was grabbing at his wound and gurgling like a trussed turkey.

Buck rolled away, survival instinct taking over. Ryan, bloody knife in hand, launched himself at the young man's face.

"Where is Joss, you red lovin' little son of a whore?"

Buck's upper body strength was stronger than Ryan expected. His use of a crutch made his right arm powerful beyond his years. He poked at Ryan's left eye and then punched at his right temple, blinding and disorientating him in one move. Pushing his assailant away and then rolling on top of him, Buck cracked Ryan's wrist hard down onto a fire-rock. The knife dropped far enough away to force Ryan to make a grab for it, so Buck used his elbow on the inside of Ryan's arm. A loud snap from Ryan's arm and a yowl from the merchant ended the match. Buck slid the weapon underneath his own torso – out of sight. Scurrying continued around the two men. Buck couldn't see or come to conclusions about what was going on, but he did know that things were coming to an end. Whoops of victory were heard but Buck didn't know who was fighting who or why they were even having this vexation, and being unable to stand on his own without a stick of some kind, shuffled himself between his now dead friend, Mark, and his drunken friend Ryan.

"I don't know where Joss is," Buck said quietly. "The last I saw him was on New Year's Eve at the saloon."

"He would have followed you anywhere," Ryan rejoined. "Christ, this hurts. What you do to me, boy?"

"Broke your arm. If we live, I'll fix it. Joss would only follow me if I had a good horse. If I recall, there weren't a great many good horses about except the MacLaren's and Pete's and they were both in the barn."

Silence.

Sand Owl stood above them, tears running down her cheeks. She pointed at Mark. Raven joined her as did Oswaka from behind – he hadn't been far away after all. The mourning chant began. Ryan moved to sit up. Buck shoved him down.

"You're at a funeral. Did you start this or was this a revenge for something?" he whispered in Ryan's ear.

Ryan shook his head.

"Was just following you because I thought Joss was with you and these fellas said they found blood in the snow and footprints. They figured natives were either up to no good or had a great feast planned. Once I told them about Joss going missing they put it about maybe they'd stolen him to use him for something evil; one of their dances maybe."

Buck sighed. "And that's where you all shared the whisky."

"The snow is ended. It is near dawn." Standing White Raven was stroking Mark's hair away from his bloody face. "You, Man Who Stands In Shadow, will stay for one moon as Great Spirit commands." He looked to Ryan. "You will not find your Joss here. You will go when your arm is straightened and go back where you came from and wait for Buck to return."

"He speaks good," Ryan told Buck.

"He hears well, too." The Raven heard the whisper.

"Sorry. I didn't mean to be un-mannerly."

"No, I guess ripping our shelter apart with your knife was a polite way of introduction."

Buck heard the irony in Raven's voice, even if Ryan didn't.

Sand Owl's teeth began to chatter. From out of the other tipis families appeared with food and blankets.

"How did they know?" Ryan asked. "Where did they all come from?"

"Fighting isn't new to us. We have been in conflict with other tribes for many years and we know what comes after a battle or skirmish. Natives are better at keeping a peace than you people." Raven took one of the offered deer skins and wrapped Mark in it with the help of Oswaka who kept showing up at the right time for a change.

"Where is Lieutenant Johnston and what's left of his party?"

"They're packing up to go," Oswaka said.

"Make sure they go south, old friend," said Raven. "I will feel safer for you when you start your way west." Oswaka hadn't done enough to earn his right to stay.

Dawn folded into the world against its wishes. It peaked its head above the snow drift at the river's edge and took its time coming into the cold day, but when it arrived fully there were bodies to be seen at the water's edge, some in the almost grey coverings of the Missouri Volunteers and others, not as many, in the dress of an outdoorsman. Weapons were lying where they'd been used and unfortunately the only long bore gun, an old musket, floated muzzle down on the ice. The snow was colored with blood spats and a saber stuck in the back of an older man's leg, his head floating on the ice and a small knife in his right hand.

"We must leave." The Raven announced the obvious.

The tribe began to pack. Tipis were struck, the wood being readied for reuse further southwest. The Raven moved very quickly and Sand Owl, once she began to move became animated and chatty with the other women of the tribe. A travois was put together and Mark laid gently on it.

"We will remove him from the sight of the savagery and find him a place on a hill to rest."

Raven retrieved the sabre from the white man's back and gave the small knife to Sand Owl. "Maybe use it to cut herbs or mushrooms or even skin small animals." She looked up at her brother with love and respect. "You would like me to help you in your work?"

"You do, anyway."

Buck felt out of place. Perhaps he could go back with Ryan. He noticed a black stallion having a drink at the river, looking for an owner, or at least some guidance with not a morsel of food as grass wasn't available at this time of year. He was a big one at any rate and there was another beast looking forlorn, lurking in the woods.

He spoke to Raven about it very briefly, recognizing that he was responsible for all these people and the organizing.

"I will send for them once we set that arm. It will be good for you to start your learning."

"So, I'm not going home, then?"

Raven glared at him, "I have told you what will happen and why. Mark has gone, my promise to him has not." He tucked a wolf skin into his leggings and helped to haul Mark's body onto the transporter.

"Ryan. Go to your healer, Buck. Sit in front of him on that log."

Cushioning his arm, Ryan did as he was told. "Do I get some of your poppy juice first, Buck?"

"I wouldn't think so. I lost more of my leg thanks to Raven and I haven't needed a drop of it." Buck actually thought the drunk in Ryan would have loved a legitimate slug of laudanum, judging by the way the man's eyes were roaming over the open contents of the healing bag.

Raven joined them. "Drink this." He handed Ryan a small cup of liquid. "Toss it back in a hurry. It tastes horrible but works well."

Buck nodded at Ryan in encouragement.

"You, Shadow. Close your eyes. Just between them you will visualize a blank page of blackness. Think about your breathing and bring it into beat with your heart. Slow all down. All down."

Buck began to feel as he did when his mind went for a walk.

"Think about the colors or movements you can see. Keep your eyes closed. When you are ready, bring the white light from above your head through your body all the way to your feet. Yes, the energy remains. Slow your breathing."

There was a silence Buck thought only belonged to him.

A finger poked at him. Raven whispered to him to open his eyes. Ryan had his eyes closed and his breathing slow. Raven motioned for Buck to stay still and watch, then he took Ryan's arm, twisted it, pulled it and snapped it back in position. Sand Owl, unnoticed, moved forward with a splint and bandage, placing it across the murderer's chest and then folding Ryan's arm she placed it in the sling shape she had created.

Ryan hadn't flinched and had slept through all of it.

Chapter 6

////////////////////////////////

"To be a healer you have to be in the right state of mind. The healing has nothing to do with you and everything to do with the Spirits. You must be able to step aside, physically and mentally. Now, we will go for Ryan's horses and send him on his way. Maybe he will give one to Oswaka for his journey, but you will not need one for a time."

"He will have to keep the black one for himself. I recognize it and I'm not sure he should have it here. It's called Buchanan and belongs to the saloon owner in Validation," Buck said. "Pete may be furious and on his way here as well, just to get his horse."

"Be gone with you Ryan O'Grady." Raven stood to make a sharply dismissive move of his arm and hand in the air above the Irishman. "Never be seen in this nation again. You carry trouble, now carry it with you back to the town you live, so it may carry your burden instead of us."

Ryan stood slowly, not knowing how strong he was, how well recovered from his bone repair, and although light headed, he steadied himself and proceeded down toward the riverbank, clicking his tongue to the stallion. The other, lighter colored bay followed on.

"How did you know Ryan was an O'Grady?" Buck asked.

"Things travel on the wind, Buck, or as they say, by word of mouth. In this case, Mark's." Raven glanced at the remains of his friend. Buck couldn't help but notice the sadness cut into him and for no predetermined reason, lent his head toward the medicine man's. They shared the same few breaths of air for a time and then came apart as gently as they had joined in their human communion, and in silence.

Raven helped Buck up to his feet, to bring him to a travois that had been built for him.

"I'll be just fine on a horse, Sand Owl."

She had been crying. Buck was aware of the tear stains showing through the cold mask of her face. Tears were warmer than skin. He reached to wipe away a stray hair, but the young woman jerked back and grunted at him.

"You are a proud one, Ma'am. I didn't mean anything. I'm trying not to give you worries." Moonfeather was floating behind her, smiling as she sometimes did when he made an idiot of himself.

Sand Owl grabbed at him, removing him from Raven's care, and plopped him down on what felt to him like a springy and unsafe mattress. Yes, it was cushioned with furs but still, it was attached to the back end of a horse which may cause a whole different set of problems. The look on his face may have told those standing around the contraption what he was thinking, but Raven took another fur (my, they did have a great many), threw it over his body and gave the horse a sharp tap on its rump. Buck experienced a jolt that made his leg hurt for the first time in days. The horse was travelling uphill so he held on tight to the sides of his moveable bed. Much laughter was heard and he realized the natives were making fun of him, so he let go and placed his arms across his chest. This was met with whoops of approval and a little applause. He grinned back at them, realizing how he must look: a skinny white kid, taller than the shoulder of a horse, dressed in old rawhides, wearing a tired slouch hat and swaddled in furs that were too heavy for him to stand in. Buck was, he suspected, a nothing man with much expected of him to prove them wrong.

He could see Oswaka at the river retrieving the bay horse and helping Ryan mount Buchanan. He watched as the two had a short argument, but it was over quickly and the right man got the right horse. Oswaka mounted quickly and joined the tribe again before raising his hand in salute to them and throwing a bag over his shoulder as he headed southwest. Buck's heart went out to Ryan. Did he know, was he aware, that Raven had come as close to giving him an Indian curse as was possible to give? Ryan, his Irish blood, would perhaps have curdled due to his inbuilt superstitious nature. Once, when he was much, much younger, he'd seen Ryan making the sign of the cross when he rode out of town with Aunt Jenny –– all due to the uncomfortable feeling his Mindwalking abilities gave people.

Looking back at the destruction caused by a gang with nothing better to do, whoever they were, combined with the pain in his leg brought Buck back to reality. Raven was walking beside him for the moment.

"Do you know anything of this?"

"I know Mark and four others were murdered and that perhaps the Missourians had the sense to run except for the seven dead. Johnston has disappeared."

"What started it?" Buck asked.

"I don't know. Perhaps food. Some is missing apart from what was left of the chickens. Some oats."

"Cowards, then."

"Hungry cowards. I will go forward to see to the others." Raven moved to the front of the line.

Buck was alone with his thoughts for the first time since his horse, Piddlin', died. He hadn't had time to come to terms with the loss of his toe, his Aunt and Uncle, or even the justified murder of his cousin Duncan. He closed his eyes against the weak sun hiding behind a thick grey cloudbank. He began to shake. He rolled to his side and was ill outside the moving bed. Moonfeather was with him and unusually spoke to him directly without suggesting something for him to do.

"All will be well. This is part of your healing. Life changes every eighteen of your years. You are not as alone as you fear. All will be provided. You will never hunger or go without a roof. You will always have enough and you will experience great moments of joy."

White Raven returned. "He is fevered. It has more to do with last night than his wound, but I will look when we get to the big camp." He walked back to the front. "Nice to see you, Moonfeather."

Buck's eyes shot open. "He can see you?"

"There's no reason he couldn't. Why? Do you mind sharing me?"

"I thought you were mine, only."

"I am a member of his tribe and always will be. They knew me before you did, so they pray for me and keep me safe and strong – strong enough to work with you."

Yells and shouts were heard in the trees to the side. Raven and others halted. They yowled in response. With Mark dead, Oswaka banished, and four others of the small hunting party killed – three of whom were men or boys – Buck hoped that this wasn't another attack after last night. It was just after noon, he thought. His stomach rumbled as if to confirm the idea. No one had anything to eat since last night's dog stew and fired chicken.

A native broke out into a clearing. Raven lifted his hands and shouted a welcome. Buck could tell Raven looked younger when he smiled. More natives joined them. There was much patting on the back and questioning. Buck held an interest for some of the women for just a bit longer than was comfortable. Sand Owl said something that made them laugh. She was helped onto a pony; a man slid off a young horse and gave Raven a quick lift. Buck hadn't realized Raven was so venerated. He turned his head to see the tribe settle around Mark's body and listen to the wail that came from the silence. A child began to cry. The natives reorganized through all their grief and began to move forward again. Buck wondered what was happening, but he had no one to ask so tried to focus on what was going on rather than what may happen later or what happened at the end of last year. He was being self-involved, but he had to be: he was on his own. He was sick again and his head was itchy, so he gave it a light scratch. It didn't feel like one of his warnings, well not one of his serious ones, but still, he gave it another scratch just in case.

This way of travelling was not the most comfortable. He would love to get up to stretch. He couldn't of course, but the thought that he couldn't made it even worse. He was hungry too, but at least he was warm. He had no right to complain. These people had done their best for him. He didn't know why, exactly. They owed him nothing. It had something to do with a promise that Mark made to Raven or the other way around, he wasn't sure. He closed his eyes again. At least it wasn't snowing. He felt the horse go downhill. It began to trot. Buck bounced along and didn't care, his mind flitting from one disjointed idea to another. He was sick again, but he'd hung on to the travois and managed to miss the furs near him. A boy showed up beside him to walk with him for a bit. It was curiosity, Buck thought. The child touched his face, looking puzzled probably, that white skin was the same temperature as his own. He went running away shouting something. Buck was relieved until a woman, probably the child's mother, walked beside him and touched his face. His head itched – just a little. She went running to the front. After a minute Raven showed up, but not on his horse. The woman was with him. Raven place his hand on his forehead and spoke to the woman, it seemed to Buck, harshly. He shooed her away.

"You are hot, like a devil, like the white man's devil. You have a fever. I know that, but she will stir up people before we get to the big camp later tonight."

"It will pass," Buck said.

"Yes, I know your fever will pass but in the meantime Chick in the Field might make your life miserable."

Buck scratched his head a bit more strongly. He grinned at the name of the large woman who had taken against him. Was she to become an enemy?

"Chick in the Field?" She was an unusually large chick.

"My mother's sister. My aunt is a good woman – mostly."

Buck flushed.

"I know it's a light name." The Raven raised his eyebrows at Buck. A smile played in his eyes for just a blink. "She feels it, I think. I may have something for you to do later." He walked back to his horse through the lessening snow with a grin on his face sharing a private joke with himself.

Chapter 7

////////////////////////////////

Chick in the Field marched beside Buck at a safe distance, her young son behind her, trying to look like a warrior. Buck thought he looked about eight years of age. She wasn't a scrawny Chick; as a matter of fact, she looked old enough to be the mother of a full brood, the boy being the last of them. He closed his eyes against the vengeance in hers. He considered the darkness behind them and saw red flashes and yellow sparks. He looked deeper for more understanding and found it. He would speak to this woman later.

Buck felt himself shifting into Shadow. He thought differently when he did it, and if he could, he knew he would move differently. He was a much older man as Shadow than as Buck. It made him wary of himself. He'd felt this older and perhaps wiser energy creeping up on him when he circled around his cousin Duncan, just before Pete saved him the sin of killing his own blood. He remembered feeling cheated at the time, but that was the Buck side of him. The Shadow side that was sliding toward him was grateful because the Gypsy was right when she said that Buck would get a taste for killing if he could experience murdering someone. Pete, of course already had that stain on his soul, purely out of self-defense. He didn't like it, and now that he was going to be a father, liked it even less.

There was nothing for him to do but wait and look at what was going on. Wailing overtook the busy unpacking noises. The relatives of last night's attack must have been told the news. His head began to itch again so he looked for Chick in the Field but there was no sign of her. A woman in rags hovered over him. Moonfeather pulled her back, speaking to her in urgent Cheyenne. White Raven came to stand beside him.

"You have fever. Sand Owl will bring you to our tipi once it is finished. Do not try to move. It is dangerous for you." He sounded anxious. "Our Chief is not here yet."

"Does that mean you're the boss man?"

"Yes."

"I can't go far, Raven." Buck smiled just a little, partly to be encouraging and partly to pretend he wasn't afraid.

"They know you are here only until the next full moon. You will be left in peace until then so there is nothing to make you uneasy."

Sand Owl came with two men Buck had never seen before. He was lifted easily from the travois into the tipi. There was already a small fire which surprised him until he remembered that other people were already here, so would have been able to share the makings of one with his caregivers. The wrapping from his leg was slipping. Raven removed it rather than wind it over the wound again.

"I'll need to look at it later and put more salve on it." He spoke to Sand Owl in Cheyenne. She rubbed her cold hands together and acknowledged words that were still unknown to Buck by leaving the lodge, returning in a matter of moments with water and using a cloth to soak it up before the medicine man dropped some oil on it and then applied it to Buck's head. It felt like a combination of fire and ice. Buck took a breath so sudden and deep he thought his stomach would touch his spine and each of the two consecutive times Raven did this Buck's reaction was the same. The medicine man began a low chant as did Sand Owl.

"Don't do that again, please. It hurts all of me."

Standing White Raven continued to chant a bit longer before he responded: "That is your little fever gone. There is nothing wrong with your leg, so your sickness must be the movement on the travois."

Sand Owl tutted in the background. A woman, not Chick in the Field, thank goodness, entered carrying a pot of something Buck hoped was edible, not medicinal. He was ravenous now.

"We have to share, boy. You will be given a large spoonful. That's all, but enough to keep you from the true agony of starvation." Sand Owl stood in front of him.

Buck was aware that not once in all the previous days had he said a thank-you. Aunt Jenny would be so disappointed in him.

"Tell everyone I am grateful for everything they have done, please, Sand Owl."

"You will have to do some work before you leave us and that will be gratitude enough."

She didn't smile because – and Buck's head itched just a little – she meant it.

Chick in the Field entered. She stood with her back to the flap, filling the whole space, greying hair falling straight down her back, arms across her ample chest, and brown eyes looking at him as a cow chewing its cud.

"It's time we spoke, Chick in the Field," Shadow said.

"What about?" She was taken aback, her assessment of him incomplete.

"The blood caused by the yellow flash of the gun and the loss of your mother who died in her rags."

Sand Owl moved away as Chick in the Field took a step forward, exposing her son who had been standing just out of the line of Buck's sight. He was a curious child, held back by an overprotective mother. Shadow didn't judge her but wondered who would pay for her care in the long run? Would the boy break her heart by running away somehow or would the boy finally accept his fate and have his own will broken?

"Will you sit to speak with me, Chick in the Field?" Shadow noticed her wince when he said her name.

"You hate your name, Standing White Raven, tells me."

"It is not a strong one, so I have…" She plopped down… "had many trials to live instead."

"Your mother's murder when you were just a young chick."

There was a long pause as she hid her face. Her son stood by her shoulder, glaring at the white man.

"That's how I got named. I was lost in a field and looking for scraps of food, just like a chicken."

"How long were you on your own, without help?"

"They tell me they didn't know I had survived until they saw the sunflowers moving in the distance and then only came to see what animal it was because it didn't seem to have a purpose. The movement was going back and forth in circles. It amused them. So, I must have been away from camp for nearly a moon in the warm months."

"Who found you?"

"Resting Bird, father of White Raven and Sand Owl."

"So, he named you on that day."

"My mother would not have been pleased with it."

Shadow leaned back to look at her: "It is a strong name, I think."

"I am nearly a grandmother. Resting Bird should have thought longer about my name." Chick in the Field tried to stand. "I'm sorry, Sand Owl, to make an offence to your Spirit Father."

"It is a name to wear with honor." Buck said. "What other young beast would survive in a field all by itself? A puppy? A mountain lion kitten? Only a bird, a chicken, could live in a field of Sunflowers. Not even an eagle chick could live as long as you did. An eagle fallen out of its nest and unable to fly would not live, but a chick was never meant to fly so it lives how it can. You lived how the Great Spirit intended. You are strong. You have many children grown. You are a natural grandmother, Chick in the Field, now go and let me rest." Shadow fell back into being Buck.

"Could I have a sip of water?" He was still hungry but knew he would not be given more.

Chick in the Field ran out of the tipi, Sand Owl bent to her fire and rose with a cup of warm tea. Chick in the Field rushed back in carrying a beaker of cool water. Buck pointed to her, smiling at Sand Owl.

"I no longer have a man. I will care for you while Standing White Raven and Sand Owl teach you our ways." Her son was still behind her and still glaring at the white man.

"Thank you, Chick in the Field. I will consult with Standing White Raven in this matter. He will know better of what the Great Spirit has in store for all of us." He took a gulp of the water but found it so bitterly cold it shocked his system and made him gasp for air, once again making him aware of his stomach touching his spine. He presumed it was hunger. Is this what starvation feels like?

Standing White Raven entered, shocked to see Chick in the Field ministering to Buck. "Too many in here. All out. Now." He held the flap back for everyone except Sand Owl who offered Buck the warm tea.

"You should have been here. Chick in the Field is now very proud of her name and it's all because the Shadow in your white man explained our father's logic." She sank down on her knees to ensure while Buck drank he wouldn't waste the tea by spilling it on himself.

The Raven sealed the door with a tie and sat down heavily. He was exhausted. Buck wondered how old he was because since last night's attack he looked older than The MacLaren and he was no youngster.

"You really are much advanced." Raven sounded relieved. "I thought I may have to send you on a vision quest, but Mark was right, you may have taken one on your own without realizing what you were doing. He said you had visitors in an ice cave. Is that, right?"

"Yup. It's how I lost my toe."

Raven snorted. "Well, you've lost more now and I'll have to get someone else to build your crutch now that Oswaka has left."

"I'm sure one of Chick in the Field's sons would like to do it." Sand Owl spoke quietly. The two men nodded at her wisdom.

Chapter 8

"Let's have a better look at your leg." Raven looked dispassionate, as if the wound had nothing to do with him and so had no interest in its progression.

"How did you get it so clean looking? There's no tears or rips. You must have a sharp saw."

Sand Owl left, shuddering as she did so: "Don't mind the doing of it, but not liking the talk after it."

"Yes, a good sword. Borrowed, of course."

"it's so tidy looking, like a new made pillow, kinda." Buck was amazed.

"I borrowed the string and the sharp needles in your healing pack."

"The one the doc gave me?"

"If that's where you got shiny sharp needles like porcupine ones."

"That's them."

"The best one was the short, thicker one that curved a bit."

The two men, healer and patient, examined and prodded at Buck's stump.

"Can I have a look in my healing bag?"

The Raven passed it to him.

"Doesn't weigh as much."

"Still looking at things. What is the brown liquid?"

"Poppy juice. It's mixed with alcohol and called Laudanum. It's good for pain and they say it keeps women calm when they most need it." Buck sounded knowledgeable but in effect, didn't have any idea that women could be wild enough to need poppy juice. It was a puzzle to him.

"Is that what you had when you lost your toe?"

"Most likely." Buck was admiring the finish of his stump. "It looks almost healed."

"Not really. It's only been a few nights since we did it."

"If I was stronger I would sit up."

"If you were stronger, you could stand up, even with your old crutch but you came to us weak and will not gather any strength until we kill a deer or a wild boar."

Buck's stomach growled in agreement.

"Sand Owl is making a sock for you out of an old blanket and some fur."

"Just one?" Buck meant it as a joke, forgetting that natives don't have the same sense of humor all the time.

"It's just to cover your stump until we can find a real one you can walk on."

"Where can you find a real leg?" Buck laughed.

White Raven didn't think it was funny. "Your people are in a war. There will be a pile of false legs somewhere. I know. Some were seen near your iron rails up north." White Raven was stating a fact he thought Buck would have known. "There were some in the grey suited country too, but they didn't look as strong. Maybe wood built, not shiny iron. Lighter maybe, I bet." Raven placed more wood on the fire.

"I will light a pipe."

Buck just nodded.

"Mark and Oswaka should be here," White Raven said.

"What are you going to do with Mark?"

"What did you do with your family in winter?"

"The ground was hard so all I could do was dig a shallow pit and pile stones on top to keep the animals away until a thaw." Buck accepted the pipe. "The wolves got to them a bit though." He returned the pipe to Raven.

"That's what we will do with Mark."

Sand Owl rejoined them, letting in a blast of wintry night air.

"Excuse my ignorance, but I thought you would build a platform and cover him with furs."

There was a pause before Sand Owl asked Buck what good it would do. "We need furs for the living. It's getting dark. At least the snow and wind have stopped. Chick in the Field is busy getting everyone ready for a feast in the morning. She thinks one of her sons will be lucky and is on his way back with meat." Sand Owl put a pot of tea back on her fire. "Who poked at my stove, White Raven?" She sniffed.

"It was getting low and we needed to smoke."

"You sound like you did when you were a child, little brother."

"I am not your little brother." White Raven retorted. "You are in good spirits. Has the man father swore to you come back?"

Sand Owl blushed.

"Ha. I knew it. You kept saying you would never have anything to do with him, but it looks like you've changed your mind."

"The hunting party has come back with two small deer. The man the Great Spirit means me to take is not there. He must be coming in last because he'll be so burdened with meat."

"He's not yours just yet, Sand Owl. No need to brag until he gets here."

A strange head poked inside the tipi.

"Meat tomorrow." The man stared at Buck for a breath, before he left.

"Just here to look, I guess," White Raven said, "I thought your intended would have stayed, Sand Owl."

"Oh, my friend hasn't returned yet," she said, "What makes you think the one Great Spirit intends for me is the one Father picked?" She stretched out on her stomach, watching her brother's reaction.

"Be careful, sister."

For the first time Buck felt he should leave the little family to themselves but wasn't able to leave the tipi unaided. An uncomfortable silence came to rest. White Raven moved closer to Sand Owl and for the next few minutes they spoke in low tones and in their own language. Buck didn't need to be fluent to understand "no," and "go away from me," when Sand Owl put her flat palm up to her brother's face. Normally noncommittal eyes were flashing and "Great Spirit" invoked more than once by each of them.

"I'm sorry about this, friend," White Raven said to Buck, "Fatherless women need more guidance."

The Shadow in Buck came to the surface: "Fatherless women need more friends, I think."

Sand Owl's jaw dropped open, her hands trying to cover her face as she squealed, nodding at the white man.

"White men do not know our ways, Buck." White Raven stood near the flap of the tipi.

"We know a little of the ways of women, though. We know that when they are happy, men are happier."

"So, you think Sand Owl would be better with a man who has no experience of leadership, even of a small hunting party?"

"My brother wants me to take Broken Path, as father did. I would be the third wife he has worked to death."

"She wants Broken Path's son from his second wife: he's so untrained he hasn't undergone a naming ceremony, so we call him Hunter of Nothing."

Sand Owl had tears in her eyes, "He found me."

"Does he bring anything to our feast? Can he kill? Does he know to thank the Great Spirit and Mother Earth for all they give us, has he been that well taught that he has seen how to behave at pow-wow?"

"I know all that, and I will show him what little he doesn't know."

White Raven swished out, leaving a cold draft of night air.

"What will happen now?"

"He's my brother. He will ask Broken Path to give me up to his son, the Hunter of Nothing. We will have to pay something but knowing Broken Path, it will be a bottle of your poison liquid," Sand Owl was visibly upset. "Why do you people make that stuff? Corn is meant to be eaten. It can make your insides angry if you eat too much, but at least your head stays clear."

"I've never thought of it like that, Sand Owl," said Buck. "I have no idea why except it makes lots of money for them that make it, and takes it from the pockets of those that shouldn't buy it."

The tent flap crashed in. Sand Owl stood. An older native glared at her. He was drunk. Stepping toward Buck, he lashed out to kick his good leg and lost his balance, collapsing on top of his stump. Buck screamed like he never had in either of his two amputations. The native was pulled away by White Raven. Sand Owl sited her tiny frame between the native and her patient. The native released himself from the medicine man's grasp and this time deliberately threw himself on top of Sand Owl. Another younger native, inserted himself into the tipi.

"Father, stop it." He reached down to the belt around the older man's leggings to jerk him off and away. "Sand Owl?"

She was having trouble breathing, the wind knocked out of her. With her brother's help she rolled over and off Buck to face the man who had saved her.

"Hunter. Many thanks." She gasped as she tried to focus. He helped her to sit forward.

Broken Path was stirring like an angry bull. White Raven pulled him down to the level of the fire and across from the others. He clicked his fingers in the invader's face, speaking to him in his own tongue once he gained as much attention as he was able.

"Is Buck in one piece little sister?" He said without looking over his shoulder or removing his focus from Broken Path. Raven was concerned that the amputation hadn't experienced any damage. Sand Owl, sitting up now, gulping in air, looked at him in the semi darkness.

"You have been punched in the eye, brother."

"Not give woman to white man," Broken Path grumbled, "Bloodline not good." He was beginning to shout and noises were heard outside as some of the tribe came to listen.

"No, Sand Owl will be given to your son, Hunter, on the day of his naming and for the price of one deer and two bottles of liquor. It is what the Great Spirit requires of us. Another woman will be discovered for you. Perhaps in the time of less snow and more warm." Looking into Broken Path's bloated face, Standing White Raven squeezed his old shoulders with both hands. Broken Path nodded, staggered to his feet and left the lodge.

Activity off all kinds fired off. Buck, still whimpering a bit was subjected to a quick inspection of his stump while Sand Owl left to get snowy ice for White Raven's eye, still feeling a little tender in the stomach. Hunter returned to the meat he brought back – two dear and a small boar, saying he would come back before the moon was fully risen with something to cook and some wood for the fire. He shooed away the gathering audience outside, assuring them there would be a feast at his naming ceremony and admitting he didn't know what Standing White Raven would name him. He also didn't know when he and Sand Owl would be allowed to be married. The crowd, mostly female left in little groups to head toward their own abodes. Hunter, slapped his thigh in embarrassed anger and went to confront his father before he promised the meat for whisky.

Chapter 9

"It is hard to show respect, Father." Hunter of Nothing was outside on a fresh clear morning. The skinning of the kills came first before the meat was shared out, an offering made to the Great Earth Mother before any member of the tribe was allowed to eat. The ceremony was a short one, but the words known by all, even the youngest. Thanks, were given for the sacrifice of life to sustain the living.

"Don't lock yourself into an unworthy union," Hunter's father said.

"Sand Owl is worthy." Hunter of Nothing stood to hang the hide over the frame just in front of his tipi. It was a proclamation of his prowess and it joined the other one on another frame that held what was left of the wild boar. Hunter of Nothing disproved his name. It was something he was good at – killing his dinner, providing for his tribe and he took comfort in it, but remained self-deprecating.

"The white man is sitting outside now." Broken Path made the comment without causing Hunter to look.

"He gives no concern to me."

"That teaching they gave you has done harm to your thinking."

"No, Father, just burdened with another name I didn't need."

"Dan."

"Yes, Daniel. He wasn't very clever." Hunter sat to clean and sharpen his knife before he began to slice the meat proper. "This Dan wasn't a Chief. He put his head in a lion's mouth."

"Why?"

"I think it was to prove his God was good to him." Some small children began to gather. "The Great Spirit is good to all." Hunter let a piece of meat fall onto the fire and then moved a cold snowy rock closer to him. "These small ones look they are big enough to eat. Will I ask the Great Spirit for permission?" He moved his knife toward them. They laughed at him, none running away.

"Why, do you think I will never eat you all up?"

"Because you are a Hunter of Nothing, not even us." Two Soups, his niece, stuck her tongue out and ran just far enough away to avoid his teasing hand but not so far as to take her eye off the cooking meat which was beginning to sizzle. The smell was attracting more tribe members to the fire. One was Chick in the Field.

"Two Soups. You are old enough to know not to speak to the elders like that." She was wearing a dignity she didn't own the day before. "You will ask Hunter of Nothing for his pardon."

"That's only because you think you will get none of his meat, Chick in the Field." Native children were never punished but this little cousin was too much to be tolerated. Chick in the Field grabbed her shoulder and marched her away from the gathering group. No one heard what was said, but everyone saw the chubby wagging finger and the sound of two slaps on the girl's backside. Two Soups was so shocked she stood still to watch Chick in the Field leave for Hunter of Nothing's campfire. The young girl was beginning to shake her fist at the matriarch's back but noticed her own mother staring at her and thought the better of it.

The first deer meat had been shared by the time Chick in the Field returned to the campfire, but Hunter of Nothing left her in charge of what was cooking before he retreated to White Raven's tipi. Buck was seated on a tree stump just outside the door, taking in the morning sun, enjoying the clear blue, if cold, air.

"You are well, Hunter."

"I am well."

White Raven was preparing for the naming ceremony, Buck presumed, somewhere deep in the woods.

"What do you think you would like as a new name?"

"I've never thought about it," Hunter said. "Do I hear Sand Owl inside?"

"Probably." Buck smiled at him. "You're looking forward to your marriage?"

"Only if she is. I still don't know if she wants me."

"You haven't asked her?" Buck was astounded.

"No. Do you think I should? It's up to Standing White Raven who she marries, now her father is gone."

"Seems to me if you ask what a woman thinks about it all before you take her to her wedding bed, the whole thing'll go a great deal easier."

Hunter of Nothing was stunned. "We don't talk about that stuff. Not out loud. You need to learn manners of us."

"White folks don't talk about it either but all I can say is that asking a woman first makes things, in general, a whole lot better. Makes sense, I think." Buck turned his closed eyes to the sun.

Hunter cleared his throat and blushing, stood to let himself into to The Raven's tipi. Much giggling was heard, a slap and then a flustered Hunter of Nothing nearly tripped leaving the medicine man's tipi. He bent down to Buck. "Thanks, many thanks. Don't know how you knew, but many, many thanks." His step away from the lodge was lighter than the one that brought him there. "I will bring meat very soon. Sand Owl does good cooking."

"Thank you, Hunter. We will see you soon, then." Buck waved him away, relaxing once again into the warmth of the day and wondering how he became so wise. Sand Owl stuck her head out of her home, to watch Hunter leave and ducked in quickly when she noticed Buck watching her.

White Raven came out of the woods behind the camp, so the timing couldn't have been better except he had Two Soups with him and was now not in a mood to do a naming ceremony, let alone a joining one. She followed behind him sniveling, covering her mouth and rubbing her rear end with her other hand.

Sand Owl stepped out to see what was happening as did most of the campsite. Buck stopped her with a low "shh."

"Chick in the Field punished her for being smart as a bee in a flower patch to Hunter of Nothing."

Sand Owl squatted down to watch. "She must have made complaint to my brother and if he was asking the permissions of the Great Spirit at the time, he will not be pleased with the silly little fool."

Buck could tell Two Soups was glad to be the center of it all just by the way she held her shoulders back and jigged gently from one foot to the other.

"Today, when the sun is highest in the sky, Hunter of Nothing will be given a new name by Man Who Stands in Shadow." Buck was appalled. It was the first he'd heard of it. "Then the new name will be joined with my sister, Sand Owl."

Standing White Raven turned to Two Soups. "The Great Spirit does nothing by accident. You will be the first to address Hunter with his new name and you will learn more of your place in this world of the Great Spirit." He drove his long medicine stick into the hard-frozen ground three times and returned to the tree stump Buck was perched on. He was now very uncomfortable, physically and mentally. He turned to look at Sand Owl who was as stunned as he, if the color of her face was anything to go by. Jabbering of women in the distance was another indication he should get out of the way double quick.

Raven came to him, handed him his stick, and instructed him to stand. He did support his arm but then it was up to him to follow, unaided to another tipi just a ways away.

"We do the men's work while the women prepare Sand Owl for her matching."

Raven told him to sit but didn't tell him how so Buck aimed his butt for the highest pile of furs and threw himself sideways. His elbow caught his weight but he only flinched.

Raven gave him no time to think. The fire was low, dried wood and herbs were added. "This is sweetgrass. I am using sage as you call it, to clear the air of bad energy. Here. It is smoking well now, move the sweetgrass around you, all around you. All directions, not forgetting up and down. Breathe it in. There is no rush to be clean." Standing White Raven supervised as he used a length of plaited sweet grass on himself. Then he brought out a small drum and began to tap on it lightly. "This is the beat of your heart. Become in tune with it, Man Who Stands In Shadow that was Mindwalker and Buck Ross."

Buck felt himself becoming lighter, like he was somehow leaving his body to fly to another world and then he was above the trees, huge green trees. He observed an eagle flying beneath him and saw wide clean waters running down to huge still waters. There were shorelines and other peoples, he turned back, not comfortable about being there and then returned to himself. Standing White Raven was looking at him, just looking. After a time, he asked: "Do you have a name to give Hunter of Nothing?"

"Many, but I think Hunter of Eagles."

"We don't have many Eagles here."

"I know, but I don't think he will stay here to hunt them."

"Where will he take my sister, then?" The Raven showed his concern.

"Do not worry yourself. They will go just a little way, somewhere near running waters."

"Running waters, always have people around them."

"Yes, many."

"It is not a life my sister would like."

"It will be hers and Sand Owl is strong."

"I don't like the name. You said you had many. People have healthy, long lives if they are given names to give them wisdom to do it. Is there a name for him that doesn't have Hunter in it? Perhaps it will change Sand Owl's future."

"Running Waters?"

"It's not easy finding a name for someone." The Raven said. "Picture him as you see him. Is there part of how he is that comes to you?"

Man in Shadow was fully present. "Is that how you saw me?"

"Yes and because of it you will be able to work wonders without being noticed. Now, about Hunter."

Raven leaned forward. "Tell me."

Chapter 10

"Hunter of Nothing will become Hunter of One," Buck announced to the gathering.

"One what?" Hunter couldn't take it in. Somehow the name sounded strong.

"One at a time. All men have a purpose. You are patient. You wait for your chance but like the gold cats of the mountains you will pounce on your prey." Buck leant on Hunter's shoulders, speaking the words directly at him and keeping himself balanced as he did so. He turned on his crutch and faced Raven. "Return to the tipi with me, please, Raven."

Raven, the teacher kept pace with his protégé.

"Hunter will become a man people will fear."

"I don't vision him as a killer." White Raven growled in deep tones as he moved a little closer.

"No, not a killer but he will do the white man's work and catch one at a time. Sand Owl will become proud and the mother of many because Hunter will live by the river edge, trading on the big ships and tracking for the companies. He will become wealthy by the way of the world, but he will forget he is not of stock to enjoy the refreshments of the white man's world."

"I will not tell him what you predict." There were tears in the older man's eyes. "It may cause him to flinch at his destiny and no man can afford to do that."

"What is my destiny, then?"

"You already know that, but we have to hurry your training. Your healing work will be needed in the spring, but not here. You have to return to Validation and then be given further direction to the direction of the sunrise." The Raven held the flap open for Man in Shadow. Light was fading and a misty cold began to creep up from Mother Earth.

Buck went to lie, to dream, only, he hoped. He would like to dream of pecan trees and fishing. He wanted to dream of Aunt Jenny and being taught his letters. A dream of having his ears boxed would be a kindness. He'd probably earned his thick ear, of course, but it would be would be a familiar thing, so a comfort to him, but before dawn he heard rifle shots and much screaming. Something smelled foul and sickening. He sat upright, finally understanding he wasn't dreaming – it was a vision. He had seen Joss. Joss was alive. Joss had joined the army at the age of fifteen, the stupid boy, a good little friend was fighting in grown-up battles. White Raven looked down at him. Both had tears in their eyes.

"How long was I away?"

"Only a few breaths. I feel sorry for you, having fierce sight like yours is a burden."

"You have time to learn some essentials before you have to go – at least one full moon time, but then you must leave for your home. Your destiny is linked to that of the boy, but not in the way you expect."

White Raven left to officiate at his sister's wedding to Hunter, knowing that as much as he would like to attend, the young man had participated in enough ceremony for one day. Buck would like to be able to see another man's vision to help him understand his own. He would also like to just leave once the words were spoken. Oswaka did it, Sand Owl was silent most of the time, but moved on when there was no need to stay and White Raven was the master of self-control. Buck wanted to learn that. There was dignity in it. Moonfeather came to him. He hadn't seen her in a long time. She was always a comfort. She would watch over him while he slept, as he must. He did. Buck slept an innocent sleep filled with childhood dreams. He said goodbye to them forever as he woke that morning.

"Oats?" Sand Owl poked at his shoulder. "Hungry for learning?" This wasn't a vision. He knew as soon as he saw her making a fuss of the fire.

"Morning, Sand Owl." He tried to say no more than was needed. She handed him a bowl of what Jenny used to call porridge. Saying nothing, Sand Owl left. This was why native people have the reputation of sneaking up on people – they don't, it's just how they behave naturally. They are a quiet race, respectful of their environment. Buck ate.

White Raven entered as Buck was struggling out of his warm furs.

"Come," he said, "I need you to be at the river, so I will help you dress to make sure you get there in plenty of time for the geese."

The two of them were used to doing this now, so Buck was organized very quickly, prop under his arm. White Raven lifted his sleeping furs.

"Sand Owl," he shouted, "Buck wants to return your furs to you now that you are a wife."

The lady, arms outstretched and blushing, reached for them and hurried on her way. Buck didn't even see which direction she had come from – the natural stealth.

"You've just had a lesson. Take nothing for granted. Trust only in the now. The past is gone; it brought you to this place, the future follows in your thoughts which will move your footsteps in the direction you need to go. If you think your destiny is to fall and trip, you will. If you think you are here to heal and you focus on it, you will heal. Think, then move. Think in good ways, not bad ones. Always think first." White Raven began to move away. "We do. It is why we are a quiet people – most of the time, anyway." He grinned at his student. "We like a feast and a celebration with music, though. Don't we, Buck? Hunter of One is still sore-headed from yesterday's celebrations."

Buck stayed silent and nodded.

At the river the ice grasped the edges of the water so tightly, the water turned a bubbly white as it stormed down the middle. "It's higher than last year, what do you think, Shadow?'

Buck was about to say he didn't know, but he would have said it without thinking, so he slowed and thought.

"There must have been a thaw upstream because I've never paid any attention unless it gave our stream on the farm much of a start and the field a flood." The two men stood to stare and think. They considered the slightly-cloudy grey sky, when both heard the call of geese. There seemed to be hundreds of them. They flew behind and to the west.

"They have been mightily disturbed."

Buck thought again before he spoke: "By what? A storm?"

"Most likely. The eagles are clinging to the top branches. We'll know more if they rise."

Buck wondered what he meant but said nothing.

"You should ask, if you don't know Buck Ross."

Buck shrugged and asked what he meant by the eagles rising.

"Eagles rise above the storm. See? Today one flies south, the other, north. They fly free above the clouds, in the warm sun. When we see them again, you will notice the storm leaving."

"I've seen that happen many times, but never thought about it." Buck was overwhelmed by his own lackadaisical attitude. Beauty and a message, a reliable message, from the Great Spirit should not be ignored. He was humbled.

"Come, I will teach you and pack for you a medicine bag, for you will need it." The Raven seemed to glide through the snow but that was a silly thing to think as far as Buck could make out. He hopped as best he could and then he thought: he asked me to come to see the geese. How did he know? Ahead a little more, his teacher entered his own tipi, one Man Who Walks in Shadow had never entered. He must leave behind his old life. His name was never Mindwalker, it was always just Buck. It was his affliction to be a Mindwalker – what others called him in the past. Now he was Shadow and he needed to learn how to manage the different abilities granted to him.

Someone had set a small fire as usual. The Raven motioned him to sit opposite as he lit a pipe. Ah, this was going to be formal, then. He closed his eyes as he waited for the sounds and smells of a drawn pipe to be created. The White Raven asked: "Are you settled in mind and heart?"

Buck nodded once. He opened his eyes. Raven asked if he had the stomach to be a healer and passed the pipe, so he could answer. Buck thought before he replied in the affirmative.

"It will take many years to learn balance in all things, to become a truly spiritual man, a Shaman. Leave it to the Great Spirit to educate you. Observe and listen to all things and above all, be loving and patient – especially with yourself." Standing White Raven cleared his throat. "You will not know until you start with a person who needs your strength."

Buck was aware enough of manners to pass the pipe back and so words were exchanged, and a plan could be put into motion.

Raven stood to reach into a cluster of dried herbs tied into a soft leather medicine bag. It was well worn, judging by the fraying tassels along the bottom. "We will visit an elder who seems to be going silly in the head as so many of us do nowadays. I will teach the family what to do with this herb."

Buck thought it looked like a shriveled elderflower.

"You will stand well behind me, listen to what I say, observe my manner and forget nothing, because I will question you on our return."

In the afternoon, Buck met more than one elder and began to think he was being shown around to settle curiosity. He sensed the Raven carried some pride in his teaching ability and recalled from his visits to church that pride was one of the seven deadly sins. He was flattered that Raven was proud to be passing on his knowledge and aware he was honored to be a student.

It was dark and cold by the time they finished their work that day. Buck was invited into the Raven's tipi again. The older man didn't have to get his fire going. Sand Owl called a greeting from outside and Raven flicked back the door flap. She came in carrying what looked like a deer meat stew and a chunk of cooked potato. Buck's stomach gurgled long and loud in anticipation. All of them laughed.

She put the pot onto the fire, ladled out some meat for each of them and left. She didn't need to ask how they were, or how Buck had got on, or what kind of day they'd had because the rest of the camp had already told her that Buck was a strange one – he seemed to glow a green color at times, like the spring color of trees. They were glad he was a quiet one – he listened to complaints and comments very well and seemed to have a good heart. Sand Owl was pleased for her brother, because he'd been needing a pupil to stimulate his own interest and abilities. The Raven had chosen wisely; acquiesced to the Great Spirit. She, of course, natural healer though she was, couldn't be taught by a man, she accepted it, but held fast to the dream she would be provided a medicine woman who could educate her. Now she was married, the Great Spirit must have chosen a different path for her. Sand Owl would have children and not attempt to heal the sick any more than she needed.

That night, after checking Buck's leg and re-dressing it, Raven took advantage of the peace of a gently snoring student to take another soft piece of leather, light a sage stick, bless his work and sew together Buck's medicine bag. He knew Buck had retained the knowledge and at points during the day had witnessed white and green light transferring between patient and healer. Raven created a much larger bag than his own. He included porcupine needles and deer sinew. Tomorrow he intended to show Buck plants that could be used as a natural cleaner for deep wounds and eventually, when the bag could hold no more, he pronounced an end and whispered an ancient blessing, encouraging his words to rise up through the roof hole and meet with the stars.

In the morning Buck would begin his trip back to Validation. It would likely take a half moon because Raven needed the time to teach him more. Hunter of One would also join them. Sand Owl would have to be left behind this time, new bride as she was, because there may be some emergency healing to do.

"I thought you said she couldn't be a healer," said Buck as he dressed.

"No, I said she couldn't be trained as a healer. She was born as one. She can no more prevent her destiny as a healer than you can prevent being a Man Who Walks in Shadow."

Chapter 11

////////////////////////////////

It appeared to the citizens of Validation that Buck had brought friends home for dinner. He was sitting on a horse Indian style and took up the middle between two natives, one who was an older man with dark hair and a narrow nose, the other, much younger, more Buck's age, straight backed, with a touch of arrogance, maybe. Buck looked directly at the MacLaren who had taken a stance on the sidewalk of the saloon, Sharps rifle in hand. All heard another rifle being cocked behind the small group. No one else was about, well not visible, anyway.

"Put that thing down please, Pete. These men are friendlier than anything in a grey coat, even if they are natives."

Pete, the saloon keeper, thin and wary as usual, came to join The MacLaren on the sidewalk. The big man, the bounty hunter who'd come to find the killer of Buck's family, had stayed on after the job was done and he looked more content now that he'd found his soulmate in the local banker and post lady. The contentment appeared to be showing in his belly – just a little, though. He was still much taller than he was broad. Buck flicked out the walking stick Chick in the Field had bullied Broken Path into creating for him and slid from his mount and slipped the crutch under his armpit like he'd never had the use of a full leg, so used to it he was.

"Welcome." Poppy Diamond banged onto the snowy street from inside her establishment, the Black Diamond Saloon. "You have taken another chunk from our Buck." She pointed at the half leg. Poppy was always direct – Midwest direct, people were proudly calling it.

Buck bashfully moved toward her, one arm out to hug her. She came to him as a mother would her son – concerned to see his hurt, but grateful to the good God that he was safe. She attributed this to the two men with him and that was all she needed to know for the time being at any rate. Buck hugged her as best he could, feeling as he knew he would, the babe inside her. There was movement, but he would suggest she not only loosen her stays, but not wear them at all if she could get away with it.

Pete took both rifles inside, The MacLaren embraced Buck's shoulders and shook the hands of the natives who thought the custom odd but were relaxed enough, probably by Poppy's reaction to them, which was one of not caring who they were if they'd take good care of one of hers. Scraping the mud and sticky snow from their boots, students and mentor entered Poppy's domain. Buck felt it was looking tired and run down, but said nothing.

The wood burning stoves brought heat to the reunion, the food, served in huge bowls with matching chunks of fresh bread and pots of hot coffee and the love felt for a returning son made the conversation easy until one of Poppy's girls, Clara, meandered into the room looking to ply her trade. Poppy clicked her fingers and the girl disappeared, but she couldn't help seeing the look of sympathy on the face of The Raven.

"You keep many girls, then?"

"No, just those who need a place to sleep and a meal in their bellies. How they pay for it is their own affair. As long as there's no trouble they keep their pallet." Poppy wasn't good at hiding her feelings.

"You did their job a great many moons ago."

Poppy blushed. "I got by, yes."

The Raven was silent, just as Buck knew he would be as he looked deeply into Poppy's eyes.

Pete was glaring at him, "Don't talk about my wife like that."

"This is a sadness still living inside her, but she's found great joy now. When is your babe going to make her appearance?" he asked Pete, not Poppy.

"In the summer – maybe even on July 4th if we're lucky." He squeezed Poppy's hand.

"Later that that I'm afraid, Pete." Buck laughed at him. "More the middle of the month, I think."

"How do you know it's a girl?"

"I can only be a little wrong, but I'll bet you it is."

"I won't," said Buck. "I think it's a girl who'll be called Jenny, isn't that right, Poppy? After my aunt?"

"The babe will be what the babe will be," It was the first thing Hunter said.

"You like the food, then, Mr Hunter?"

"Thank you, yes." He was looking at the bottles behind the bar.

"You ever been in a Saloon before?" The MacLaren was resting his boot on the brace of the table.

"No, I have not."

"You've gotta work up to the hard stuff, but I can offer you a beer to see if it gives you a pleasant time."

Pete looked aslant at Poppy for a brief second and then rose to fetch a small glass of the beveridge.

The doors of the building were suddenly blown open, not by the wind unless the wind had the name of Shona Haggerty, Ryan O'Grady or Ian Grant. All were out of breath, covered in bits of snow and ice, glowing with health and cheerful as mice in a grain bin. Gloves flew in all directions, scarves at the bar area to see if they could catch a warmth by the fireplace under the rifles, coats properly placed on the coat racks, Poppy had insisted Pete build for her, so there would only ever be one big puddle on the floor rather than one under each customer's chair. Buck was rising as Ian got to him first. There was the back slapping as expected, the how are you, the look at the leg and the guilt for having asked but it was all over in a hurry. O'Grady was heard, under the noise of it all, including the promised glass of beer which Hunter winced at, apologizing to the medicine man for his bad behavior that long-ago night. A head was bowed. Nothing was said. The Raven was in the moment. O'Grady was in the past, still. Shona got to him, finally, but gave him only a short hug. She had tears in her eyes. "I have a letter for Ryan." It was on Army paper. He fell into a blank chair just behind him as he received it.

"It's in Joss's hand, so it can't be all that bad." Ryan was shaking but he ripped it open without tearing it.

He read a bit of the beginning to himself before he started reading it to everyone else.

"Dear everyone, I know Ryan would read this to all of you, so I thought it would be cheaper just to send one letter.

I am fine. I spent some time in Cairo, Illinois where General Grant was my commanding officer. I saw him riding his horse once. He looks all loose on it – like he was just hanging on or something. Even so, he looks to be a good sort. I am only a private. I have a friend called Edwin. We both had the medical tests. Tell Buck not to waste his time when he becomes a doctor, with rubber gloves. They're just plain sore. Edwin's been given the duty of cooking bread so he's a good friend to have, because if a man can find bread he can find a coffee. A couple of weeks ago the Army found out I was a good shot so my Lieutenant, made sure I got one of the new Henry rifles. You most likely know about Fort Henry and Fort Donelson by now. I was at both. One was just a silly thing because of the river being so high but the other was hard, long and noisy. I couldn't hear myself for nearly a week after it was over. One or two of us had the bloody ear.

We privates and even some of the corporals, don't really know what's going on half the time. We just get pointed in a direction and told to shoot or run up a hill and then shoot and then it's all merry hell and what hell probably smells like. Not sure a body can breathe in hell, because it must stink as well. As you can figure it, there's plenty screaming and yelling but there's also whooping when we win. There seems to be enough men, though. I couldn't tell you how many, but it seems like thousands so most of the time I feel real safe. At least they don't aim at me if I can see their backs.

We're taking a boat south tomorrow, I think. I can't tell you where, really, but I do know we're going to get off in a different State – probably Tennessee. I think we're in Kentucky right now. If the Rebs hadn't run away at the Fort we wouldn't have to chase them, I reckon. I suppose if they keep this running away from us thing going, we'll be in Atlanta or even Richmond by the summer and the whole thing will be over.

Please, would someone send socks? Edwin could also do with some because he's got no kin that give a damn. He's a good buddy and gives me extra rations when he can. You can just send it to the Army. My number is 104/K/1862.

Take care of Buchanan and Vengeance for me.

Best Regards, Joss (but they forget to use the O and just call me Grady. Took your name, Ryan – hope you don't mind).

Shona and Poppy were hanging on to each other. The girl that had been trying to drum up trade was sitting wide-eyed at the bar, a pink knitted shawl around her shoulders to cover her bosom as she crossed her pale arms, and stared right into Buck's eyes. Tears ran down her cheeks, but she made no sound.

"Buck," said Ryan, quietly. "Please go for him. Please see if you can get him back. He's lied about his age. I don't know what he did to make the army believe he was eighteen, but either he was fast on his feet or the army recruiters were seeing him in the dark." He looked up at Buck, pleading.

"Buck can't go, Ryan." The MacLaren rumbled his opinion. "He's too eaten up already – just look at that leg."

"Yes, he can." No one noticed Doc Fraser and the good Reverend Parker come in while the message was being read. "I believe whoever did this surgery has done a superlative work repairing his leg. If he can ride a horse, as he obviously can, he can ride a train. All we must do is get him to St Joseph in Missouri and he can ride all the way to St Louis in less than twelve hours, I believe. The country is opening, all. We must take every advantage while we can."

People moved about now as they came to terms with the truth of a war that, until this afternoon was so far away. Joss gave them a focus on it, a reason to participate. They would set their minds to it.

"Come to see me Buck. We'll have to find some decent clothing for you. I believe Mary may have ordered some worsted wool, grey if I recall and with any luck I can come across a pair of good boots for you." Ian was being ever practical.

No one thought for a minute that these boots hadn't been worn by one of the clients now six feet under. Ian only buried people in the clothes they wanted to be buried in if they'd paid for it, otherwise, they got a shroud and he sold on the outfits to help affray his expenses. "We can't have you visiting the army in clothes that aren't at least business like."

Buck was silent as was White Raven. He was thinking. The Raven kicked him gently on his good leg. "I will go but I will not leave for seven days. It is the best way to time my arrival with meeting Joss."

"Your mind been for another walk, then?" Ryan asked.

"Yes, Ryan, it has. Where are the horses?"

"You noticed."

"Of course. What do I tell Joss?"

"The truth. The Army's got them. No choice."

"I will find one, maybe."

"Maybe."

Poppy filled the food bowls, but silence is not good for the digestion, so she tried to serve conversation as well.

Hunter did a polite burp, "I don't like your beer. Sorry."

"Keep it that way Mr Hunter." Pete snorted a laugh and patted his shoulder.

Chapter 12

It was the right time of year to find a bed in the Black Diamond. As soon as it was made clear to the evening ladies that their ministrations weren't required, Buck and his native escort had a comfortable night in the three rooms above the saloon, taking full advantage of the heat rising from below.

"This cannot be a healthy place to live all the time," said Hunter first thing in the morning, as he sat in a wooden armchair to receive his breakfast of bacon, eggs, hash browns and a pancake or two.

"No, most unusual. I wonder if there were other things living in my bed last night." The Raven brushed down his sleeves as if to check but he picked up a fork anyway.

Poppy had a hot pot of coffee in her hand. She slapped a mug down on the table. Buck watched her from half way down the curving staircase. How she managed to pour a perfect mugful of hot beverage without taking her furious eyes from The Raven and without spilling any, amazed him. It was a practiced art. The Raven showed nervousness by looking down. Poppy snapped the lid shut. "There no creepy crawlies in my linen, Sir."

"No, Ma'am," said a contrite Raven. Hunter took a sip of the coffee she had already poured for him but wasn't good at hiding his amusement at his elder's embarrassment.

"Eat your bacon. Buck, what are you doing hovering on the stairs like an eagle? Your breakfast's getting cold. I remembered you don't like eggs, so you don't have any. There's a couple more pancakes. Hurry up."

Buck hopped to his seat, grateful for it because he felt his stump to be on fire.

"Leg no good today?" Raven was stirring the small bowl of sugar. "What's this?"

"It's called sugar. It's for your coffee if you want to add it. It's sweet."

Raven dipped his little finger in it and brought a tiny bit to his mouth, but he squeezed his eyes shut to judder a bit.

"No. Not like that one bit. Not good for me or anyone. What good does it serve?"

"I don't know. Do you, Hunter? You went to a proper school and got proper taught." Buck asked.

Hunter put a spoonful into his coffee. "I like it."

Buck never had, except when it was in a candy or an ice cream, but he didn't like it melted in coffee. He might try it again, sometime.

Once again there was a silence as the animal that sacrificed its life was thanked – in Cheyenne of course, which brought one or two of the girls out of their rooms and stopped Poppy still as she came out of the kitchen. This was a good thing. It gave Buck a chance to look at her pregnancy in the light of day. As he expected, there was something amiss. It looked like the unborn was lying across, not up or down. He remembered promising her he would be here for the birth of her daughter. If he was to find Joss for Ryan, extricate him from any of the trouble he was in and get back from wherever he had to go to get him it may be a promise too difficult to keep. If he was going to go, he'd better make a start.

"I'm going to the General Store today. Maybe Mr Grant has some cloth that can be turned into a travelling suit for me." Buck checked that Poppy wasn't looking before he picked up a slice of bacon in his fingers to make a long gift of it to his tongue.

"We will leave when you do. The spring moon will be with all of us as we travel," Raven said, "you in your direction, us in ours – for a time, at least."

The saloon door banged open, throwing in Doc Fraser. There was no wind. My, February with no wind. There remained enough snow to melt from the rooftops, but with still air it couldn't whip around. The whole winter was so mild compared to last year, but if spring was too early the frost may not have had time to kill off the bugs that attack the crops. Buck wondered what part of him made him think like that. His mind hadn't wandered for a while, perhaps because he was tasked with a true mission this time. Not even his head was itching. Validation may finally have brought him some peace after all this time.

"You're well, then, everyone?"

"Fine, Doc. You?"

"Better than my best. Buck, I may have found you a spare leg." His eyes had the sparkle of a child's with a Christmas toy. Ian says he could organize a fitting for you later."

Hunter belched. Doc wasn't used to honest table manners. "Hunter is paying a compliment, Doctor Fraser," said Buck.

"Sorry, not used to being around a white world anymore." It was the best apology Hunter was willing to make in the circumstances. Doc shrugged, no doubt thinking something dark about savages.

"There's not many people about yet, if you can come now." There was an urgency Buck hadn't noticed so he rose to excuse himself from his companions. "I won't be long. Will I meet you in the livery or would you like to come with me?"

Raven joined him while Hunter vanished to see Ryan in the stables. Doc was right, there really was no one lurking or even peeking through the lacy windows. So the three of them swung down the middle of the single street in the direction of the church, long coats and furs defining their professions: two trained healers, one apprentice. The ground remained hard in places, but little icy puddles were forming in hoofprints and wheel tracks. It meant there was the beginning of a thaw.

On arrival at Ian's General Store and Mortuary, Buck's heart turned. Mary was waiting for him. He didn't want her to be there and wondered what she wanted. He took his hat off, manners always showing through. If he wasn't mistaken she may have given him a quick bob. His head itched. He scratched it, just a little.

"How's the farm then? Paying its way I hope?"

"We're doing fine, thanks Buck," she informed him. "Rent will be on time."

"Come see this Buck," said the doc.

Buck had trouble leaving the eyes of Mary's hard stare. He'd never noticed before that she never blinked. Neither did a wolf.

"Look," instructed The Raven. "It's very fancy."

It was lightweight despite the wide silver trim around the thigh grip. The hinge between the soft rubber padding and the cup ready to receive Buck's stump, was just loose enough to let his knee bend naturally and it had a carved foot shape on the bottom, not a stub. The calf of it was made of a soft red leather and the inside had a polished wooden cavity to nestle a stump.

"Sit, please." Ian offered his office chair, the one with arms, placing it between the haberdashery counter and the upright bolts of fabric. The light came in through the door and windows, but to be hospitable, Ian turned up the wicks of the two wall lights. Buck was taken aback, the permanence of his condition finally punching him in the gut, but he did as he was told. Doc removed the light dressing Buck had wrapped on himself before he came down for breakfast but he couldn't watch as the bandages were completely unraveled and the doc began to redress his wound.

"Did you do this?" He asked The Raven.

"Yes. Without fuss. Clean and quick."

"It shows. What a beautiful job of stitching."

"My sister, Sand Owl, but she used the needles in the kit you gave Buck."

"I thought you stitched me." Buck's head jerked toward him so their eyes would meet. Raven remained calm.

"Sand Owl isn't allowed to heal, remember?"

"The curved needle was the best, you told me."

"That was what she told me to tell you."

Doc reached for a cotton handkerchief and a fine woolen sock lying on the counter. He slipped the cloth over the freshly bandaged stump and then held it in place with the sock.

"You ready?" He waited for Buck to look him in the eye. Gently, the prosthesis was slipped over his thigh and onto the stump. A silence held the attention of everyone as the final, gentle push whooshed home. After a minute, the doc asked Buck if he felt up to attempting a stand. Raven nodded and assisted him by handing him his stick.

"Look at the lace holes in the silver trimming. All you need now is some sort of ribbon so we can, if need be, tie it on through the loop of your trousers or something." Doc was thinking out loud but he was also enjoying himself as he watched Buck balancing. Ian moved the chair in front of him but with the high back facing him and Buck grasped it while he took his time adjusting to his new equipment.

"You're such a big man now, Buck. You've chosen the right time of year to arrive home though. Do you remember old Mr Pelowski?" Ian said.

"No. I'm not wearing a dead man's shoes," fearing that the old fella had passed over.

"I was going to say that since you haven't been here to make the boots and shoes, he's taken over. He's the one that polished and refined that half leg in case anyone would need it and now look. The Lord certainly does work in many mysterious ways as they say. Mary found your old shoe-making things and gave them to him. He has made you a pair of high knee boots he thinks may suit your needs, using the templates you left behind and Mary herself would like you to try on a travelling suit she has roughly stitched together."

Mr. Grant looked the part of a tailor with a long-folded ruler wrapped around his neck. Mary stood in the background, arms folded across her scrawny bosom.

Buck was sure that Mary had charged a good price for his tools, but respected the fact that her father still thought of her as a generous little girl, so said nothing.

"I'm so sorry," Buck said. "How much do I owe you for all this?"

"Just do your best to bring Joss back. It's what all of us want."

Ryan and Hunter had arrived while the negotiations were in progress. It proved how warm it was. The wood stove wasn't on and there was no substantial draft when the door opened so no one had noticed their arrival.

"Come with me for a minute, please Buck. I need to finalize my stitching and now that we have a machine it should only take a day or two to organize. Try not to scratch your head, please. I'm not that bad." Mary's eyes hadn't changed but with Doc's help he returned to the back room, the very one where she and her father had fought the sickness at the end of last year. She pinched him and hauled him around without saying a word more than she needed. He started doing a breathing exercise Raven taught him to stop himself from scratching.

"You need socks and undergarments as well. I'll see to it but, I will give you an accounting. We do, after all, have a business arrangement." She smiled with her mouth. Buck's head felt alive and knowing it would irritate her, he used both hands to scratch. He didn't smile, though. She pushed and pulled at him, fixing pins in places including the length of his stump. Not once did she flinch or show any type of friendliness.

"That's fine – you can go now." She swished out before him.

The MacLaren was there, taking up the whole store. He hadn't changed. He was just one of those people who could warm an empty room by his presence. Or chill it, come to that. Customers came and went, trying to pick up as much gossip as they could as they received their change.

"I'm taking you to St Joseph, Missouri by wagon where I'm going to help you get on the train where you will get off at St Louis. From there you can use your common sense to find Joss. The army will most likely be that far south by then: somewhere in Tennessee at least and near one of the rivers, anyway. He talked about boats in his letter don't forget…"

"…you're awful excited, Benjamin MacLaren," Buck stated a fact. "It's not your usual way."

"I'm too old to join up so just feeling a bit of envy for your adventure."

"Aye, an adventure that could get Joss and Buck killed, so you are not going too, Benjamin." Only Shona could speak to him like that. She wasn't loud about it to embarrass him, especially as she'd just turned up.

"I'll need to see you at the Bank and the Land Registry before you leave, Buck." He acknowledged her order.

Outside, he saw The Raven and Hunter on their now refreshed horses ostensibly taking them for exercise. It made him anxious to leave the store, so he asked Doc to help him walk Shona back to her offices. Everyone else adjusted themselves back into the day they had planned. Ian shouted out to him to come back in the afternoon because Mr Pelowski would be available to fit his new boots that very day. Buck waved his hand in response. Mary hefted the suit cloth under her arm. Stopping to choose some buttons that had been worn by one of her father's customers – brown leather – she watched the odd party of natives, the doc, a redhead and Buck wander away.

"He's even stranger than he was, Pa. Hope his mind doesn't go for a walk when there's a bullet looking for it." She sat down heavily on the nearest armchair.

Ian didn't say that he was more worried about her mind than Buck's. It probably had something to do with losing her mother and siblings. He knew he'd done the best he could. It would suit Mary fine if Buck was killed. Who would she pay rent to then? Ian was aware, in the new silence, of the sound of the sewing machine. He knew she'd arranged that Pelowski would make her shoes for the next year or so. Did she make the same deal for her husband's footwear? Ian wasn't sure she did.

Chapter 13

The livery was empty without Joss. Buck got the doc to assist him as far as inside but was managing fine manipulating his leg now he had fences and stables to lean on. His back was sore with it but otherwise he was comfortable. He hated the damn thing.

There were only two horses left, one old swayback mare so the farmers could bring in what little harvest was left after the various raids that had been carried out – one or two by the Confederates when they were feeling ornery and one by accident, by the Union forces because they thought they'd seen grey uniforms. At least the water pump wasn't damaged. The town was hanging onto itself by prayer and the Grace of the Good Lord. Buck had only been with the native people since the middle of January, but it was obvious there was no life in the place. No young blood, no breeding blood, as The Raven said. He shuddered. It would mean when the war ended the fields, rivers and forests would be overrun with those anxious to breed again. Rabbits would have to look to their laurels is what he implied. Some took it as a joke, others, not so much. What does a native know, anyway? The gate behind him creaked. There was nothing there but at least a movement told there was life about somewhere.

"Buck?" Ryan spoke from deep inside the steading.

"I'm wondering about your arm."

"Yes. It's very good, considering."

"Considering what?"

"Your people could have killed me."

"Yes."

The air smelled warm and moldy.

Buck was getting extremely good at being native. He stood still, seeming to be a head taller than he usually was, making Ryan uncomfortable.

"You are sorry for your drunken act, then."

"Oh now, look, Buck. I'd take it all back if I could, but don't make me feel worse." He did, he felt like a child who'd been caught with his hand in the molasses.

"No, you're right," Buck said, "you couldn't feel worse, so we'll let it go. You left your knife behind." He offered Ryan the hilt. "It has been cleaned. Any message for Joss?"

There wasn't much hay in the barn, but Ryan found it to sit on.

"Slip my knife into your good boot, sir. You may need it but if you don't, please let Joss have it as a gift from me."

Buck leaned on an upright, not willing to admit he may need a hand to get up again. It also made sure he would continue to look down on the man who had killed Mark. The Raven wouldn't approve, but then The Raven didn't know Ryan. Buck wanted to make sure the Irishman didn't start bragging about how he'd killed an Indian. Ryan was able to start trouble if left to his own devices.

"He has to come home. He is missed."

Buck slipped the killing knife into his boot. It was a solid one, the blade about eight inches long and tapering into a half inch point. Instinct told him it would work well.

"Will I also tell Joss he is loved and that once again you are sorry for treating him like a no account?"

Ryan tried to snap to his feet but slipped on the wet straw. Buck caught him with one hand, the other grasping a harness to keep balanced. He held on to his shirt collar and bringing Ryan's face closer, he said: "You never did him any harm, I admit, but likewise, you didn't do him much good. Once he'd learned his letters you stopped him and put him to work. I hope the army has discovered his talents. They could make him an animal doctor if they chose to."

"Maybe, but who would pay for it," Buck, surprised by his own strength, flung him back where he came from.

"Ryan, you are not the person Joss would come back to see and I don't blame him. This conversation I will hold between us so now we will remember it." He was relieved to leave the heavy atmosphere. "You still hanging on to his Ma?"

"Leave her out of it. She's better than in many a long time," Ryan snapped.

Buck ejected himself from the livery and limped back to the saloon. He needed a coffee. Doc Fraser had the same idea, so they joined together in the frosty morning air – healers from a different branch of the tree. "What a shame you had to sleep through the operation on your leg, Buck. It would have been an education for you because once Raven – is that his name? – told me how he'd gone about it and the fact that he had chopped it rather than sawn it off but still managed to control the bleeding, well, the procedure must have been fascinating. The two of us had a great deal in common..."

"...why wouldn't you chop it than saw it, Doc?" Buck asked the question as he held open a door to the saloon. "Butchers do it cleanly with their beef."

"Well, he is a native after all."

"Yes, and from what I've read of your medical books you've still got lots in common with the doctors in the days of Henry the Eighth. What a good thing you've got ether, and laudanum these days." Buck was grinning. Doc had forgotten what a good looking young man he was.

"At least you've come out of things well, Buck."

The saloon wasn't full, but Poppy came to them while wiping her hands on a clean white apron. This meant she'd been baking, not slaughtering chickens or the like. "Coffee?"

"You should get one of those Samovar things that Rachel the Gypsy used. Then you wouldn't have to be running back and forth, but yes please Poppy and try to put your feet up for a bit, will you."

She chuckled as she flung a cloth over her shoulder, returning to the kitchen using a walk that looked like she was more pregnant than she was.

"I worry about her, Buck."

Pete came from the back room dusting snow from his clothes. "Some of the stuff fell loose from above me. We're melting, out there, for sure it's too mild. Got enough firewood to keep us going anyhow; just checked to make sure in case March goes normal on us." He smiled at them his greying moustache leaving his top lip, while he poured a shot of his best and downed it before Poppy arrived with the coffee. "You're off to Tennessee by the telling of it."

"As soon as my clothes are ready and The MacLaren can find a rig."

"Probably in the morning, then."

"I'd thought a week, but as The Raven says, the moon will light our trip and there's no reason to delay now the spirits have spoken. I said goodbye to Ryan already."

"I bet you did." Doc and Pete exchanged a quick look. "How did he do in his arm? He said some native attacked him."

Buck took his time as he answered: "Which is why our friend, Mark, is dead."

"Mark? The one with all the turkeys at Christmas? He attacked Ryan?" Even Doc didn't think it was credible.

Buck looked down at his coffee and swilled the liquid around the mug. "Must have been an accident, I think." He fixed his eyes on Pete.

The door banged open. "Mr Buck, Mr Buck."

Mr Pelowski enjoyed making an entrance and he was waving Buck's new boots in the air. His scarves (he never wore less than one, even in July) waving around like an extra pair of arms. "Come. See. Your tools, and I hope you don't mind if I get from Mrs Tom used to be called Miss Mary. I use them to craft you new boots to match with new leg. So, you sit there where I can see – there's not enough light in the store – and we will see what we will see."

He knelt in front of the young man. Both his knees cracked, making the Doc wonder if he was getting enough to eat, or was it just age. At any rate, the sound echoed against one of the wood burners now that it wasn't currently in use.

"Haul up trouser leg, then Mr Buck." With a bit of fussing and clicking of his tongue, Mr Pelowski nodded, used the table as a standing brace and knees clicking again, he told Buck his leg would make Captain Ahab proud. He fussed so much he lost one of his scarves onto the floor but after removing Buck's normal rawhide boot, replacing it with astoundingly, a matching red leather boot that laced up on the inside and then using a looser version of the same to place securely around the prosthesis, Buck matched, up to the knees.

"Good thing Raven didn't take above your knee Mr Buck." Mr Pelowski patted his work very gently. "You most likely better smart than Ahab, anyway. Least you don't chase after revenge." Buck's awareness of Pelowski's true calling was made manifest to him in that moment and the old man knew to say nothing.

"Who's Captain Ahab?" Poppy asked. "Unless that thigh bit gets drawn tight the whole thing'll start to chafe, Buck." She moved toward the silver filigree. "See? This isn't attached all the way around. Means a cord should be woven through it so you can tie it to yourself, Buck." Poppy motioned to one of the girls.

"Take my old corset, rip out the stays and bring me the cords please." She turned to face Pete: "Who's Captain Ahab?"

"Wasn't he the guy in the book about the whale?" Pete asked Mr Pelowski who nodded.

"Didn't know he was legless." she finally sat down.

"Ahab lost his leg to the whale. He spent the rest of his life getting even. Great for the author, lousy for the whale, waste of time for the man. Innit that right Buck?

You got better things to be gettin' on with." Pete sounded fierce.

"Well, whatever happens, you to be careful my laddie." She leaned forward to him. "I need you, don't forget you promised to be here for the birth, and I want my Joss here as well. I want who I love all around me. I'll feel safer."

"I'll tell Joss that very thing if he gives me any trouble. It'll make him run back here faster than a cat with its tail on fire." He covered her hand with his and both were aware of a slight shock. Neither of them mentioned it.

Polly's girl returned with two white cords. Poppy thought for just a minute and then leaned forward to weave them in and out one on the left, the other on the right. Then she drew them together and tied them. "That comfortable?" Buck stood to test it. Applause was heard. "Take a bow then Poppy. You're a damn genius."

"Watch your language, Mr Ross." She did blush with pleasure, though.

Later, and after meal of stew and potatoes Buck leant on Doc's arm to get to the store. Mary was finished the suit. He tried it on, she nipped and tucked again, the men sniggered as Buck swaggered in his first ever grown up suit, grey with a black houndstooth he was told. It was itchy, he told them. Get used to it, you're a man now, they rejoined. Mary got madder and madder. Eventually, Ian presented him with his first ever bowler hat. He removed it from a tall proper box and brushed the fabric in the same direction with his practiced swirling wrist and hand.

"You need a haircut," Mary said.

"No. I remember what happened to a man who let a woman cut his hair. The one in the Bible. I'm going to tie it back with a bit of leather, but I'll cut if I want to, not when I'm told." He did exactly that, placed the hat on his head, stood in front of the long mirror and watched tears form in his eyes. "This isn't me. It's Joss, but it's not me. I will get him and remind him." The MacLaren handed him a polished pipe with a matching bag of tobacco. Pete gave him a silver box to hold some store bought matches or even some loose change. "I've always found it better than cold money lying in your pockets."

"I'm sorry you don't like it, Buck."

"No, Mary, it's not that I don't like it, it's just that I'm not used to anything but leather and rawhide. I am grateful that you did such a fine job – especially the buttons."

She had the grace to blush at that comment and wondered if he knew where they had come from.

"Wear it back to the saloon, then. I dare you."

"I will wear the suit you made me to face the whole Confederate Army, so what makes you think I wouldn't wear it to see Poppy and the girls." With that, and remembering to duck through the door, he swung his way down the street again with the help of the doc.

Hunter and Raven were returning from their exercise, horses more settled. He ignored their laughter now that he was so obviously a white man. Mr Pelowski was waiting for him. Poppy and the girls, and Reverend Parker along with Ryan were ensconced at the bar. They stood to applaud and cheer. Buck was mortified but Mary, whose husband Tom had just arrived, was proud as a sheep with triplets, so took a large bow for her handiwork. Buck stuck his hand out to the man. He was as rundown looking as ever his uncle had ever been and as his heart went out to him, he was certain sure that his decision not to marry Mary was the wisest move he'd ever made.

Chapter 14

"Pelowski did a grand job on your prosthesis." The MacLaren said as he eyed the young man up and down. "Mary did a grand job on your suit as well." He pulled a bit at Buck's jacket shoulders. "Good thing Ian had a well-fitting shirt in stock. Suits you fine." Buck felt like a cow being judged for its breeding potential as everyone stood around him.

"He needs proper gloves to match so we dug some from our Papa's old chest. They should be big enough." The two ladies from the old laundry marched and slid over the bare street. The Raven's horse, not normally skittery, moved away suddenly, not being used to the sound of a screeching woman. It was thought they were both deaf and had to out screech each other to make their opinions heard. They were tolerated though. Hunter couldn't take his eyes from them. All the women he knew, even Chick in the Field, didn't screech like that.

Poppy came hefting a basket of what was no doubt some cake and biscuits. Pete followed with a much bigger hamper.

"I'm sure there's food in Tennessee, Poppy."

"Well maybe last year, but now the war has taken a real bite, maybe nothing good." She slung her offering on the back floor of the buckboard. It was a fine enough day to release the covering, but since the first port of call was only about six hours away at Fort Leavenworth, the men didn't bother. Doctor Fraser came out with some extra bandages and a tourniquet for inclusion in Buck's medicine bag. The Reverend Parker was told by Shona not to take much time with his blessing. She had tears in her eyes as she allowed The MacLaren to give her a peck on her cheek before he swung aboard the rig. She handed him his best black hat, feather in situ. "Be home safe." She murmured.

Ryan surprised them all. He came gingerly toward the heroes, bearing two items people had chosen to completely forget about. One was Ryan's mother. She struggled, did Aimee, but she got there. With her arrival came the guilt of forgetting all about her. It was always taken for granted that if Ryan needed any help for her he would ask. In Aimee's arms was a long black wool and leather trimmed winter coat.

"Silk won't be needing this anymore, Buck. You should have it. Maybe Joss will recognize it and know it's someone from here wearing it." Aimee's voice was stronger than her body looked to carry it.

"I didn't know you had it."

"No one did. It's a good thing though. Especially today. Will you take it?"

Buck reached for it, immediately sensing it didn't belong to him but he didn't think he should let down Joss's mother, so he took his hat off to her and said he was grateful for the extra heat at this time of year. He thanked her for her special consideration. Ryan continued to support her frail body as she turned to go to the livery.

"Come for coffee, Aimee, if you have the strength," Polly said.

Aimee smiled a bit but shook her head gently and continued her way. The Raven, watching from his horse, held the bridge of his nose in the fingers of his two hands, while he bent his head forward and down to hum a healing prayer. He didn't need to know the ins and outs, he just needed to know help was required so he sent his healing through the air, with the intention of helping the bedraggled Aimee and the situation she was in. Buck slipped the coat on. It moved against his trouser legs, seemed to slide down his arms like a snake shedding out of its old skin and then swept the toes of his feet, just skimming along the earth.

So, there he was then: a young man in a new suit of his own, wearing the coat of the man responsible for murdering his whole family. He'd lost half a leg and was risking more to pull a friend from what was most likely to be the worldly definition of hell. Buck Ross, Mindwalker, healer of body and mind but struggling to come to terms with the spirit of being a Man who Stands in Shadow.

"I didn't know you were as tall as that bastard, Buck." He came back to the present.

"Neither did I, Benjamin MacLaren." Buck swung easily onto the buckboard. Moonfeather watched him. He'd forgotten about her. She never showed displeasure, but she was capable of showing concern. Buck raised his hand in acknowledgement to the people who loved him, as The MacLaren headed out of Validation. The two natives whooped only a little before they turned their backs, the white audience cheered a bit more and the screeching sisters cheered loudest, whether in competition or out of joy, the adventurers didn't know. Buck lifted his palms to the Great Spirit. Hunter and

Raven did the same before they turned their backs to return home.

"Are we really going to Fort Leavenworth first?"

"Clever boy. No. Too far south maybe. We'll see the lie of the land before I make that decision. Whatever happens we must be in St Joseph in two days, and we can actually do it if we just keep going at a sensible pace and the weather stays with us."

"Where'd you get the horses?"

"Ah, there's some stuff a passenger shouldn't ask the driver in case the passenger has to answer a question. I am glad your native friends take such good care of you." He winked. Let's just say they chose a good time to take their three horses for a bit of exercise."

They passed the tired looking chapel. It needed more than a coat of whitewash next spring.

"The less I know, the better, then." Buck drew his collar closer to his chin. He jumped. "I've stuck myself with something." When he drew his hand away there was a blob of blood on his finger, so he gently investigated to see if he'd been bitten by a beast of some kind. The buckboard lurched around until Ben found a pair of frozen tracks in the mud and it could settle into a safer movement.

"Stop doing that, Buck. Whatever it is will be easier to find in the dark when you can shine a light on it. If it's steel, maybe just one of the lady's sewing pins, it'll show itself."

Buck touched his chin again. The bleeding had stopped. It was odd, though – being stung by Silk's old coat. Was that man always going to be around him? He shoved the thought aside while he pulled his hat down to consider a territory he'd never seen before, even with his short time studying with Doc Fraser.

"We're quite some ways away, then."

"Never thought of you as the nervous type, Buck – especially as you've been through so much."

Buck was using both hands to hold on to his place. His head jolted back and forth between the frosted breath he expelled. Ben seemed to sit like a rock.

"Try to relax into the movement, Buck. Don't fight it so hard. Find something solid to focus on or you'll be sick and trust me, you don't want to feel that way on the train."

"You been on one?"

"Yep. Early last year, just before Fort Sumter. Was one of my travels to get to the west."

"You still gonna go?"

"If Shona will come too. No point a man going west without a strong woman to share the dream, Buck. What about you? Even with that duff leg you can go west."

"Most likely, Mr. MacLaren, most likely, but there's a part of me that needs to go to Boston yet – I need to see what I own, my inheritance, I guess."

"Not sure how Boston would take to you until we've sorted this war. I forgot you inherited the burden of a distant land."

"I'm also a first generation American. Maybe it's why I feel called to go further. Perhaps, even to the old country." Buck became aware that his buttocks were skinnier that he thought. "Can we stop for a bit? I need to stretch my leg."

"I never took you for a softie, laddie, but if you're that sore, well alright. The horses have been working harder than either of us." The MacLaren slowed the team in what appeared to be a thin stretch of wet grass

– they could get a drink and he could give them a bit of hay to chew on. It wasn't too cold for them, but neither were young, so were glad of the extra feeding. "You need help to get down?"

"I don't know." Buck stood on his whole leg at first, intending to jump and land on his half one. He thought it through and changed his mind. He held onto the frame and swung himself down. The MacLaren steadied him.

"Good dismount, Buck. Next one will look like you've been wearing that thing all your life."

Buck lifted his pant leg to see if any damage was obvious.

"I didn't know it was red leather," said The MacLaren.

"I don't know where Ian got it, but it's very light wearing and look at the silver filigree at the top and bottom. Poppy figured out the use of it. See, it's the cord from her stays."

"I know there's a foot at the end of it. Does it have toes?"

"Only three wedgie shapes."

"Are they pretty?" A gun clicked behind them. Benjamin straightened with his hands in the air. A resigned moan escaped him.

"They're Union, Benjamin." Buck said as he turned slowly to face them. They were not in uniform of any kind.

"How'd you know that, boy?" The bushy grey beard felt to Buck of a man used to spending time in hiding, but not of one that ever had a true home. A hat of many different types of fur appeared to grow from his head and his long winter coat was obviously patched together from the discovery of many left behind in the bushes and now gathered to create warmth. A leather belt tied the middle. Watery blue eyes peered at Buck.

"Experience tells me that a Grey wouldn't have the decency to give any warning." Buck answered, remembering his night in Raven's camp and thinking that his head had given him no warning so there was no real reason for concern. The MacLaren was staring at him. "Put your hands down Benjamin. These boys need food and we have plenty to share, isn't that right?" The Shadow had just made his first appearance to a white man. The MacLaren would be the first to share that Buck and Shadow were housed in the same body, but thought differently.

Ben let lowered his hands slowly. Only one other was signaled to join the man with the beard. He was a bit younger. Buck opened the smaller basket of food Poppy had made, showing it to the strangers. "Coffee?"

That word alone relaxed all of them. Guns were stashed, blankets thrown over the horses, conversations of family and their whereabouts were discovered.

The men, brothers, were from Topeka, making their way there to finish some business with the rest of their family before taking a steamer up to Cairo to sign on. Their cousin, Bully Carlson, was nearly out of business because the government had stripped him of all his horses. There was a rumor he was so heartbroken by the piddlin' amount of compensation he received, that he was going to fight for the south. Aaron, the younger of the brothers, much skinnier dressed and not nearly as bearded but with the same blue eyes, commented that Bully would make a fair-sized target for any army's guns so perhaps he'd be better just to stay home and admit to being too old, anyway. Buck only asked if they had a cup between them, because the coffee was ready.

"Yeah, the only horses they left him with was the new born colt and his dam," said the older one.

"Army not happy the colt not old enough, though. He's a right fine black, Bully got them in a trade for fresh team. Called the young one Thunder, after it's sire they said."

"Good God. Is that what happened in Topeka." Buck's mug of coffee nearly burned his lip.

"You been to Topeka, then?"

"No, but my late cousin Duncan had a horse called Thunder. We'd always wondered about it."

"Sorry for your loss. Was it the war?"

"No, just bad luck," interrupted Ben. "What's the fastest way to St Joseph that you know about?" He didn't want Buck's troubles to become public knowledge.

"You're going in the right way of things. Just keep on until you find a fork, bear left down river, such as it is, you'll find a passing place at this time of year so go over the first one you get to, have your dinner and set off in the same direction in the morning – should get there in plenty of time for the train."

The MacLaren stood slowly as he cocked the pistol only Buck knew about.

"How did you know where we were going and for that matter, why were you skulking around the trees?" Buck's head still wasn't itchy, but he did have a curiosity.

Neither brother moved one little bit. "You can tell you are country folk: you talk loudly to make sure you can be heard in the next field. We followed you through the trees. Who's Poppy, the woman who made the food, cos let me tell you it was damn fine, and we thank you for sharing it with us. We, MacLaren, would like to continue on our way to Topeka without any fuss, if you would be so kind."

"You're not scratching your head, Buck."

"No reason to, Benjamin."

He stood up carefully.

"We don't know your names."

"Last name is Carlson, obviously. This here is Jem and I'm Henry, like the rifle. Should have told you before we ate your vittles. Sorry."

Jem stood slowly, his hand on his right hip. Ben waved his pistol at the lad.

"Time both of you left, don't you think?"

Buck levered himself into the rig and reached for the rifle Pete left under the seat. He placed it across his knees, taking the lead from Benjamin.

"If it wasn't for this damn war we would have met as strangers in need of each other. Nowadays, we have to take sides and it puts us agin each other. Not Christian."

Henry Carlson didn't look back, he just left, taking his brother with him.

"He's right, you know," said Ben. "Country doesn't work as well as it used to. Doesn't run as smooth." He flicked the reins. The horses were glad to be moving again.

Chapter 15

Buck watched Jem and Henry trudge their way to the south through trees covered in frost but there was a path of sorts, through thicket and bramble that was unnaturally mown down. He wondered what could have caused it. Benjamin MacLaren organized their team, slowly nudging them forward on the suggested route.

"Those boys knew what they spoke of, didn't they," said Ben as he flicked at the reins. "Look, a ford across the river."

Buck drew his breath. "I always thought a river would be a wide, busy thing."

"Oh, my Lord. I forgot you'd never been this close to running water before, well apart from the stream beside the farm. Hell, boy, this is only what they call a tributary of some bigger one somewhere. You wait 'til you see the Tennessee River or even the Cumberland, let alone the mother of them all, the Mississippi."

The horses didn't hesitate to plod through the water. Buck took it as a sign that if the beasts weren't worried, he shouldn't be and besides his head wasn't itchy. Moonfeather stood on the other bank laughing at him. He was glad Ben couldn't see her.

"Once we cross we'll stop proper after we take the turn the brothers told us about. I think we can risk a fire."

Buck said nothing, because he was listening to the water under the frosting of ice. There weren't many birds at this time of year, well not many small ones. Spring would mean the arrival of robins, the tiny red-breasted spirits of courage. Jenny told him they showed up in winter in Scotland, but were nowhere to be seen after the daffodils came out. Maybe they all came here for spring.

"Where is your mind, Buck?"

"Nowhere important, just going for a daydream, not a wander." He grinned at the older man.

The wind was getting up as the sun began to go down, so not willing to be caught in the open as they were now crossing what appeared to be a crop of cotton that had been cut back hard, they cajoled the horses to pick their way through it as safely as they could. There looked to be an old lean-to on the other side, so Ben aimed for it in the hope that it would offer protection for the night.

"We must be well out of Kansas by now." Ben had to raise his voice a bit, just to be heard through the jangling of reins and gusts of wind.

They came to another road once nearer to the lean-to.

"Would you look at that, Buck? It's a serious house."

It stood two floors high, had a row of three windows holding large panes of glass to match each other, top and bottom, a porch in a semicircle and a juicy wooden door that was no longer doing the job of keeping people out, because it hung only on its wide top hinge. They rode closer to shout a hello. No one answered.

"Stay where you are, lad." Ben slid Pete's rifle to him, butt first, as he slid from the rig. He crept toward the red brick house, his own Henry rifle gripped lightly in his right hand. The wind covered any crunching sounds that may have been created by stepping on old leaves or skims of ice covering a puddle. He walked up the steps of the porch and entered the house. A pistol fired from behind him – too close to his head for comfort. Part of the door shattered. He spun to face the noise. Pistols were slow to reload unless done by an expert, and it was likely that an expert would be travelling with a pair. On the other hand, an expert wouldn't have missed. Pistols didn't have a huge range. He saw Buck standing in the rig, the rifle aimed down at a skinny black woman hovering below the porch. If only she knew how unsteady the kid was, but she appeared to be in shock, whether it was because she missed her target, or just because of the noise, MacLaren didn't know or care.

"Put that damned thing down, woman!" Ben was angered as he marched over to her and grabbed the thing from her hand. Buck remained standing. "Relax, boy, I've got her," Ben shouted.

"Yeah, you do, but you haven't got that bunch." He used his rifle to indicate more people sneaking into the open from one end of the building. They were dressed in cotton cloth, some of which was ripped, most of which looked like they'd been tied into. A woman with a babe on her hip, stood in the middle of the path, staring at the invaders. Two men stood holding pitchforks as if on guard.

"Where are the owners of this fine house?" Ben asked, loath to acknowledge he was obviously speaking to slaves and unwilling to refer to them as property. "My friend and I are only travelling through and would

like their permission to visit with them for one night."
He removed his hat as he put the pistol in his belt and
placed his rifle back in the buckboard. Buck had the
sense to lower his gun as The MacLaren approached the
group. "Have they done a runner, then, your masters?"
Buck got down slowly to soothe the horses. He hadn't
seen the vein in Bens' neck throb like that in many a
long time – as a matter of fact not since Silk held a knife
to Joss's throat. The throb meant as much to Ben as an
itch did to Buck except with Ben it was a sign of anger.

"Have you been abandoned to yourselves, then?"
He looked at the young woman who knew how to fire a
pistol.

Quietly she said: "They left after church last Sunday,
Masa. They gone North."

"So, over a week then?"

"Yes, Massa."

The babe began to whimper, the girl holding it
handed it to the woman who'd tried to assassinate Ben.
Much shushing and patting of the child's back went on.

"You got milk for that child, Mother?"

The woman shook her head slightly.

"Buck, get down. We're going to the kitchen of this
place, we're going to stoke the fire and we're going to
have a feast. I'll bet there's some good things in the
pantry that these folks have been afraid to touch."

The young woman led the way mumbling about how
unhappy the master would be, strangers coming into his
home, even if they were the right color.

"He wouldn't be happy, Sir," One of the men said.

"No. He probably wouldn't, but he wouldn't like me
to shoot him dead either if he bothered me while I was
eating. Come with me, you all look like you could do

with a feed. Buck and I will take full blame if the son-of-a-bitch has the guts to call me out. Meanwhile we'll all have full bellies and a good warm night of sleep." He returned first to the rear of the buckboard to grab hold of one of Poppy's hampers before the woman who shot at him led them to a small kitchen in the rear of the house. One thing he was sure about was these black people would generally do what was asked of them and sure enough, they followed his lead. Buck worked silently with one of the younger men to sort the horses, taking them to a clean, empty stable behind the main building. There was however, hay and straw bales. The young man fetched water for them as Buck sorted the feed. Buck said they should go back to the house.

The young black man said, "Yes, Sir."

The words made Buck's blood run cold. "My name is Buck Ross. What's yours?"

"They call me Boozle."

"Howdy, Boozle."

They walked side by side into the kitchen, Buck wondered where the name came from.

"Look, Mother. Buttermilk. Would that do for babe?" Ben could sound right motherly, Buck thought as he watched the woman grasp at the bottle. She wasn't all that sure, but she wasn't going to turn it down, either. The MacLaren spread the goods on the sturdy kitchen table.

"Good, now, do I go through here for the dining room?" He slid open what looked to be cherry wood doors and found, a large kitchen containing a massive black cooker and oven, rows of pots all shining to look never to be used, skewers and ladles and a floor of highly polished stone, probably a dark grey granite.

A multicolored rug was placed at the foot of a rocking chair. He laughed so hard, his nose began to run. He used his massive hanky – the one with his initials embroidered in it by Shona and so kept safe inside his breast pocket. Another girl followed him and wiped up after his feet as he walked. He wondered where she'd come from. She was nearly toothless but only about fourteen or fifteen maybe. She did have hard brown eyes though. He looked at her. There was no footstep present. "Thank you, lass, but there's no need. Please, we'll concern ourselves about mess after we've got food in us."

Eventually, he moved on and found through the next set of doors, the dining room with a table large enough to seat ten or twelve. The good china dishes were well displayed in a cherry wood case, the most delicate tea cups and saucers hidden behind glass. The fireplace was clean, but, unlaid. Soot formed a light layer on the hearth.

"Gentlemen, if we leave the ladies to see what they can find to feed all of us, surely we can build a decent fire and set a table. Tonight, we will eat as best as those in the White House and enjoy it that much better because we know the toil is honest as is the food all to be eaten by a free people."

"Nice speech, if it were true." A young man had his arms crossed, glaring. "Why did you laugh at the big kitchen?"

"Because it is so stupid to have one room for one purpose and another for show– it's just a waste of space, when it comes down to it. Got any kindling for the fire?"

The young man pulled a large bit of paper from his breeches and handed it to Ben most likely presuming he had a flint of some type. The paper still felt warm but the hole in his clothes it was protecting, must have prickled with the effect of the chill air. Ben opened the obvious letter.

"You can't read." He looked at the young man, noticing the hard eyes that matched the sharp jaw. He was maybe a half breed he was so light skinned. He also had the longest skinny fingers with one fingernail missing from the middle finger of his right hand. "What's your name? Ezekiel Johnston?"

"How'd you know that?" The brown eyes darted around the room looking for escape.

"I see what's happened here. The Johnston family own you and gave you their last name before they left. Is that right?"

"If you say so, Sir."

Ben took the single step he needed to put his hand on Ezekiel's shoulder. "This bit of paper frees you from your bondage. You are no longer indebted to them and no longer their property. Now you can decide your own life, and may the good Lord keep you safe. Did anyone else get one of these?" Ben began to fold it again, the red seal with ribbon attached hanging at the bottom of the document. He returned it.

"All of us, Sir."

"How kind. None of you read, though." Benjamin was disgusted by the callousness of the Johnston's behavior.

"No, sir. We just hanging on to them in case the Masa wants them back."

"My name is Benjamin MacLaren, Mr Johnston." He extended his hand. It shocked him to realize that he could touch a rougher hand than his own, and how cold it was. "I'll leave it to you to tell the rest of your family. Ask my friend Buck to join me when you see him, will you? He's pretty good with a fire."

Ezekiel wandered to the kitchen door, paper in hand. Just before the door closed he heard the weeping and one man saying it wasn't true and the other asking what they should do, where would they go? Ezekiel gave Buck Ben's message, so limping he joined his friend near the fireplace. Ben was managing to get a light with one of the paper flowers that was left behind. There was a stuffed blue jay in a dusty glass covered jar – very fashionable, he assumed – so tossing it into the fire along with the rest of the contents he managed to get a welcoming flame going. It was getting appreciably darker outside.

That night felt as near to a Thanksgiving as people could get. Poppy had provided two loaves of bread the likes of which had never been seen before by some and certainly never tasted. One was a yellowish color, braided, and the other just plain, but large. Butter, the pistol shooter (now truly embarrassed) had churned but never been allowed to taste, sent that lady, now called Simone Johnston, into what can only be called a passion of ecstasy when she licked in from the bread. The girl, name of Jezebel, held tears in her eyes as she began to see and take in the reality of the situation. No one was going to stop her eating this food. No one could prevent her from staring at beauty. She gently touched the linen cloths and silver forks and knives. Then, little Jezzie, as her friends called her, poured gravy on her chicken and potatoes. Two guinea fowls had been hanging in the small pantry. They were now stripped to the bone, each party guest receiving a fair share. The carcasses would no doubt be used to create a soup of peas and beans with maybe a bit of bacon for flavor. The good china held carrots and corn, potatoes and beets and the bowls were circulated as quickly as possible.

In the center of the table, a large fruit cake, purloined from the missus' cupboard under the stair, where it had been hidden from the staff who'd made it, was waiting to be fired because the MacLaren, who knew about these things, had poured a bottle of brandy over it. The celebration of the cake would end the feast.

Ben held the babe – a girl called Sunny, by her mother and Mary by her owners – in his lap to give her mother a rest after feeding. He was truly in his element. Buck watched the scene.

"Not one word when you get home. Understand, kid?" Buck nodded but couldn't help the grin that matched his feelings. The MacLaren wanted to be a grandpa. My, what would Shona say to that.

The fire started to die as did the conversation – comfortably, sleepily. Simone fell asleep at the table. It turned out the man who had been glaring at Ben and confronted him with crossed arms, and now called Ezekiel Johnston, had jumped the broom together with her. He lifted her to take her outside to the lean to, where they'd been bunking down since before their owners left. Buck asked them why, on tonight of all nights and knowing they were safe to do so, he didn't take his lady upstairs to one of the proper rooms. This started a rush. Boozle raced for the room above the dining room. He couldn't believe he was climbing the stairs and gave a rendition of Climbing Jacob's Ladder. Jezzie crept up to the maid's room. The other rooms were just too big for her.

"I hope he can dance better than he can sing," Ben said to Buck.

"You didn't light the cake."

"Better if the brandy has a chance to soak in, anyway."

Simone and Ezekiel took Sunny, their daughter into a room opposite the one Boozle chose.

Buck and Ben adjourned to the magnificent dark wood study they had found earlier. Well, Ben found it. He'd laid a low fire and covered it with ashes to keep it in. They fell asleep in a glorious soft leather chair each.

A crunch from outside awoke them as the sun rose. Feet were heard scurrying upstairs. In the long, drive was a herd of cattle. They were being driven by Union Soldiers who didn't bother to look up to the house after they realized, probably there was no one living in a place with a swinging door. Inside the house, which oddly, was called Serenity, every single occupant stayed exactly where they were until the herd passed about a half hour later.

The group gathered back in the big kitchen.

"All of you can come with us if that's what you think you want to do. We are going north after all and you'll be in same company."

Ezekiel and his tiny family decided to go south to the next fields to see if her sister still lived. The others decided to make for the troops that just passed – they'd heard they could sign up to fight. Buck stuck his hand out to each of them before he was boosted up to his seat by Ezekiel.

"That was like flying. Thanks. May all of you fly free as well."

Ben flicked at the reins. The two parties split.

"It seems every time we meet someone we lose them."

"Just say a prayer for that lot, Buck. We did the right thing by them."

"Poppy would be pleased," said Buck. "How much longer till we get to St Joseph, then?"

"Flat land now, according to Hugh, remember? We'll be there for lunch I think."

"Didn't anyone at the house know?"

Ben looked at him. "They never left the plantation except to get there by cart. They didn't know where they were, let alone where they were going. They only know, really, that north is better than south. Mostly, that's just a prayer for them. Hope they remember that cake though."

Chapter 16

The men kept their thoughts to themselves in the morning light, feeling as if a spoken word would be an intrusion into the peace God granted them, so when the long, straight road arrived in front and the forest began to disperse, it was a shock to be back into the real world. It looked like logs were sliced in half and place flat side up to ensure wheels would balance without slipping, even in the hint of ice. It must be the first week of March by now and it was an odd month – one day freezing and the next like spring was turning to summer. Ben enjoyed seeing the adventure beginning to boil in the blood of Buck's veins. His eyes peered into the distance, not noticing the people in front of him.

"Noisy place, a city, isn't it?" Ben stated a fact.

"It doesn't smell good either, but is that the train I have to ride on?"

The giant stack was belching smoke, the engine never being allowed to die, its lungs heaving, and what sounded like its stomach rumbling.

"That's your way to Joss, yes. I'll see where we can park up, so the horses don't get spooked. You slide off here and I'll meet you at the ticket office along a bit. Can you see the sign sticking out?"

"Good thing I'm tall, Ben."

He opened Poppy's carry box, now nearly empty, to retrieve his native medicine bag and old clothes.

Throwing them across his body and over his good shoulder he slid down using the crutch Broken Path created to lean on. He wouldn't be able to use Ben's assistance after this, so he decided to strike out on his independence.

"All I need is my ticket, is that right?"

"That's right, laddie."

They stared at each other.

"You have it, don't you?" Ben asked.

"I got the confirmation of it, yes. Miss Haggerty did it on the wires, so all I have to do is pick up the real one at the office here." He paused.

"Correct. No worries." Ben watched him from above. "Good luck, then Mindwalker, and make sure you don't go for a walk anywhere you shouldn't."

"Thank you MacLaren. Stay safe if you decide to visit Topeka, and when you see that man called Bully, say 'hey'. Look at the wall in his stable. He will have something for you. I will be safe. I will stand still in my own shadow for so long, people will forget I am there. It will be as if I was never there in the first place."

Ben juddered: "I wish you wouldn't do that. I hate when your voice changes and you make predictions I know will come true. Whatever happens, I will look for you. Scuttlebutt will tell me more than the electric wires."

"We'll see everyone soon," Buck chose to ignore the comment and lifted his hand in farewell as he limped toward the ticket office.

He was aware of being stared at and that was fine because it meant no one would speak to him. Once he got past the small crowd of gawkers along the platform (a sign said that was what he was walking on – East

Platform) and was efficiently served by a man very like Ian, he asked if he could board.

"Dat's vot ye pid te de, de eet."

Buck just smiled at the accent and said: "Danke", as he re-joined the steadily building mob of travelers. What a good thing he'd live in Validation for so long. Many languages passed through on the way west. Some of the words stuck with him.

Back on the platform he watched the busy at war of army uniforms, shouting, squealing of pigs, neighing of horses, bellowing of cattle, cracking of the occasional whip, shouting of orders, banners, music from more than one band, always in competition with each other, General Excitement followed by Private Poverty in the shape of a pair of unsupervised grubby little, nearly toothless, children sucking on a hard tack biscuit each, with the box perched between them on a munitions case. Why they should be hungry was beyond Buck. This was the wealthy north, on its way to subduing the poverty-stricken rebels, after all.

He found his way along the two carriages allotted for civilians, so swinging his way up the two steel steps he ducked only a little past the gates between them and under the door frame. He always thought the inside of a train looked much like the outside but there were seats that looked as comfortable as those in Poppy's saloon. Maybe the next twelve hours across the state of Missouri wouldn't be too bad. There was one seat he knew would be suitable to allow for movement of his leg, so he headed straight for it, just one step ahead of him. Grateful his stick had a hinge between the underarm rest and the two pronged foot, he folded it and wrapped it within the straps of his bag. He tucked them both out of the way of other people, under his chair.

It's a good thing he was organized because the train's whistle blew and people on the platform hugged each other, wailed at departing backs, held onto their children, threw flowers on the rail, shouted orders, loaded cases further down, moved the band away from the back of the vehicle and loaded horses. He saw Ben looking anxious standing in the buckboard, so he nipped to the steps he'd just come up and waved to him with his hat. Ben removed his MacLaren black hat and bowed his head. Buck spoke to him with his mind and mirrored the gesture. In perfect timing they replaced their headwear. The anxious side of Ben slipped away. His mission was fulfilled, so he sat to turn the team away from the melee.

The bands started playing again just as Buck resumed his seat. Somehow, without noticing, other people were making their way down the aisle toward him, one woman was not dressed for the journey – massive skirts and furs – she would probably take up two seats at least. Buck's head itched a bit. Most folks were quiet, perhaps even apprehensive. The train jolted forward. The steam got up. A man in a square hat and matching uniform with silver badges and buckles blew a sharp whistle and waved a flag. The train jolted again. More crying and waving of special little handkerchiefs happened. The poor man it was directed at was most embarrassed, Buck could tell. Maybe it was his mother and sister. It would be a different thing if it were a sweetheart.

The train jolted and then chugged east. A young woman let out a little scream. Buck relaxed. This was much faster than any horse he'd ever been on. The fields picked up speed as they went past. Dying trees, limp bushes became an instant memory. Cows in a field ran away. A man sat down in the chair opposite him. They were of about an age.

"Howdy."

Now Buck knew why his head was itchy.

"Afternoon."

"You look like a damned native" The man was hiding something – his eyes looked like a cow chewing its cud – vacant.

"My name is Buck Ross. I'm a Kansas man." Buck spoke quietly, forcing the man to lean forward.

"You going to join up?" The man's eyes twinkled now. They reminded Buck of a ferret's before it struck. A familiar odor came from his shiny black jacket that was just big enough to come edge to edge with its buttons. The trousers weren't an exact match, the crease of the knees worn out. The new white shirt appeared incongruous, the collar tips hiding the worn and weak collar of the jacket. Was this man looking for a fight or was he already in one of his own – survival.

"Not much good without two legs." Buck lifted enough trouser leg to show the top of his prosthesis.

"Nasty looking thing, that, right enough."

Something about the comment reminded Buck of his late cousin Duncan. The man was nearly touching Buck's prosthesis. There was a glint in his eye. Was he attracted to the silver or the wound?

"How'd it happen?"

Buck leaned a bit toward him as if wanting to share a special secret.

"Got into a problem with a guy."

The stranger pushed himself back. "Ah. He still got both legs, then." He folded his arms and grinned.

Buck pushed back into his own seat before he shouted over the noise of the engine: "Yeah, but he's also six feet underground." Buck felt his eyes go colder when he thought of Silk, and the stranger touched the rim of his hat before he stood to wander along the aisle, speaking to people, encourage the little lady who appeared terrified of the speed. She cried as he left her for someone else to speak to, but he patted her shoulder first. Buck's head was still itching, but it was getting worse. He decided to dig his other hat out from his medicine bag but putting it on didn't help. He could only wait for developments. Maybe it had something to do with that woman's skirts, after all.

The train jolted and jolted again. The woman with the skirts grabbed the rail in front of her They lifted long enough for Buck to get a glimpse of red and grey silks. She appeared to adjust her bosom. The colors did not match with the blue Union she was wearing on top. His itching stopped. He found the source. The woman was a sympathizer but not dangerous, just stupid. He would keep an eye on her. She was the type that would be picked up by a field worker of some kind or color – probably in a covered coach of some description. He let his imagination run a bit wild. Would her horses be matching? A grey pair, maybe?

The train got back up to speed again, Buck had a nibble of Poppy's chicken and bread and fell asleep with his bag on his lap until the man came back to look at it. Buck calmly reached out to pinch him on the skin between his thumb and his forefinger. The stranger's legs collapsed beneath him and he was so shocked he forgot to breathe for a second.

"I was worried your bag might fall from your knees."

"I wasn't. I wasn't even worried you would manage to steal it from me. I have met you many times, under different names. My late aunt Jenny would call you Satan."

He let go of the finger and pushed him away. The noise of the train and the now failing light of the day made the other passengers believe that Buck had prevented the fall and was helping him up.

"My mother says that the Godly find the Godly and that Satan finds his own."

"It looks like we've found each other."

"Let battle commence, then, Buck Ross."

"Aye, in this life, or the next."

The train blew its whistle and the lights were turned down in the public coaches.

"Yes, Malcolm Andover. Don't keep me bored though. I enjoy amusement."

"How do you know my name?"

"You make a point of telling everyone, and I listen. I listen to most things I feel will be important one day."

Buck pulled his hat down, tucked his stick and bag between him and the coach side and closed his eyes. He felt Malcolm move to sit opposite. He was already bored with the events. One Duncan in a life was one too many, but this creature? It was probably a good thing he'd had experience of one. It would help him to know that Malcolm couldn't be trusted to wipe his own buttocks let alone tell his left from right.

He was surprised he slept all night. It meant he could stretch and perform his ablutions where all the men did from the back carriage. Malcolm was gone for the time being. Perhaps he was in the other car. Buck wasn't concerned. The day was only just cloudy and so not as cold as yesterday. He reached up for a scoop of ice that had been forming all night. It was a much larger piece than he thought it would be. The woman was still upset by the movement of the train and could be heard whimpering still. He held the ice in both his hands and offered it to her.

"You're the man who helped Malcolm last night."

Buck smiled. What a good thing she didn't know why.

"Yep. Have a lick of this before it drips all over you. It will settle your stomach."

She took it in one of those hankies that were profuse these days and sucked the water through the fibers as she looked into Buck's eyes. She was like so many women these days – tucked in all over but the eyes always under full control.

"My name is Lizzie. I already know yours is Buck. Malcolm told me."

"Known him for a while, then?"

"Only about as long as you. He seems a decent sort, not a gentleman, of course – the whiff of mothballs let him down I think."

Buck remembered. Ian used them in the morgue clothes to keep them intact before he could air and sell them on, usually to the prisons as the finish of a man's sentence: a graduation outfit.

"Where are you travelling to after St Louis then, Lizzie?"

"Papa is in the army, so I'll meet with him and then go to my aunt in Boston. What about you?"

"Well, I too have business with the army, but I will have to let them tell me what to do. I'm sorta under orders."

"How exciting."

"It will be if I don't follow them."

Chapter 17

//

Buck took the opportunity to change out of his new suit when the train stopped to take on water. Lizzie flinched when she saw him. Buckskins didn't come into her world very much without giving rise to rough ideas.

"I've only changed my clothes, that's all. The world is going to get wilder, I'm thinking," he tied back his hair and then slid back into his seat which he needed to do to pin his pants leg back before he slipped on his prosthetic.

"No, it doesn't hurt, in case you were wondering."

"Did you really loose it in a fight and is the other man really dead?"

"For a young lady, you ask a great many questions but yes, he'd done me and my family a wrong. He paid for it the way he expected to."

"You condone murder."

"No ma'am, but I think he must have. Ask my parents, my aunt and my uncle." He stamped his leg deep into its home and looked at her. She had green eyes. Nice. Buck liked green eyes. Not thinking, he smiled at her gently, not realizing it would make him look pleased with himself. My, those green eyes could flash.

"Having enough trouble in the country without wanton murders adding to the lists." Lizzie turned her eyes to the now dirty window. The silt and ash from the engine was circulating around the cabin. Most of it was settling on people's feet. There was a light mist of it hanging in the air. At least there was a residue of warmth added to the body odor of those hanging about. It was a good thing the carriage wasn't full this time. The government was making noises about sequestering all the rail tracks for troop movements. That would leave the Confederate States short, but things could still be done at Corinth unless of course the Union blocked it. Buck had been listening to too much gossip, he was sure. Surely the Union wouldn't have to come that far south to stop the war. No, it wasn't possible. Was that what Joss meant in his letter? Was he going to Tennessee? His head started to itch. The train began to slow and chug. A whistle blew and then another, this one from the train itself. Another chug. Buck's head jerked forward and back as did Lizzie's and out of the corner of his eye he saw Malcolm standing, holding on to a luggage rack above him.

"We're here, little lady," he said, leering down at her. She ignored him.

Lizzie was tying her green bonnet under her chin as the train gave one long squeal as it screamed into St Louis, Missouri. She was forced to let go of it to prevent her falling into the seat in front of her. Buck moved to halt her.

"Would you like a ride to the river, Buck?" Her eyes pleaded with him to accept. "My father or one of his staff is coming to pick me up and nanny will have a picnic of some kind."

"I'll gladly take you up on your offer, miss, as long as you have a person there who is able to protect your reputation."

"That's why nanny will be there – to protect yours, Mr. Ross." Malcolm couldn't resist the jibe.

"Don't paint me with your colors, Malcolm Andover." He didn't feel the need to look at the man.

"Yes, thank you. Buck? If nothing else, your company would be appreciated. Can my father and I help find your family, do you think?"

"How did you know that's why I was coming?"

"A man with a bad leg doesn't drag himself all the way from the middle of Kansas just to see a war. No, he'll come for a stray dog, a stray horse or a stray member of his family, so I presume your quest is a human on." She stood up to attempt to dust her dress and fold her parasol. "I wish I could leave this stupid thing behind. Parasols are worse than useless in the winter."

She had an old-fashioned way about her. Buck liked it. He hadn't come across many mannerly ladies in his time. He helped her get down the two steps. If it was possible to see a busier city, Buck didn't want to. Was it true that St Louis was being called the Chicago of the west? Bands were playing, doctors were selling patent medicines from home-built painted stalls; cure all's from the gout to the earache to the skin rash, one bottle sorts all ailments defined by the genius of medical science in this day of miracles, and just for the price of a nickel, "yessiree, just five American cents. One drop in beer or water will cure you by the morning: guaranteed". Buck wondered if it would cure a missing leg and smiled to himself as he moved slowly past the buntings and banners, children and boxes, foodstuffs, dogs snarling for scraps, cats winning the arguments because they could climb, women shrieking at their husbands, casks of wine being rolled and finally Lizzie tweaked at his elbow to shout, just in time for the train to give one last belch of steam, she could see her Papa's rig. She pointed as he read her lips. Malcolm, he noticed, watched them go behind the long low building meant to be in use for railway stores. Lizzie broke into a run. A thin black woman about ten years older threw her arms around her and the two of them danced together like long lost sisters.

"Come meet Nanny, Buck." Her green eyes sparkled. "Papa can't come but Emmett is here and we're under orders to meet Papa on the river."

"Nanny, this is Buck. He's been careful of me on the train. Oh, my. There's that poor woman that cried nearly the whole way here. Looks like she's got a young man to meet her. I hope it's good news. What do you think was making her so tearful, Buck?" Lizzie stopped for breath. "Buck's to come with us Nanny. He's on a search for someone and I'm sure Papa can help."

Her bags were being removed from the train as she spoke. Buck lifted a hand to help the man who was most obviously Emmett who kindly asked if Buck had anything apart from what he was carrying. Buck said he had not. Emmett, a large man, wearing a tired looking Cavalry uniform, reached to lift Lizzie into the wagon. There was something about him that looked heavily burdened. His greying beard and moustaches drooped over a bluish set of full lips. What a good thing it was getting to the end of winter he remarked, as he swished her into place. He also gave Nanny a boost up.

"Emmett is my adopted uncle, Buck. He's got his own business in Illinois."

"You need help, sir?" Emmett's dark brown eyes woke up though – perhaps because her remark made him remember happier times.

"No and I thank you for the offer Lizzie, but my burdens are not yours. I will find my way."

"Don't talk like a native, Buck. Come with us. See if life can be easier for you than it has."

Lizzie's green eyes had a determination in them he hadn't seen since Sand Owl made sure he ate his bowl of soup after more of his leg was removed. Women of all tribes must be the same. Aunt Jenny, Poppy, and Shona could be included. Mary? No, not Mary.

"I'll get in on the other side then. Would you mind me riding shotgun, Emmett?"

Emmett's brown eyes were twinkling. "That ok with you Lizzie?"

"Buck can sit where he likes, Emmett, don't be silly."

So, Buck pushed up on his crutch and swung in ass first.

"Sorry, man. Hadn't noticed." Emmett said.

"No reason you should."

"Bull Run?"

"Nope." Buck laughed. "Just a murderous son of a b..." He remembered the ladies just in time.

"The son of a bitch Mr Ross is referring to, got the bad end of the deal though, didn't he Buck? Six feet under you told that slimy Malcolm creature."

Nanny drew her breath in like a snake before it spat: "You have spent all your life in a soldier's camp, missy, but I thought I'd helped you to understand that gentlemen don't like ladies with mud on their tongues." It was whispered but the air was frosty enough to carry the words to the men in front; neither chose to acknowledge the comment.

"Which Malcolm was it, Buck? The one I saw trying to hide from me behind the railway stores?"

"Malcolm Andover," Buck replied.

"That's what I thought. Just out of Leavenworth last week. Wonder what color he's chose, grey or blue?"

Maybe Buck's instincts about the smell of mothballs and Ian's sale of old suits to the prison service wasn't as far-fetched as he thought.

Emmett flicked the reins. The horses had always been a team and were used to noise, so they moved steadily forward and down a road Buck hadn't noticed. It was a larger version of the one back home except there were more stores, three hotels, two saloons, a couple of brick buildings that looked like they had a government use and on the corner of a street they pulled up to, a bank building that seemed to curve around the corner. People trotted quickly out of the way of the horses, chatter could be heard coming from inside the buildings as people entered or left them.

"Mr Andover will choose the side he thinks will fall for his charm and make him the most illegal money. I wonder how much he'll get for his suit?"

"You're a quick study, Mr Ross."

"Used to have a cousin just like him."

"Good thing it's not full spring yet," said Emmett. "One day soon, all that frozen horse hockey is going to stink out even the Confederates in Arkansas." No one appeared to have made an effort to clear the streets of muck.

"As long as I don't have to smell it I'm happy," Lizzie said.

"Don't you like horses, Lizzie?" Buck was making conversation.

"Don't mind them." She was staring ahead, her mind on other things.

"Your Papa will be glad to see you safe and sound after..."

"... my mother dying," Lizzie finished Nanny's sentence.

"I was in Topeka the night of the fire, Buck. She had been unwell for some time. It was too much for her. She had a stroke." Tears joined her words.

Nanny held her for a bit: "You did the best you could, angel. I know you. You would have done everything you possibly could."

"Many kind souls helped me, Nanny. Many kind souls."

"Sometimes people find the good in themselves when it's needed."

The wagon lurched as it made another turn, this time out of the city of St Louis, Missouri and northeast on a rutted road. Once the wheels found their way, Emmett could speed up.

"You seen the Mississippi River before, Mr Kansas Man?" Emmett's back straightened.

"No, Mr Emmett, I haven't. I've been told she's not only the mother of all rivers, but the lifeblood of the country."

"Well, this much I can tell you, once you go north on a Mississippi steamer and meet the folks in Cairo, Illinois, you can tell people you have lived." He grinned at him. Even the downturn of his facial hair didn't move, though.

"Why Cairo?"

"That's where Papa is. It's a confluence of rivers – the Ohio, the Tennessee and the Cumberland. He's one of General Grant's quartermaster sergeants. Didn't I tell you?" Lizzie showed her pride, as indeed she should.

"No, but I'm glad the spirits made us meet, because that's where my friend Joss went."

"See, a stray dog. I knew you were one of the great protectors. You have an air about you."

Nanny stared at her.

"Tell me about this Joss then. Why are you worried?"

"He left home without permission and he's only fifteen. He wanted to sign up and he did. We've got a letter already."

A silence entered the wagon like a ghost entered a house.

"It's not likely he'll be in Cairo, then," Emmett said.

"No, he was writing from Fort Donelson. He wanted socks, of all things."

Emmett halted the wagon. Nanny and he exchanged looks.

"You have to come with us. Your friend, Joss, is it? He'll be going south as we go north. The fastest way to find him will be by river. The closest one to Donelson is the Tennessee. There are trains, I think," said Nanny.

"True," said Emmett. "The thing is you can't count on who's running them anymore. No, you'll have to come with us to Cairo, take a boat, if you're allowed, along the Ohio River and then catch a scow or something, anything to get down the Tennessee River."

"That's a good idea, that way you can see Fort Henry and find out where the army is most likely to stop marching."

"There's a place called Savannah down there isn't there, Emmett?"

"Yes, Lizzie, just opposite Pittsburg Landing – the place with all the high cliffs. You may be able to get off and check around there, Buck."

He took off his beloved slouch hat to run his hand through his hair, trying not to scratch in front of the ladies.

"That would be very kind. I thank you."

Emmett clicked the horses forward again and the ghost came back to the wagon. This time it was Moonfeather, but only Buck felt her.

Chapter 18

And that's what happened.

Buck rode with Emmett, Nanny and Lizzie, the heartsore Lizzie, all the way to the Mississippi. It wasn't that far considering how far he had come. Lizzie suggested he put on his good suit of clothes again because he was going into civilized country. He would have to look to be a man of substance even if he had none, and perhaps he could do something less ostentatious about his homemade swing bag. She looked at it as if it were alive and going to bite her. That, fortunately for Buck, was the time he decided she was bossy. Not as greedy as Mary, back home, but not willing to accept his inconsistencies, so why should he accept that from her, it was normal to have a slave in Nanny and to be on the Union side in a middle of a war to stop the misuse of other people.

"Plenty northerners have slaves, Buck. The difference is in the way we treat ours."

Buck felt Emmett twitch when she said it. Nanny sat still, facing straight ahead as they moved closer to their destination. It was a bright day, not too cold. Traffic picked up as they got closer to the docks, if that's what you could call them, as Emmett said.

"You wait 'til you see Cairo, lad. There's a sight. Landings, docks, plenty of sailing ships and more than a few Ironclad boats – the pride of the fleet they are.

If we're lucky, the *Tyler* and the *Tigress* will be lurking – *Tigress* being General Grant's ship. A proud steamer, big and powerful." Nanny tutted at that remark.

"I don't know. You men are always fussing about which machine is bigger and better. Bigger guns, faster bullets, balloons that carry a man above, so he can spy out the land. Lord have Mercy on us poor souls who have to keep your dinners warm."

Emmett pulled up his team, asking everyone to stay put while he organized a trip north.

"You'd better take Buck with you," Nanny said.

Buck was keen to go for a look, so he slid down using his crutch for support.

"You'll have to get a proper one from the hospital, Buck," instructed Lizzie.

"This was made for me by a dear friend. I will not part with it for the sake of a good looking one that gives people the impression I was wounded in this war." Buck was at the disadvantage of looking up at her, but he did a double-quick turn to escape the glare he got.

The men wandered through the stacks of goods all crammed together by an invisible quartermaster and suddenly came across an office that had its own history. It was solidly erected, two floors high, red bricked and windows painted white. The door was solid, had brass fittings, hinges and a double heavy lock. Two steps led up to a porch on which men discussed prices and smoked pipes. They all seemed to be high dressed, so it was a good thing Buck had taken Lizzie's advice and put his suit back on.

"This where I get a ship north to Cairo?"

"Well, you can get on here. Your help – he nodded at Nanny – can get in another line."

Buck's head began a gentle itch. He removed his bowler hat and bowed his head. Then he took a step up to extend his right hand. The fool took it and when he opened his eyes he was flat on his back lying at the bottom of the step. Buck observed him to ensure he was conscious and breathing before he ushered Emmett into the office. The man behind the desk was obviously shaken because he had been a witness to someone flying through the air.

Buck smiled at him: "Four to travel to Cairo on the next available steamer, if you please. Is that right, Emmett?"

"Guess so, Buck." He was stunned too.

The man told them the price and once again Buck's head itched: "Is the price higher because you see a country boy?"

"No, that's the regular price."

"No. It isn't, and you damn well know it." Buck glared him down. Emmett folded his arms across his chest.

"What do you think the price is then?"

"Exactly what it says on the board outside, not a penny more. Five dollars a head, two meals extra if needed. Twenty dollars it is, then." Buck passed cash over the counter. The clerk said nothing. He stamped the tickets and told him he'd better hurry along because the steamer was due to leave in the next hour.

When they left the building, Nanny had brought the wagon to the front door. "You had bit trouble, so I thought you could do with some help." Once again, she took her seat behind Emmett.

"The Lord moves in mysterious ways, Mr Buck. If you hadn't been here I'm not sure how we would have

got all the way north – well not in safety anyway,"
Nanny mumbled.

"We're not there yet, girl."

"Where'd you learn to do that, Buck?"

"Combination of teachers, Emmett. Fisticuffs with my
cousin Duncan, pressure points from a native called
White Raven and the best of all, really, a great man called
The MacLaren. He's the one who taught me to duck."

The whole group laughed out loud for the first time
in many days.

Emmett encouraged the team forward through the
drovers and butchers, the loose troops, the hawkers and
the men with cures. One man had set up his camera
machine. He was taking photographs of the ships and
the people looking busy. Every once in a while, a lady
with her maid would come into his view so he would
ask if they would like a photograph of themselves. The
lady would pass a bag or a parasol – both on one
occasion – to her maid and then take it away giggling.
The maid always pretended she wasn't fussed with not
having a photo of her own. Lizzie noticed. Buck noticed
her noticing, as did Nanny.

"Papa can take it to war with him," she said to
Emmett.

"Don't let it take long. We have to stash the team
and the wagon before the ship leaves."

"You boys leave us here and we'll meet you on the
boat then. Can I have two tickets please Mr Buck?"

He handed them to her: "You can pay me when you
get on board."

He knew she was expecting him to take care of the
fare and ordinarily he would have done it, but it hadn't
been talked about and now he only had pennies left.

Emmett helped both down. They ran off after the photographer who appeared to be closing for the day: "That'll be something to do with the light probably," Buck said.

Later, Lizzie was seen to be escorted most gallantly by a man in a naval uniform.

"I'm not sure her Papa would like the look of that," Nanny looked glad to be taking up the rear because perhaps it gave her time to assess the gangway lurching a bit in the wash of the other steamers. On the way up the gangway she nervously responded to each shift of the ship, clutching onto the railings.

Buck watched Lizzie test the deck of the ship with her toes before she committed herself to stand on it. She leaned heavily on the arm of the sailor. Oh my, he thought, clever girl but I better rescue you from yourself because I don't think you really know what you may be getting yourself in to.

"Lizzie, darling. You got here. Well done," Buck held his hands out.

"This is Ensign Leveler. My friend, Buck. We've just met."

"Yes, I gathered that." Buck extended his hand but this time, because his head wasn't itching he just shook the one presented to him by the sailor.

"No, Buck. I meant you and I have just met."

She turned to the Ensign, "Buck was on the train with me."

"That's good to know I can leave you in safe hands miss."

Nanny joined them, ever so slightly out of breath: "Is this your personal maid, miss? If not, she'll have to go to steerage below like all the others."

"This is my Nanny. She's always with me," Lizzie was horrified that she may be parted from her.

The steamer's whistle blew and orders to cast off were heard. The ship moved, and the rain started – just a spit but the ladies hurried for the salon inside. Buck took the parasol and luggage.

"I'm going to steerage to help Emmett make sure the horses are all right. You two stay together. I'll come back later to make sure you're alright."

"You can't go to steerage, Buck," Nanny exclaimed, "you're white and you'll just get in trouble. Emmett's wearing the right uniform."

"Hadn't thought of that, I told Emmett I'd be back once I'd found you."

"I'll go. You keep an eye on missy, here."

Buck sat in the chair Nanny left, and his head itched a bit. This wasn't right.

"Do you want the money, Buck?"

"I'll need some of it back, yes. I only have pennies left after paying the twenty dollars."

"You paid twenty dollars?" Lizzie leaned forward to whisper the question.

"War prices."

"I can give you ten right now but we'll all need some food money, won't we?"

"That's good of you but not right now in public. These people are all desperate themselves or they wouldn't be here and paying various sums. Wait until we can get back outside and be more private."

They relaxed into their leather armchairs. Tobacco smoke filtered through from the smoking and bar end, tea and coffee were served. Lizzie stopped the girl and asked for some. It was two dollars fifty for coffee and a ham sandwich with mustard. She said she would have two.

"War prices seem to come in even numbers; no such thing as ten cents anymore," she said.

"Why did you order two?"

"I was hoping all of us could share."

"You are a conundrum, Lizzie. One minute you try to tell me I don't look swank enough with my homemade but honorable crutch and the next you show concern for your fellow man."

"I always wondered what a conundrum was. I like it – being one, I mean."

Chapter 19

It stopped raining, so Buck took the opportunity to escape from the mostly female company of the salon. Women can in general, talk about anything to anyone. A woman would make a great spy. She was born with the natural ability to glean information from anyone, but perhaps she would need to be a little trained in discretion. The war was still in the exciting stage, so people weren't rightly sure how to behave. The southern women on board were more brightly dressed and had more float and flounce in their demeanor than the more Presbyterian northern ladies. Buck heard a voice in his head. He couldn't see Moonfeather, but it was a feminine voice with feminine attitudes. The voice told him to be careful but to look up, so he did, just as an eagle rose in the sky ahead of him. The climb was matched by another. Many witnessed the event as they both disappeared into the pure blue sky, above the clouds now. They plummeted to earth together, linked and squawking, screaming, tearing apart before they dove into the Mississippi River. He remembered the lesson White Raven gave him about eagles flying above the storm.

"It's an omen," Lizzie found him, holding his forearm tight.

"Looks like it, but they'll find each other again, don't you worry," Buck repeated what Moonfeather told him.

"You sound sure."

"They can't live well without each other."

"That's a good way to look at it, Buck," she patted his arm, slipping ten dollars into his sleeve knowing no one would notice because of the stir created by a flurry of geese and maybe even a swan. He put it in his pocket. "Dinner, Mr. Ross? Steak and onion stew is on the menu, followed by some kind of fruit pie."

Buck hadn't realized how hungry he was, "what kind of steak, I wonder?"

"I thought it best not to ask about the main ingredient of each course. I'm going to offer it to the Lord and pray he makes it taste good."

The engine of the ship gathered speed. The river had a smell to it as it was flushed through the paddle wheels. The noise was like a controlled waterfall – soothing. Buck was fascinated to see the wheel turning and would have stayed out longer except for the offer of the first real meal since he'd left Validation. He would like to sit somewhere that wasn't moving, though. The twin smokestacks blew black dust into the air as they released a bellow – so much for the fresh air. Another steamship was rushing toward them, leading what appeared to be a fleet. Buck starred along the deck and behind him: their ship was leading another two of their fleet. Lights were visible in the cabins of the whole flotilla, engines were throbbing, wash was heard slapping against the shoreline, throngs of excited people lined the edges, watching what they must have presumed were warships because a collective moan was heard when it became obvious the fleet was an accident of formation and full of civilians pretending nothing untoward was happening in the world.

That night he slept in a blanket Lizzie found, and curled up against one of the soft chairs. Tomorrow, late afternoon, they would arrive in Cairo. Lizzie would be reunited with her Papa. He could be on his way. She had been kind to him and he was grateful, but he wasn't old enough to give her what she so obviously wanted – marriage. No, time to go.

The next day, cards were played, more smoking and drinking occurred, more ships were seen, one ironclad which created a stir as it steamed past them, south. Ships horns blew at each other in salute. Passengers oo'd and ah'd, trying to see the name of it on the hull. War could be so exciting when it came down to it.

By late afternoon Buck had seen enough of the great Mississippi to know he wasn't keen to see much more of it. It was getting choppy now, perhaps from the other vessels or maybe from a cold wind that seemed to be building up. Lizzie was also tired. She was remaining mannerly, but only just. The only way to properly cope with a trip like this would be to have your own cabin, she informed him. Buck thought of the cost. If the fare was $5 each on the mezzanine level, what would the upper decks be? Either way, he thought, there would still be the Mississippi to contend with, beautiful and wide as she was, a river can turn into a wild beast if there was enough wind and rain, Emmett had told him so.

There was a blast of the horn. The ship passed under a heavy looking bridge, rusty looking woven iron. The engines screamed as the wheel reversed and then the Captain let his ship float into a dock area where a tug came out to nudge it into place. Buck ignored Lizzie plucking at his sleeve.

"Look, there's Papa. I'm here," she shouted, and she jumped up and down. A man in a Second Lieutenants uniform waved frantically at her.

"I thought he was a Sergeant."

"He was when we last saw him. Mother would be so proud."

It was the first time she mentioned her mother.

The ship docked. Immediately the gangways folded out and the gates were opened to discharge the passengers, Buck noticed Emmett and the team meet with Papa. Nanny arrived from somewhere. Lizzie hadn't noticed she'd been missing all night and now, when she got off on the same gangway as Lizzie, no one made an overt fuss although he was sure he heard a tut or two from some of the older worthies. They were, after all in the north.

Lizzie ran into Papa's arms. Buck stayed on board. Moonfeather said she'd forget him. Moonfeather, it appeared, was right. It was the first time in days he began to relax. He folded himself into the shadows of the passengers who had spent most of their time in the bar area. They seemed to be heavy set men, bulging with self-indulgence. A few were tall like him even if they were ten years older, so he managed to fit in. He knew if he stood still long enough he would vanish so that's what he did, and it worked so well that he saw Lizzie looking at where she left him, not thinking that he would have changed his position even if was only a few steps away.

Moonfeather told him to keep going. He needed to go up the road past the army recruiting center and find the next ship, the one sitting on the Ohio River. He took his enforced time getting there. His bag was plucked at many times, making him stand still while the offending party changed their mind when they realized they'd been caught. Buck used his blue eyes to extraordinary affect at times. He found it amusing. The bands that were playing sounded tired, the bunting around the recruitment center looked lackluster probably due to the melting winter weather, the roads were beginning to soften, the horse dung just beginning to ripen, a pack of dogs scrambled for scraps of meat at the slaughterhouse, Corporals and Sergeants bellowed over the noise of it all, women picked their skirts above their ankles to keep them away from the daily dross as they crossed a street for an errand. Finally, Buck found his way to a dock. He wasn't used to the sight of ships and he wasn't all that sure he wanted to be. How many rivers did this country have? It seemed like every ship the United States of America owned was floating in front of him.

"Here. You. Buck, is it?" Lizzie's father found him. "Where are you off to, do you think?"

"I have to get to Pittsburg Landing, Lizzie told me."

"You're looking for someone, she said."

Buck nodded, observing the newness of the Second Lieutenant's uniform and how uncomfortable it must be around the neck and armpit area. The hat seemed to be loose, though. Glancing down at the man's feet made his heart go out to him. Lizzie's father would never really be an officer: he was still wearing the boots he enlisted in.

"Yes, Sir. His name is Joss and he's only fifteen and needed at home."

"Chances are he knows his own mind, son."

"Chances are you're right, but I made a promise I would try to find him and that's what I'm doing."

They were being shoved and pushed as the conversation was going on and Buck was shoved so hard he fell toward the officer.

"I'll organize a seat on one of these steamships for you. Come into the office for just a minute."

"I'll be fine, Sir. You see to your Lizzie."

"Yes, well, Lizzie is catching up with all her friends and one of them was engaged to be married so there's nothing but women's talk going on. Besides, I need to thank you for taking care of her and to pay you the $5 she still owes you." He handed Buck coin. "Lizzie can be careful with money, if you know what I mean."

"That's good of you, Sir. I'll need it to pay my fare south."

"You'll also need a piece of paper that'll let you get on a ship south at the Tennessee River. I can do that for you, but I'll need all the seals and signs, so you better come with me before it's too late and you'll have to stay here in this God-forsaken town for a night or two. The fleet looks organized today but..."

They squeezed past the crowd, down one street with all the people heading toward them and then up another where there was hardly a soul. In a brick building with a wood burning fire in the middle, and a desk and chairs placed as required with no idea of proper decorum, sat Lieutenant Johnson. He was removing his sword from its scabbard.

"You got another recruit there, Bob?"

"Not unless we're taking one-legged men." Bob, Lizzie's father, indicated a chair to Buck. It was near the fire, so he was grateful but sliding into it, said nothing, sensing there was tension between the two men.

"Prove it."

"Prove what?" Bob asked the Lieutenant.

The Lieutenant rose from his seat behind the desk, grasped his sword, pointed the tip to Buck's leg and repeated his demand.

Buck stood: "I am not in this army. I do not owe you a response to your order. I will show you because you are drunk, and I know you are not worth the argument." He pulled up his pant leg and unclipped his prosthesis, causing it to thud onto the floor. Unfortunately, the sock he normally placed over the stump of his leg fell off with it, so the scars were obvious to everyone. The Lieutenant puked on the floor beside his desk.

"I'm giving a pass to this young man, just so you know. You can countersign." Bob, Lizzie's Papa, shoved the paper in front of the flustered officer who did what he was ordered to.

"Get organized please. I haven't filled in your whole name yet."

Buck sat in the chair, placed his sock back on and straightened out the lining of his false leg before slipping it on and then stamping into it. The wood in the fire jumped with the floor being tested in such a manner, sending sparks up the flue and filling the air with the sound of crackles and the smell of fresh smoke. He told Bob his full name and that is how Buck Ross made it to the confluence of the Ohio and Tennessee River, was nearly saluted by a young private who let him on board a ship called the *Tyconn*, simply because he thought he was wounded and this was carrying medical supplies.

There must be something in the family line of Johnston's. It was a Johnston that had thrown up the first time he saw it. This was a proper soldier, though.

Buck expected more of him. A proper suit was paying off. He found a place to sit on the upper deck – out of the way and with a great view of the reddening sky as the sun began to set.

Chapter 20

///////////////////////////////

THIS IS JOSS O'GRADY, JUST SCRIBBLING WHEN I CAN.

I held on to the handle bar of the door frame as the train jolted into the platform because I'd learned to stick up for myself at stations. It had been a long way from Fort Leavenworth to here. I'd walked a lot, accepted a couple of rides and finally, accomplished my goal when I stepped onto this train. Most of the time I had trouble standing up due to the lurching and tossing of this black beast. Being skinny can make a body sore. Used to be I wanted to ride one of these.

Now I was in the busy town of Cairo, Illinois, the great junction for the congregation of the northern Union Army and Navy as it turned out. We crossed over the iron bridge across the Mississippi (Edwin thinks) but I never wanted to see another bridge like this, ever – I could see myself dropping down into the icy water not really understanding how the train could ride safely on the two ribbons of steel. Missouri turned out to be a real big state and I'd been a passenger long enough to know that the ride was never smooth, so it was always a good idea to get a hold of something if you were caught on your feet. On this January dawn, now the trip was ended, all aboard were keen as hungry dogs to make their mark on the war.

I'd never heard or seen anything like this: the noise, the smell, the colors of red, white and blue trying to fly in a non-committed whirling wind, trying to wake up, as it were. The bands were warming up and beginning to play the Star Spangled Banner and other ditties, the steam engine blew its last belching note and the wheels screeched on the ice-cold tracks.

People stink, mostly. People stink worse than a horse on a summer day, especially if they're corralled together like this. Leastways, all horses know they smell and feel a whole lot better if they have a scrape down. Take that lady over there. It's so hot in here she looks like her face is going to peel off, so she puts on more of the powdery plaster stuff and then dabs a mite at her neck, pretending she's not having a good scratch.

The train stopped finally. I jumped down first, Edwin right behind me. Now, I thought I'd got used to all the city noise but oh my Lord, it was all going on and the sun wasn't fully up. I could see breaths of cold air coming from all over the mouths of men, horses, dogs and hogs. The mud at least was hard now, but wagons were caught in ruts and the swearing that was heard would have sent Miss Diamond back home in the Black Diamond saloon into one of her red fits.

She'd say, close up with one finger wagging and the other holding a rolled-up tea towel: "You so drunk you swear, you too drunk to care. Out and home to your Mama or whatever woman'll put up with you 'cos I damn well won't." No one dared to tell Poppy Diamond that damn was a swear word.

I met Edwin while stopped in Columbia, Missouri. He was doing what I was doing: escaping the boredom and going to enlist in God's Army. We only looked each other up and down and found each other to be pleasing: skinny, slim, fair and hungry. I had the height of him, though; just a bit. We were always hungry. We knew we would be fed in the army because we'd heard tales of great steaks and corn pone. One thing the army was good at was feeding the men, we'd heard. As men of the midwest I didn't feel the need to talk more than was necessary and neither did he, so we fell into comfortable way of things. I had pilfered some of Poppy's cake for the journey and Edwin had stashed cold meat. We ate once a day on the five-day trip to Illinois.

"How old are you?" asked Edwin.

"Old enough." I stared out the window because I thought I could see water, lots and lots of moving water. I wondered where it came from and where it was going. Did it care?

"You ain't no more than sixteen, I reckon."

"Like I said, old enough."

"You ever seen a dead man?"

"Yeah. You ever seen a river?" I didn't feel like talking about how Mr Silk died.

"Old enough to be put to good use then." Edwin nudged me in the ribs. "I think that's the Mississippi River."

So, we left the train behind, forcing through the crush of people, the slurry on the roads, the loose dogs and skitter-arsed horses. The air clogged up the nose somewhat. The windows of the lines of stores on the byways still had ice patterns in their corners that looked like they'd been forming and reforming for days.

We pretended we were warm as we scouted for a recruiting office. There were many of them, we'd overheard on the train. It was better to sign up to a new regiment rather than one with experience. Ohio was a good one to aspire to. Bit of both, it had been whispered, until the man who said it became aware of our eavesdropping. He'd snorted at us and turned his back but now we'd overheard. we went looking for the Ohio bunch. In the event, the Illinois regiment recruiting office enticed us with loud speeches about courage and damn Rebs, but most especially the hot bowls of free soup. All we had to do was stand still and wait 'til all the speechifying was over. It didn't quite work that way, of course.

We got into the line for the meal and were told to go back to our momma. Edwin was tougher than he looked. He said, flat out, that if he was tough enough to stand still in all this cold, listening to some old speeches he'd heard a hundred times before, he'd earned his meal and besides he needed to sign up.

"You need to sign up, kid? You need to? You don't want to, you need to." The man Edwin was squaring up to had four stripes on his blue army jacket, two above and two below: the shape of the Mystic gypsy eye, come to think of it.

"Yes, Sir. I need to." My friend nearly broke his neck staring up at the man.

"First, get your ranks right. I am no flibbity officer. I am a Sergeant Major, so you will do what I say and when I say it."

"This is my buddy, Joss O'Grady. I'm Edwin Patience. We both need to sign up, Sergeant Major."

The older man, dark trimmed hair but bushy matching eyebrows framing a pair of large brown eyes meant to intimidate, but wasn't successful. Bluster and bullying behavior doesn't stretch past what the boys could see behind him inside the recruiting office: a glowing wood fire and a table laden with eggs and bacon with uniformed men sitting around it, some even enjoying a smoke, but not one an obvious officer.

"Before you can have any of that you have to earn it." The duty Sergeant took up the door space as he closed it in front of them.

"How old are you, boy?"

Joss told him he didn't know for sure: "Probably eighteen, maybe more."

"You got no papers, then?" It was normal these days – too many diseases, too many orphans.

"No. Sergeant." I tried to straighten up but once I'd seen the food my stomach turned into a washing mangle out to deafen those nearest.

"Where'd you come from?"

"Kansas."

"Well, a true-blue state anyways now that you've made your mind up. Lots of volunteers from there." The Sergeant looked him up and down. "You ain't even grown any peach fuzz, lad and you're too small to tote a musket, let alone one of them rifles."

I shifted back and forth in the frosted mud, pretending to adjust the weight of my pack. It was pretty near empty now. I noticed the man's blue camp hat was so tight on his head it carved a second set of eyebrows above the overgrown ones and the jacket was on him so neat I was reminded of Poppy's Christmas turkey and even in this cold, steam coming from his mouth, he was sweating like he'd just been basted.

"Where do we sign up?" Edwin's voice was becoming high-pitched in the cold.

He stamped his feet in the cold but to the Sarge it sounded like impatience.

"You. How old?"

"*Sixteen, nearly seventeen. Birthday on January twelve of this Lord's Year, 1862.*" Edwin sure had spunk about him.

"*So, seventeen tomorrow.*"

"*Train must have made me lose track of time. Must be tomorrow if you say so.*"

"*Come with me, then. I'll sign you up if you don't mind doing real Army stuff until the war ends.*"

He opened the door to the office to let them in. We couldn't take their eyes off the food.

"*Sit.*"

We sat at the long bench running along the wall of what turned out to be the kitchen. The men already present looked us up and down but said nothing to us.

"*You will do as I say, when I say so. No chatter.*"

Edwin reached for a streak of bacon.

"*No. If you want to join us you must learn rules. Army even got rules for wiping your arse, if either of you can read it in the manuals.*" He stood in front of them.

"*Reach for plate.*"

We did.

"*Reach for one fork each.*"

We did.

"*Now, reach for two rashers of bacon, each.*"

We did.

"*One large spoon of mama's soft scrambled egg each.*" Edwin did.

"*No thank you. I don't like egg.*" I looked up at him as would a schoolboy who hadn't done his arithmetic.

"*You need to join the army, you need to obey the rules. The army is good and kind enough to provide you with eggs, you will be grateful and you will eat.*"

I gave myself a small spoonful. Edwin more than made up for it.

"Eat. You have fifteen army minutes."

"Means you gotta eat in a hurry, boys." A voice filtered to us from the kitchen end.

We ate as fast as we could, not needing encouragement being we were both so damn hungry in the first place.

"Forks down. What a waste. Clean your plates into the pig shed out back, rinse them and return. You have one minute."

That was the fastest quarter hour I've ever known but we didn't argue even though we weren't sworn in yet and could have walked out, but it didn't occur to us, and within that minute we presented ourselves back at the table. Other recruits filed in, looking shocked and bemused by the surroundings, but all looked older and taller.

"With me, gentlemen."

We followed our mentor back outside. Once there was a bit in my belly I didn't feel so ornery toward him.

"Over there you will find the doctors." He indicated a solid looking large structure that may have once been a hotel. "Take these slips to him and you will get a full medical, including a check of your teeth. If you pass, and I'm sure you will, come back here, I'll get the Captain to give you a once over and then we'll swear you in and give you a job suitable to your nearly seventeen and probably old enough. Can either of you bang a drum?"

I couldn't but then I learned the second unwritten rule of the army: never volunteer.

"I'm pretty good with a Jew's harp, though, Sergeant Major."

"*Excellent, son. If you can blow on something you can blow on a fife.*"

"*I'm real good with horses. If you think I'm too young to shoot a musket, I could clean stables.*"

The Sergeant Major looked straight at me. I hoped he was impressed.

"*Keen little fella, gotta say that for ya. You got a strong suit, Ed?*"

"*I know my letters and numbers. I can run like the wind, if I get enough to eat, that is.*"

"*Army don't like its recruits with a smart mouth son. Let that be the last I hear of it. Now, be gone but if you're away for more than an hour I'll jump to the conclusion you've buggered off.*"

So, we wandered over the road, avoiding ladies with long dresses, hems covered in frost, kids with snotty noses, men in tall hats and walking quickly as if on important business, slapping our hands like other men on business of some kind and Edwin stopped suddenly in front of me so I nearly knocked him down. He was staring toward the river again.

"*Look,*" *he pointed,* "*what is that?*"

"*Another engine of some kind. I can see smoke coming from one of its chimneys.*"

"*That, young man is one of the pride of the Navy: a ship named the USS Lexington.*" *One of the busy men stopped to speak. He was slim and grey bearded in a uniform of blue and had gold shoulder bars on his long jacket with what looked like an oak leaf on them.* "*When you're old enough, maybe you should join the navy.*"

"*Thank you, Sir but the Army is going to give us a job today and we really need to be doing something.*"

The navy man laughed out loud, "are they going to let you peel potatoes?"

I was mightily offended: "No, Sir. If we pass the medical test, and the Sergeant Major says we will, Edwin is going to be a drummer and I'm going to play the fife." The Navy man then took us seriously and shook each of our hands. "I wish you the grace of God and the very best of luck." He turned his way and we turned ours.

I don't think they really gave a damn about whether we had papers to prove things like age. A man with moustaches out to the end of his sideburns and all a tinted with nicotine stains to match the yellow of his gnarly fingers didn't even look at us when he asked our names. He wrote them down as he saw fit to spell them which is how I turned from O'Grady to plain Grady. He didn't hear the O. When Edwin said his name was Patience, he was renamed into Perfect. Neither of us thought it was worth the remonstration, especially as we were trying to avoid being found by relatives until we'd become heroes and felt they should be notified. This corporal (we saw the two stripes) shoved a piece of paper at each of us and pointed down a hall while he shouted, "next" to the man standing in the street.

"You ever been in a building this massive, Edwin?" I whispered.

"I think it's a Post Office because I can see all the parcels and counters."

"Hurry up gentlemen. This army waits on nothing, let alone strays." A medium sized and newly shaved man with long dark wavy hair and sad brown eyes, probably just a bit older than Buck, back home, tried to fill a high doorway. We trotted toward him, in step, as it happened. "A couple of naturals, then," said the first lieutenant I'd ever met. "Come in and undress to your underwear. Then file around in order – you can see the numbers and I only hope you can count to six because then I say whether you stay or go." There was a long line of men, none of them looking very comfortable, especially as they came out from the screen at station three.

The room had beds, screens, a cold looking wooden clerk's desk and set of chairs all in steel. It hadn't seen a lick of fresh paint in many months by the look of things.

"Take your clothes with you if you want, but otherwise just leave them in a pile here." He indicated to what had probably been a long parcel counter in its day. I dropped mine. I'd get better ones soon anyway, if someone had a mind to steal them that was just fine. I kept my boots though. I'd seen what the corporals were wearing and I saw the Sergeant Major and the Officer were still wearing civvy shoes so it must be allowed. Edwin didn't drop anything.

"Down to your skinnies, lad."

"Haven't got any, Sir."

"You're telling me you're stark naked under those pants?" The officer whispered closely into Edwin's ear, turning every head in the premises and creating smirks in some quarters and scowls in others. "Go straight to screen three but only in your pants, mind." Some of the smirks became grins.

"I'll lend you mine if I can go first, sir." It was the only thing I could think to say.

"You don't have a spare pair, then?" I felt the Lieutenant's eyes baring down on me as a buzzard would eye up its dinner.

"No."

"No, Sir."

"I'm not in the Army yet, Dr Slocomb, so no, I don't have a spare pair to lend to my friend." I read his name badge, and noticed a steel thing hanging around his neck. I think I remembered Doc Fraser having one at home and listening to Silk's chest with it. More than anything, I surprised myself at my mouthiness. Edwin just took off his coat and jacket but there was no undershirt to be seen as he sat to remove his shoes. He stood as tall as his nearly five and a half feet would let him as he stood at the first station to be weighed and measured. The room began to buzz again and I took his clothes from him while the paperwork began. In that way we followed instructions to the letter. I held his clothes and then he held mine. I got my teeth checked, by a different doctor, pushed into one of the cold steel chairs while I put one knee over the other and then got clobbered with a small mallet to see if my knee reacted, yet again by a different doctor. I still think it's a silly thing to do. If the knee didn't jump then a bit of me would be dead, wouldn't it? The screen was next, and I think I heard Edwin yelp. I did not find this to be a comfort because Edwin was a tough little sprog. He had come all the way here, in the middle of winter wearing no socks or underwear, and if he yelped then it was incumbent on me not to let him down. Whatever was ahead, I would allow myself a yelp. Looking a funny shade of white or green I wasn't sure which, Edwin retrieved his clothes and then left for station four, which looked to be a running and jumping exercise. In station three, Dr Slocomb asked me to drop my drawers and hang on to the frame in front of me. This forced me to *bend a bit. I yelped twice and I still don't know what he was fishing for up my backside. He wore a rubber glove while he did it but I'm not sure it helped. I limped out like I'd seen some of the others do. Edwin was dressed again so I did the same.*

At the running and jumping station we did fine and then we had to have our breathing tested and our heart listened to: the only doctor who explained anything at all was most likely so deaf he wouldn't be able to hear a bad heart. He looked so old that he must have fought in the war of 1812 and maybe even the War of Independence. He had a mouthful of teeth that looked like he'd borrowed them from someone else. If I ever had a granddad, he'd have been just fine because he smiled and cackled his way through the whole day.

At station six, Dr Slocomb was waiting. He passed both of us and moved us toward the clothing section where our Sergeant Major was passing out the uniforms. Edwin and I were partly excited but thanks to screen three, warier than we'd been an hour ago.

"Shirt, trousers, socks, drawers and vest, cap – looks like you're in the 41st Illinois today. Could change, of course, as you're needed, but a proud regiment in good standing, to lend you their name; see you keep it that way. Here's boots to you. Polish them, even if they don't fit. Don't lose anything or break anything because your pay will be deducted as you replace it and all bits are part of the uniform – right down to the buttons. If any bits of your uniform are missing you will be considered out of dress and will be placed on special duty. Good reason to take care of all your gear, trust me." Sergeant was official sounding. "Sorry no room for you at the barracks but there's something doing and I have a

feeling, just a feeling mind, that we'll all be going down river to Memphis very soon so learn what you can lads. Keep your mouths shut and your ears open: best advice I can give you except to say before I swear you in you have to fill out your last will and testament and write a card home about your pay account."

"I can't write home. I don't have one." Edwin looked the Sergeant Major in the eye.

"Invent one, then, laddies because I don't believe you and as for you, Grady there's something you left behind in Kansas so here you are and put on your uniforms first – over there near the door, just in the men's wash area. This used to be a post office and bank."

We opened a heavy door into a room that looked like it belonged in a church or some such. It had high stone with swirls in it ceilings, all white with soft grey, and open cubicles and washbasins with what looked like plugs in a hole and steel taps. We could hear the echoes of the other men, some of whom knew what the equipment was all about and showed how the sinks worked and then and roaring noise of water came from one of the cubicles.

"That's a toilet. They flush away your muck and you never have to worry about it again," Edwin knew about these things apparently. "We had one in the backyard on the other side of the kitchen."

"Sounds like you have a good house."

"Yes, and lots of slaves but no one was ever really pleased about things. My sister got married away in Louisiana just to get away from all the yelling. Do your boots fit?"

"No, but my feet are too small for the rest of me: always have been. Probably why I get along so well with horses – I can't kick their sides all that hard."

"Look," Edwin said. "Have you ever seen yourself in a long mirror?"

I sidled up beside him, trying to keep hold of my pants because they were the only thing that kept up my underwear. The elbows on my jacket were nearly down to my wrists. There were many more of us in the washing come changing room, so we swapped jackets and trousers until we all managed to find more comfortable gear. My cap fit fine. I didn't think I looked like a soldier. I got closer to that mirror because I wanted to be sure that my suspicions of growing a beard were well founded and they were. The red of the Irish was showing on my chin. It was soft but it was there, so I made my mind up to grow it, especially as it was winter and maybe I would be warmer.

Sergeant Major sent that yellow tinged corporal to get us, so we fixed to sit at each corner of a desk, but the front door was blown open forcing us to grab hold of the paper. It had been a while since we'd heard any of the noise from outside and the sun was setting, telling us that we'd been inside for quite a while, which was good and warm but when our corporal ran to close the door he stopped solid. "Oh, Lord, that's General Grant," whispered Dr Slocomb from behind us. "Knowing he's in Command and seeing he's in Command are totally different things boys. Now you've got something wonderful to write home about. You can begin to tell your folks you're ready to be a hero."

I wrote my card to Ryan because I knew he'd share it with everyone. He may even try to take credit for making a man of me. I told him about the General and to say to Buck now that he was doing his healing training, to avoid rubber gloves because they didn't make a blind bit of difference. Then Edwin and I were sworn in and I finally had to salute Dr Slocomb who was at pains to ensure I knew how, especially since the General was in camp. My stomach growled a bit. He gave Edwin and I a chit for some food so all we had to do now was to find out where the cooks were hiding.

"You'll be peeling potatoes there tomorrow boys so make it quick."

We thought he was joking. No one in the army makes jokes about food until after they've eaten it.

"When do we get a rifle, Sir?" I saluted as smartly as any recruit could.

"You, bonny lad, will be given arms and ammunition once you've passed your drill exercises and not one minute before, unless you're required to be fresh cannon fodder." I decided Dr Slocomb, a Captain, was a shit from that moment on. If it was true that soldiers complained about their officers, I was going to start with him.

Chapter 21

///////////////////////////////////

If it hadn't been for the business of the day, the peeling of the taters, the chopping of the beef and the toting of the bales of hay the noise would have kept me awake all night, but I slept like a hound dog at high noon in the sunflowers. Sarge told me as I was good with horses I'd most likely be good with pigs and cattle, so he gave me extra duty he said was a privilege. I never met a pig before. They seemed to know what was coming, death or dinner and scooted about accordingly so there were times I got covered in stuff I didn't care for. I did my duty, either way. After the first couple, slaughtering quick across the throat in the company of the butcher who had the knack, big man that he was, of holding them still.

"Remember this when you're in the field, lad," Sarge said. I worried I would have to stick pigs instead of rebels once we got south.

The bugle woke me, but the bugle player sounded suspect most time, probably because he'd been imbibing like everyone else. I don't like the stuff. I don't like what it does to folk.

Cairo never had a moment of peace. People were playing music and dancing jigs 'til all hours and much drinking of whiskey was carrying on. Ladies of the evening worked from dusk until the first fair light of a frosty dawn. Their doors were always the cleanest because the mud was deeper in front of them and if a boy had a mind, he could earn an extra quarter just cleaning the boots of the clients. Edwin worked all the hours sent to him. He wanted to send some extra money to his sister in Louisiana, but he knew he couldn't because it would look like he was aiding and abetting (what that means we neither of us really know) the enemy.

Each day starts with roll call and inspection. This is good because we have to muster in Regiment, so we got to meet our fellows. Most of us know each other from the same town or city, but those of us who started as outsiders stayed that way. Edwin and I don't make a fuss of this circumstance as we knew enough already not to try to stand out. In my case I am killing pigs and milking cows. Edwin is peeling taters and learning to bake bread. Both of us are getting good at our jobs we think. Sarge Harrison and his corporal, Andy Fellowes, as it turned out, didn't disabuse us of this conception, so we mucked in when ordered and saluted when in doubt.

After inspection, as most people probably know, we drill. Up and down, up and down, round and round and shout and roar the order until our bodies could guess what was coming before our brains guess it. Edwin and I had wooden rifles. We took it badly until we saw we weren't being singled out. Only half of us had all the equipment we would need to fight Johnny Reb. We are pleased that we have powder bags and regulation Army backpacks.

"Put you boys together, we'll make a soldier out of one of you." Sarge went away laughing, his droopy drawers begging for a good shot from my old slingshot, unfortunately left back home.

There is worse than us though. A golden curly-haired boy of tubby features, double chinned, with long lashed blue eyes who always pants and smiles in a bashful way, never manages to hold himself in one piece. This is Thomas Van der Horn. Since I'm no longer an O'Grady, and Edwin in no longer a Patience it is a miracle Thomas' name came through in the altogether. The other thing is that his shoes fit. He is one of the few to carry a complete US Army uniform and kit, although the powers that be have neglected to supply him with actual ammunition and that is a very wise thing because Thomas couldn't hold on to all his equipment at the same time.

He comes to inspection last. At that point one of the officers would call attention, knowing there was no reason for starting before it got to his place in line. Then Thomas would lose something to the ground. He would pick it up as the officer glared.

"Right face," would be bellowed and we would obey. "Forward march."

Thomas was placed at the end of the troop because it meant no one would trip over or must avoid a dropped bayonet or powder bag. His badges always seem to be loose and his hair, although short, escapes from under his cap making it appear to creep up his forehead unannounced. His moustache, though. His 'tache, justifies his whole existence in the 41st Illinois. It is more than full, it is alive – not with timorous beasties or any such thing, no, Thomas wears it like a flag. We can see his glorious thick moustache before we notice the size of the rest of him. It is full of ambition and underlines the chubbiness of his pink cheeks, framing his bashful smile and acts as a megaphone to his soft but sonorous voice. As much as he is told to remove the grin from his face he is meant, for the rest of his natural life, or at least the natural life of the 'tache, to fight a losing battle with it, so the officers eventually accept the fact that Thomas may be a good luck mascot. The rest of us enjoy his good natured company.

After drill we do chores. It is the usual army thing. Edwin and I buckle down and get into it, but we wonder when we will be sent south. Ships slide in and out of the Mississippi and the Ohio, carrying loads and animals and then disappear, going somewhere without any of us. The weather isn't helping. I think it must be easily the beginning of February by now and the noise of Cairo has changed.

There is still a buzz but it's a whispered one and the shopkeepers, bankers. lawyers and large hospital on the Mound change the mood. Things have slowed down and the party atmosphere is lessening. Cairo is developing into a small city instead of a large temporary town and the attitudes of the people more sharp, astute (this is a word the butcher used about me and I like the sound of it) and less forgiving.

A whistle blew from one of the steamboats. It's deep and insistent, more like a warning roar of a mountain cat. I got tingles on my skin when the others joined in, one after another. Then, the gangways dropped. We were called to muster. I've never participated in a throng that big, but the training worked except that the poor bugler hadn't practiced the call and we aren't used to it, so I ran to dig Edwin out of the kitchens. The muster was formed by one soldier telling another and common sense. Sergeant MacDonald shouted the form to. Our Lieutenant rode toward us on an ordinary looking chestnut mare. I have the opinion that he'd brought it with him from home because it is skittery and looks a mite aged. The ships stopped blaring.

"Gentlemen. By this time tomorrow we will be boarded and on our way to Memphis, Tennessee, stopping at Fort Hood on the way. Your service to your great country is about to start in earnest. See you do your duty."

Edwin and I stood in the front of everything. I remember a murmur started. We nudged each other. Eventually the bands – all of them at once-- started to play Johnny Cope and a cheer was heard. I took the chance to glance behind me: there looked to be thousands of us now we could be seen together. General Grant, rarely seen out and about these days, rode along the ranks to show his solidarity I suspected and took a stance on that proud white military trained horse of his, one that did not skitter or even twitch its ears and the Lieutenant dismissed us, which we did, in actual military order, maybe because our General was watching or more likely, because we all had the same mind. We drilled in formation and soon we would fight in formation. We needed each other.

Sergeant Major Harrison awaited us at our tents.

"Your names and ships are posted on this notice board. (He used the tip of his drill stick to point to the obvious.) Look where you're going and get all your gear together. Those of you with kitchen duties will board last." This meant Edwin and I were likely to be apart for a bit.

I don't have a brother but the wrench I felt must have been very like the real thing. I was standing in the back of the line to see where I would be berthed when the Sergeant came up to me: "The animals will stay here, Private Grady. I hope you didn't form any special attachments."

I have no idea why he leered at me. "Clean 'em out and feed 'me up. I've still got a job for you."

"Am I ever going to be in the band, Sergeant Major?" I wanted to stop butchering innocent animals. At least the Rebs could defend themselves.

"Oh dear no, Private. I've got to get you a musket and powder and ammunition before we depart."

Edwin overheard this: "What about me? Do I get a real gun?"

"I thought you would have figured it out by now that if the Army found you to be willing and good at something it would swing one of two ways – it would keep you at it or change you to do something you hated. You absolutely shine as bright as the sun on a June day with your bread making. Must be some kind of anger built up in you the way you punch those poor loaves." The Sergeant Major stopped himself from patting Edwin's shoulder.

"No drum, then." Edwin came equally close to stomping his foot.

"Don't take bad to it. Drummers are easy to come by. Nine-year-olds can learn drum patterns but good bread makers are worth every penny they're paid and more to go with it. Army's being kind to you, Private Perfect. Be grateful." The Sarge walked away smiling to himself.

"I'm on the Tigress, *Joss – the General's ship."*

"You must be a bread maker good enough for the General."

I confess I am a little in awe. I looked at the roster through the snow flurries that had just started. I'm on the Ticonderoga. *It sounded like a native name. As long as it didn't sink because I don't want to learn to swim in water this cold. Even the edge of the fast Ohio River had an edge of ice on it.*

"We're going to be separated, then."

"Don't go all mushy on me, Edwin. I'll always be able to find you. I can smell bread from a mile away and as long as you keep baking, I can keep looking."

He laughed at me, but we'd been together for a long time now and it wasn't easy to part. "We're in the same regiment, don't forget. The army will have to get us back together just to be able to count heads at muster."

We were about to shake hands when we heard the crash of a falling packsack. It could only be one person. "What have you got in that thing, Thomas?" We had always wondered why it appeared to be so heavy, suspecting food and cakes of some description. Remaining shy, Thomas showed us a big – for lack of a better word – black Holy Bible – those letters in gold nearly worn off.

"I'm a Lutheran." As if that would explain everything.

"Well, what boat are you on, Tom the Lutheran?" Edwin managed to maintain a serious face.

"I'm being held back a day for the Tyconn, *Cincinnati's medical supply ship."*

"Maybe the doc will need a hand from the almighty." I gave him a playful jab on his shoulder. He gave me a cold stare in return.

There was a silence between all of us. Each shook hands and then formally saluted each other as we parted or three different ways.

Chapter 22

////////////////////////////////

The good Sergeant Major Harrison caught up with me just as I thought I could have a stretch on my bunk and a minute to think. Next thing I knew I got into line to be handed an 1853 Enfield Musket Rifle. She was in good condition, but my heart didn't sing to her – old and trusty as she may be. I hoped the Rebs weren't so lucky in their arms. We heard from scuttlebutt they tended to fight with squirrel guns. I wasn't in a real hurry to find out. I didn't mind guns because they had a use back at home and I had a good eye as The MacLaren had told me, but this long, purpose built for killing machine I was inspecting outside in the cold of the parade ground, surrounded by about 30 or 40 boys and men feeling as flummoxed as I, brought home that I would be ordered to shoot and kill another human. The army sounded great from the outside looking in but now we, all of us, knew why we'd been drilled up and down to sideways and back. There were a few making noises about whipping those damn Rebs but mostly we clicked at things, blew down the bolt hole, removed the ramrod, looking at it from both ends as if the action would make a difference to our eventual accuracy and were grateful to see a Second Lieutenant (they were Ensigns yesterday, so now they seemed to be growing on the regiment as fast as weeds in a cornfield) who rode by on a squat little horse to shout out "attention".

Once we were standing still, not sure how to hold on to the equipment – at least we knew what all the straps on the packsack were for but not where they were supposed to be used – a gunnery corporal came past to hand us powder and shot. He suggested we put it in our shot case. "Keep it dry men. Keep it dry."

"Now," the Second Lieutenant shouted. "You have been gifted a weapon by the United States Army. It will, if you baby it and take great, loving care of her, save your scrawny little lives. You have from now until sundown to learn how they work. You will fire three balls while standing and three lying down. There are your targets. You will be given no more ammunition until you board your transport." He jumped from the horse and handed it to a black man who took its halter and trotted it closer to the river edge and, I think, the USS Cairo: well away from an area where there was bound to be lots of noise. I respected that thought for the horse. While he was away, the Officer set up, on hay bales empty cans and bottles. He mustn't have been out of the ranks very long or he would have ordered one of us to do it for him, but I discovered that this opinion was wrong: if one of us had moved from our spot we would have had the advantage of the others by knowing exactly how far away our targets were.

"If one of you came here your mind would remember how far you had walked and this meant an unfair advantage so no, I don't want any help, but thanks for thinking of it as I'm sure all of you did." He brushed his cold hands together. "Now. Front row down. Rear stand. Pay attention and this drill will be the first of many."

A clattering was heard as the ranks found their places but after the second shot from all of us a unit mindset in. Even the Lutheran, Thomas van Der Horn was only a little behind.

For the next half an hour or so we followed a drill that consisted of, "bite, spit, ram, tap, fire." It was quite a simple thing to do provided I didn't think too hard about it and didn't stop to get the taste of gunpowder out of my mouth, move out of my place to get away from the stink or cloying of the smoke. All of us were rubbing at our eyes and I tell you now, it's the worst thing possible. Better to take a blind shot through the tears than take no shot at all. There were only about fifty of us at one time as it turned out – 25 in front, 25 behind. It seemed an efficient way of doing things. I couldn't see Edwin anywhere, but he wouldn't be given a real gun until tomorrow, probably. I guess it depended on when his ship was leaving. We were dismissed, for which I was grateful because I was choking with fumes and my eyes were needing a rinse in clear snow if I could find any. New in the day, the water butts would remain frozen over. I was overheated and shocked just a little. I hung my rifle across my chest and bent for a bit that wasn't muddy or full of animal pee.

"Private." It was my Lieutenant, Mr Wright. I jumped back into position and saluted without having to think about it: the best way to be I decided. Thinking too much made the day a long one. He saluted back.

"Come with me."

I followed directly behind him and in step – another thing I didn't have to think about. This pleased me greatly. It meant I fit in better because I was still aware I could be sent home if they ever got real fussy about my age. We marched behind the Post Office building and down a street before turning into a building that looked like Ian Grant's General Store at home.

"You remember your Second Lieutenant from before?"

"Yes, Sir." What was this about? He saluted me so I nearly relaxed because he wouldn't if I was being sent home.

"My name is Stirling. Your rifle is a mess already."

"Sorry, Sir." I was a mess to match it, but I'd only been off the field for a matter of minutes. I caught myself thinking and stopped.

"You will go into the rear of this building. You will clean it and you will scrape most of the mud off your uniform. You will then have a bowl of this ham soup (I wondered if I'd met the donor) and rejoin me in one hour back on the quadrangle." He saluted again by way of dismissal. Lieutenant Wright escorted me past all the sweets and candies just to make sure I wouldn't be tempted before dinner, he said before he asked me if I knew how to clean my gun. Ever since Edwin and I had arrived we had carried cleaning rags and fluids with us. We'd found it re-assuring that if we had that kind of equipment then we would one day get a gun. Army always runs in reverse. We were used to it. I was of the opinion that women would organize it better, but I kept that one all to myself.

After a while I cleaned my boots and shirt cuffs as best I could before showing up to the front.

In the near distance I heard firearm drill again. Lieutenant Wright was relaxing in a large leather chair, but pointed to the soup tureen. There were china bowls and real spoons making themselves to home beside the meal. Lieutenant Stirling was sitting behind a solid desk, cleaning his pipe.

"Take a chunk of bread with it Private. Your buddy, Edwin makes a great loaf."

I ladled a quantity of thick soup into the bowl and looked for a place to sit.

"You're a soldier now, boy. Soldiers sit where God gives them a place. The floor of the store is warmer and softer than anywhere you're likely to be for a long time so take full advantage, man." He grinned at me. I sat to eat soup that was beginning to get gloopy as it chilled. Edwin did make good rough bread though.

Other men came in and out. One asked the Lieutenant if, "I was the one?" I didn't look up or acknowledge the voice in any way and I'm glad I didn't because he went on to say: "Better feed him up a bit in case he gets a twitch at the wrong time." I knew not to volunteer for anything, but the Army didn't always see things that way. Sometimes it volunteered you and I had a feeling I was about to be given a job I wasn't going to like.

The guns died down from the parade ground. I was scraping the bottom of my bowl to stall for time.

"Don't stand, boy. Just pass me your gun so I can make sure it's clean before Lieutenant Wright, or worse, Sergeant Major Harrison, sees it. They're having a hard enough day. By the way, wipe the gunpowder from your mouth and if you've got a bit of cloth, give your teeth a swipe of Godliness."

"Gun clean, then?" The Sergeant Major was back and I could see what Lieutenant Wright meant. He was covered in ash, stinking of gunshot and reeling with loud noise.

"Gun, then, soldier." The Sergeant Major reached for it, so I stood up and to attention as I handed it to him.

"He can clean a gun, Stirling."

"Good news then," Lieutenant Wright looked at me, slapped his thigh and told me to follow him back to the parade ground. Once again, I fell in behind and asked no questions.

The black servant was busy setting up three targets of a pyramid of tins, all a various distance.

"Can you climb trees, Private?"

"Yes Sir."

"Fine. Right fine. Climb that short oak one, near to the top but not quite. When you get there, load and fire in your own time at that tall pyramid near the General's boat.

I must have been looking at him like I'd seen bad men in the fireworks.

"Now, Private."

I scooted up that tree ever so fast and loaded and fired even faster, aiming at the middle can. The pyramid fell.

"Back down, Private."

I hate going up things that are high, so I was so glad for the relief.

"Now, lie where you are and aim for the one to your right. You do know left from right. I know you do because you are always in step. Load and fire in your own time."

"Fine. Now stand and shoot straight at the target over the other side of the fence."

"Sir?"

"Can't you see the hay bale with the red flag on it?"

"Just used to seeing tins, Sir. Sorry sir.

"Load and fire at will then, Private. Sometimes in war your target will change."

I shot his damned red flag and made it dance a little.

"I'll see you tonight on the Ticonderoga, *Private Grady. Might be able to give you special rank as a sharpshooter or maybe even skirmisher. You know the difference, Private?"*

"No, sir."

"Sharpshooter marches with his regiment, skirmisher walks on his own, spotting for trouble ahead or behind – bit like a bird, really – flies free. Shame you don't have any papers of age though – could be the only thing stopping you."

Chapter 23

////////////////////////////

The man with the great white head of hair with matching beard and moustache that shook our hands and wished us well on our first day, was standing on the pier leading to the boat I was to be taken down river on. There was to be lots of us it seemed – thousands it looked like. All these blue heads moving in front and behind. None of us were marching really good. It was something we had to learn better, said the boys from the seventeenth who appeared to know all things soldiery. Most of us got on the big wood ships and I don't mind saying I didn't like the way it moved, all up and down and side to side. I could hear the water of the river slapping into the side of it and worried it would reach over to get at me.

"That's Admiral Foote, Private Grady. You see and mind your manners. He's a great man, a great man just as all your officers are." Corporal Andy was proud of his knowledge of things important. "Close your mouth Private. You're showing your ignorance. Find a place to stand."

Lord it stank. There were seven ironclad boats, specially built in accordance with the Admiral's orders they said. The chimney was belching black smoke and the iron cladding looked as if to shake itself apart. Snow began to fall and the wind was picking up some, just in time for the sun to start setting. I looked at the line behind me and wondered about Edwin. The wheels weren't turning yet but I think all of them were most anxious to get going.

"I was supposed to be going on the Ticonderoga, Corporal."

"You got the an old wooden instead, just be grateful you ain't walking. Only soldiers with something special to offer the General have this privilege. I'm not sure how you wound up here either, so just be glad you're getting to the fight and move along. Now."

The walkway bounced and slid but it was just wide enough to let me catch my balance. The steamship was shuddering with anticipation. Men were encouraged to walk on one at a time and not to dawdle. We found room for ourselves by moving to the other side around the top path. Now I know these are called the deck and the gangway but back then I was even more innocent of things than I knew how to be.

A bunch of us found some steps and chose to go deep down to escape the wind and cold. What was worse I didn't actually know: the heat or the cold. I was more used to cold, being from Kansas, so I took the chance to return up top.

Sailors, wearing their dinky little brimless caps threw thick ropes to men on the shore of the Tennessee River, there was a shout, echoed by another shout and the giant wheel of the ironclad USS Cincinnati began to turn. The ship's whistle blew right over my head and like all Army men, I looked for cover. The sailors laughed at us, especially as the other ships in the mouth of the river blew signals at each other which meant, I suppose, good luck or well done.

All of us that had never been on a ship before, took a time to accept there was no land to rest on. Wherever *we wanted to rest was not going to rest under us until we got to wherever we were going. It was odd. I wasn't in control of my life anymore. The feeling that my fate was no longer in my own hands wasn't a pleasant one. It put fire back in my belly, the fire that got me to leave Validation. Now that fire wanted me to be a skirmisher. I wasn't built to march in step. No, if I was to fight I would, but if the Good Lord had given me the skill to shoot straight He must have His reasons, and who was I to argue with Him? I made my mind up to it. All I had to do was act the part. The army wouldn't argue if I did the job right.*

All any of us were sure of was that it was getting dark, it was cold and being it was only the beginning of February, we weren't going to see any better or feel any warmer until at least April and the Lord alone only knew where we'd be when that happened. I was glad to be standing in the back of the boat, watching the land until I saw it disappear. We were going south and because of the rain, the General decided not to march us that way just yet. The roads weren't fit for taking wagons, guns and other essential supplies like food. Food made me think of Edwin. Was he busy baking bread somewhere?

The sails above our heads snapped and flicked over our heads, catching the wind and driving us up the river. We were going against the flow though, so the boat was forced to gyrate a bit. I'm sure there's a sailor's name for it because the men made the movement look so easy. Their drill was much more complicated than ours. All we had to do was march and shoot. They had to sail as well. No wonder they had names for us; none too polite, I assure you.

We were getting excited now. Some of us were sent to find a place to sleep and others stood watch. I dozed for a bit, but Corporal Andy kicked at me before dawn to tell me it was my turn to look out. He took my place and the heat I'd built up under what a sailor told me was a gunwale. I don't know whether that was the right word, but I'd been out of most of the wind at any rate. As soon as I stood up I felt sorry for myself. The rain was like slices of ice cutting into me. The greatcoats we'd been issued were good enough, but the caps needed some serious lining of wool and I missed even a horsehair rug because the blankets we had were made of shoddy so got soaked and smelly real quick. I couldn't see a bit of light anywhere. The river was in full spate they told me. There had been heavy rains, so trees and loose wood was getting in the way of the flow of the ships. Every once and a while something crashed into the side of us. Once, a sailor came up beside me, stuck a long pole into the water and shoved aside what looked like a rocking chair.

"Poor grandma won't be doing her knitting tonight then," he shouted to me over the wind.

There were only three hundred Army on this boat, the rest of us of the vanguard including the gunners and their artillery were understandably concerned for their powder even though most of it was stored safely below. It wasn't unheard of, they told me, that a transport ship could be blown up if it took a hit from, say, a Fort onshore or even another boat. I disliked their attempts to rile me. I only looked young enough to believe everything I was told.

The corporal nudged me in my ribs and nodded toward the shoreline. The trees onshore gave way to a formation, an unnatural conglomeration of edifice. All on board heard the engines of the ironclads but no one said anything. I felt our ship lean toward the target of our endeavors as men came to look from the opposite side. Not a body spoke. I wondered if there was a different Fort *to come or were we just going to wait for daylight. We kept going though.*

A couple of days later we anchored all the ships just below the Fort *we were going to give a seeing to. The sailors got busy cleaning decks and that wasn't much use because the rain came down really heavy. It bounced from the decks and the height of the river got higher as it got faster. I witnessed lumber, fences and even large trees go past us almost as fast as the ironclads could go.*

One morning, I heard my first cannon shot. It came from the shore I think, passing through the pantry of the Essex, *they told me. Not the kitchen, no, so I was reassured* Edwin *couldn't be involved. He shouldn't be on the* Essex, *of course, but then I should be on the* Ticonderoga. *I'm not sure if anyone was hurt.*

The next morning – we can even do a drill on board a ship because that's what we were put to doing – it was foggy. Kansas isn't used to fog, and neither was I. When I hoped no one could see, I tried to catch some, but I couldn't, not even with both hands. Fog is a curious thing. It went away all by itself just before we were to eat. Oh my.

Four of the big ships, the Essex *to my right, then the* Cincinnati, *the* Carondelet *and then the* St Louis *formed a line abreast of each other to head for Fort Henry (yesterday's edifice). It looked like the* Carondelet *and the* St Louis *were stuck to each other. We came behind and then the first shot from the flag steamer, the*

Carondelet *with a Rear Admiral Walker led the way by firing the first shot at the Confederate Army. Now I didn't know any of this as it happened, of course, I just found out later when it turned out that the river was a pro Union and probably the best soldier of the day. It was so high, that most of the defenses of the Fort were washed away so it took only common sense to give up before anyone got injured or wounded, which they did, in a gentlemanly fashion except a few escaped leaving none too many behind, which our boys, being of charitable mind and nature, in the name of Christian charity, cared for with willing hearts, knowing it may have been some of their own. And that was the end of Fort Henry, they told me.*

There was not much for us to do then, so we had a bit of tack and were allowed coffee from the galley (hark at me – knowing the names of things) but then, just around the bend a ship's horn was heard. Steaming onto us came the Tigress *– General Grant's very own headquarters. All the rest of the steamships returned the salute. We stood to cheer along with the sailors. We must have made the General proud. We were fair to bursting with it at any rate.*

A tug boat went to fetch back the Admiral, probably to have a discussion with the General, and we thought we would all be back in Cairo in a few days, having done such a good job. The sun was going down, so the cold was coming back but at least it was dry.

The tugboat came to our ship to pass what appeared to be orders to our Captain and then continued its mission to the rest of the fleet.

We would march across to the Cumberland River to set up camp for action in a few days. We saw the

Carondelet *and the* Tigress *get up steam to return to Cairo for further arms, ammunition and above all, troops. We were brought closer to the opposite shore and downstream just a little to a village called Dover or some such where we were landed in daylight the next morning. My legs were wobbly. They reminded me of how Silk walked when I saw some of us get off the boat. How was I going to march?*

Chapter 24

So, by the next morning we were offloaded and marching to another Fort – Fort Donelson. I still didn't know where Edmund was, but these things happen in war, so they say. Fort Henry wasn't any real trouble, so all of us had a lightness in our step, glad to be moving, anxious for the next day.

Sergeant Major Harrison showed up from nowhere to tell us that First Lieutenant Wright needed to give us a full inspection within the next thirty minutes or so, just to make sure we were still paying attention to detail and the regulations. My gun looked clean enough on the outside, but the rain must have done damage to the interior. It would be easy enough to sort my kit because I was wearing it, but my gun, my musket rifle I chose to call Mary – because the woman I named it after was just as vicious, with her glowing exterior and a deadly gut – needed some taming.

My comrades sat on logs or tree stumps immediately, cleaning and polishing exactly because our lives depended on it. I didn't know so many trees existed in the world – Kansas had lots but whatever state we were in now had thousands more. I wonder why some of them wear green spikes and the others have only bare branches. Some of the people travelling through Validation to go west told tales of lush green leaves and that they only showed for half a year. I hope the trees I

184

saw were just asleep because they looked as if they would be a crowning glory one day.

The Sergeant called us to attention just in time because we were all starting to warm a bit and relax more than we should, so we formed up. I noticed a string of well-fed horses up the way. Lieutenant Wright mounted one, a heavy bay. There were a great many of us I guess, and he had to see us all. Then when he finished looking at us from above he dismounted with grace and elegance, not disturbing his mount one tiny bit. Only the animal's tail twitched. The two loved each other. It made me feel kindly to the man. He walked slowly down our ranks, hands behind his back, only occasionally physically checking the equipment we carried until he got to me.

"Rifle, Private."

I passed it to him as I was drilled to do, giving him a sharp salute. He checked down the barrel and assured himself of the mechanisms' dryness, sniffing it, even. He looked me square in the eye before passing it back, or at least tried to but of course my eyes were focused straight ahead, according to army protocol.

"Name, Private?" I sensed the man beside me brace himself in case it was his turn next.

"O'Grady, Sir."

"Not Grady, then?"

"No, Sir. Recruiting officer forgot about the O."

"Your ancestors are Irish?" It was a politely formed question.

"I think so, sir."

"Report to my tent after this inspection, Private. I have a job for you." The Lieutenant saluted and checked a few more before he declared two to be a disgrace to the great Army of the Union and especially of the Army of the Tennessee let alone General Grant who would be ashamed, so ashamed. The two men so admonished were also to be given special assignments but they were embarrassed, whereas, I was anxious. The Lieutenant remounted the horse that had been held for him by a man that looked old enough to be his father but no less proud in his private's uniform than I was.

"Thank you, Sergeant Major, a good turnout. Prepare to march as ordered and don't take your time about it. The sun is coming up good and warm, so it should be a great day for a walk." He saluted, sharp and clean and our Sergeant returned an equal one.

"If you're Irish, you'll be peeling the Lieutenant's potatoes for his dinner, most like." Edmund was back.

"Where were you?"

"I can't honestly say but it's good to be back here even if it's only for a minute before you have to report in. I'm so good at baking bread they want me to keep doing it because some old French General said an army marches on its stomach." He was pleased with himself and that's always a good thing.

"You get to eat lots, then?"

"After you see the Lieutenant come visit me in the rear of the line." He said this close to my ear as he made to fasten my haversack tighter.

"Thank you, Private Perfect. I may have stumbled if you hadn't noticed that loose strap." I said it loudly enough that the others in my line could hear, then I marched to the Lieutenant's headquarters and snapped to attention, announcing I was expected. My officer invited me in. Sergeant Major Harrison stood while the

Lieutenant sat at the folding desk covered in papers, some of which had red seals fixed to them, others were telegrams. Telegrams were only received by important people. I would like to get one of my own one day. If it held good news, that is. I saluted.

"You are an exceptional shot Private O'Grady." The Lieutenant pushed back from his desk a bit as he replaced his pen in the inkwell. "There is something in you that keeps you calm. Have you seen many corpses, son?"

"My share, I guess." I didn't know what this was leading to and wished he was from somewhere sensible because he sounded almost foreign.

"Seen a man killed by another?" This gave me pause. Silk crossed my mind. "Seen enough death thank you Sir."

"Kansas born?"

"As far as I know, sir."

"So, you'll know all about bushwhackers and Jayhawkers."

"Yes Sir." I wanted to shift my weight.

"Bloody Kansas, all right."

"This war has taken over that one, though."

"How did you get to be such a good shot Private? At ease, by the way."

I was grateful and wondered if he'd been reading my mind: "Winters can be hard, turkeys run wild and there's lots of them. Rabbit and hare live in the open woods above the livery where I sleep."

"Easy to pick up a shot on a turkey, then?"

"They're pretty stupid when all is said and done. They move in flocks and if one gets lost it starts looking for its cousin or something." I had a giggle at that one, but not too loud, suddenly remembering where I was.

The Sergeant cleared his throat after a second or two.

"Sounds like the way a Fed would act in a dense wood, don't you think?"

"Guess so, sir."

The Lieutenant stood up, I snapped to attention as I'd been trained. "Come with me, gentlemen, please." He led us down the line, a bit until he got to the ordinance that had arrived on the last transport ship. Standing by a long box, he removed a brand spanking new Sharps rifle.

"Sergeant, instruct this man in the use and care of this fine instrument of war and do you see those others, standing by the canteen? Take them under your wing, keep them out of trouble until I can form them up properly as sharpshooters before we arrive at Fort Donelson. You will act as a skirmisher, though, Private O'Grady. You're too young and too small but you're a Kansas man so most likely an independent son of a bitch. Something in me says you don't march too well to a drum beat." He saluted us and left me in shock as he swung back toward his tent.

"Good officer, that," Sergeant Major said to himself as he watched our First Lieutenant leave us alone to think.

Cannon were heard from a distance away.

"Sounds like Admiral Foote has started on the defenses, so we should be able to make short work of the enemy." My Sergeant Major is experienced, I think.

Things were getting lively now. I couldn't believe the beauty of the rifle in my hands. She looked and felt as if she was made for my hands and my hands alone. This rifle was no Mary, this was like Poppy Diamond, all straight talk and no messing about.

"Under orders, lad. Move it."

I watched most of my division begin their march away, all of them cheered by the sound of our guns and the warming sun. Chatter was not normally tolerated but I suppose there was no enemy about and they were about to walk their way to a break in a field, so the wagon could join them for food. Things settled quickly. At the rear of the line was that very wagon and sitting on the back of it was Edmund who looked worried when he saw me so proud with my new Sharps. I snapped out of my dream for just enough time to wave a short goodbye as he did for me. We didn't know what was ahead and both of us knew it was a good thing. If anyone ever knew, the chances were they wouldn't get out of bed that day and that would be such a waste.

"O'Grady. You taking your mind for a walk?"

I gasped at that phrase. I hadn't thought of Buck, The Mindwalker, for a very long time.

"No, Sergeant."

"You gone all pale around the gills, lad. Are you going to pass out with the great honor the officer has bestowed on you?"

"No, Sergeant, just wondering what the bullets look like."

"Well this little thing was invented by a Frenchman called Minnie. It's called a minie ball. Ya load the rifle the same way you have been, but this little beauty can travel as far as a mile and the kick of the stock, if you hold it gentle but firm shouldn't hurt you one little bit. Now, that's the talk I've given to the rest of these men and now we will get started cleaning them, grinding the powder, not too fine because we don't want the gun so kindly bought for you to blow up in your sweet little

faces, and then we will drill and march, drill and march until we get ahead of the boys that just left. From now on, gentlemen, your number one goal is to be able to fire three shots a minute and to do it accurately. You will be the elite of this man's infantry. Pick up your gear and go." Not once did he raise his voice to the thirty or so men in front of him and do you know something? We already felt special.

Chapter 25

The sun was up as my group of sharpshooters headed down one of the roads the scouting party found. It was so warm some of us left our winter gear by the side of the road. There were two of them actually, according to report. I wasn't worried which one I was on because it was at least well-defined and had a solid surface. Small pockets of ice glistened in frozen wagon tracks, so the rough spots weren't much to avoid. I kept my feet dry, anyways. The army only gave us two pairs of socks and I was wearing them, trying to keep my toes warm. Wasn't working all that good.

Funny how we marched now. None of us knew each other of course and only one of us did the three shots in one-minute trick. He seemed as surprised as the rest of us, though. Tall guy called Gus, apparently. The Lieutenant was on his horse and didn't take up the rear. Sarge marched beside us in the front. Every once and a bit he would speed up for a few paces and then drop back to normal march. Without being ordered, my troop just followed. I carried my Sharps across my left shoulder. It was loaded in case I needed to use it. I'm not sure if I felt safer for its presence. I did feel comforted by the men around me, especially since I was not the tallest of us.

Shortly we came upon the supply wagon Edwin was marching with. He wasn't riding it now, so I got a chance to send a greeting just as Sarge started his trot march business, so Edwin couldn't catch up to me to ask the question I saw in his eyes: "What are you doing with that rifle?"

I'm glad though. I still had no idea why I had it. Questions like that can cause you trouble in this army, maybe all armies, even the rebel army. The whisper was they didn't have any real guns but then Bull Run happened. Maybe they had more than we knew. I think both sides learned lots about each other that day.

I kept up with my squad until Sarge halted us in a clearing, telling us to sit and eat if we had the need; good thing we'd been ordered to pack biscuits and fill our canteens. Other men joined us from the regiment we'd just left behind on the road. I heard them before I saw them. My, gear can clunk around. I heard tin mugs, squeaking halters, chatter of expectant fellows, a bit of laughter and a little of swearing at the boots. I was amazed at how much breath I could see as it left the mouths of the army and puffed into the air. It reminded me of that breath of the train.

The Lieutenant dismounted. He ordered those men carrying musket rifles to act as lookouts. Removing his gloves (I hadn't noticed these long blue riding gloves before now) he walked to us, waving us to stay in place on the ground.

"No doubt all of you are wanting to know why you've received these rifles." He squatted. "You are not the only skirmishers, but you are mine. Two of you I will officially promote to sharpshooter after the next argument with the enemy. Our orders are that once we arrive at our next target, a place called Fort Donelson on the Cumberland River, you will find vantage points *suitable to your own strengths as a shooter. You will know better if you can shoot the enemy from a tree or a rabbit hole. I will not order you against your instincts or the training and experience you had in your life before this one. I am telling you to observe and to prevent any of the enemy from encroaching on our camp tonight. In the morning the full infantry will give you support as will Admiral Foote who by the sound of it has started without us. Any questions?"*

For some reason, everyone looked to me. "Sir? You want us to hide in the bushes or the trees and pick off any intruders?" A man sitting beside me roared with his own brand of humor, slapped my hard on my gun shoulder. The officer looked at me, though. "Yes, Private O'Grady. Tonight, may be your very own turkey shoot."

"It would be different, killing a man though." I felt sick.

The Lieutenant stood up: "Try to make it a clean a shot as you would for a turkey." He began to pull his gloves on. The man that laughed at my question passed me a coffee and released my own mug from my packsack, probably to use for himself.

"You don't think about what you're doing to a turkey. You distance yourself, let your training take over, breathe in through your nose and relax as you focus. All over and dinner is served. Not pleasant but better than losing a meal. Try to think of tonight's duty as only that. All over and better than losing a war." For the first time I noticed the Lieutenants' hard blue eyes. He saluted, turned and waved at one of his aides to come over with a message of a sort.

Now, you're not going to believe this but the man that laughed at me that time was called Hugh Deadman.

"Cold son-of-a -bitch, eh? My name's Hugh." He thrust his chubby looking hand toward me. I shook back. "Bet that bastard was a banker before he got here."

"Don't know any real bankers."

"Keep it that way, kid. Trust me long before you trust a banker or a lawyer."

I felt exposed for my own inexperience.

"Where you from?" I asked.

"Not gonna be your buddy, kid. We're gonna be brothers-in-arms for as long as this fight lasts, or the good Lord takes one of us home."

Hugh let me keep his mug of coffee and took my mug with him into the woods where I presumed he was going to relieve himself. Pop. Pop, pop – from the trees he entered.

"Get up that tree, O'Grady." Sarge hissed into my ear. "We'll cover you."

Others in the regiment were ducking and diving under bushes and searching into the opposite woods but Sarge thought it was a good idea to send a Kansas farm boy up a tree, presuming I guess that all young, skinny men could swing up a tree like they were born to it. I am not happy up things, looking down at the world moving around me, but ordered I was and ordered I did.

"Don't cock your rifle 'til you get there." For the second time that day I was slapped on my shoulder.

Keeping as low to the forest floor as I could, I scrambled on my elbows and knees. A swimming movement, they'd called it in training, not knowing that some of us couldn't swim, but we learned fast enough. I for sure did on that cold February day.

"Hurry up, Private." I heard Sarge getting excited.

I came across a tree, but I wouldn't have climbed it even to shoot a turkey – there was no cover, only bare branches. I stayed so still for a time. I saw movement to my right. There was Hugh. Lying and bleeding a bit. I didn't see him breathe, but then that's not what I was there to do.

Remembering the Lieutenant's words, I focused on my turkey and distanced myself from the target. The Fed was stupid. He made more noise squatting on his two legs and coming toward me than if he'd been crawling like I had. I waited. When he made a noise, he stopped to look at it. I moved my gun every time and Praise the Lord he made lots of noise. Finally, I cocked my Sharps. He heard that one. He was on the other side of Hugh. We saw each other like the day had just dawned. I fired – a clean shot. Sarge raced past me.

Hugh was gone, just plain gone. His neck was missing in the front. His eyes looked at me like he had something else to say. Sarge went to the Reb next. Then he came back to me.

"Clean shot between the eyes, Private O'Grady." He squeezed my shoulder. Three times in one day. It was making me edgy. I sat with my back to the tree that wasn't worth climbing.

"Good thing you're not regular army, son. You disobeyed an order and showed intelligence beyond your years. Now you're going to find out about the real bad side or army life. You have to report to your commanding officer who will want to know exactly why you didn't climb that tree."

I nodded as I replaced my cap but then an ague affected me, so I lurched two steps away from him and vomited my coffee and biscuits. I kept at this until I turned dry and finally slid down the trunk of that damned tree. My head was swimming in circles just as I'd seen a dying trout do back home and I finally felt sympathy for it.

"Here, Joss." I looked up at Edmund. "It's only water but it'll do, won't it?"

I took the cup and nearly tossed the contents back like I'd seen the boys do in the bar back home, but Edwin prevented me.

"If you chug it back you'll be sick again and the Lieutenant wants to see you to congratulate you I think."

"I heard three guns go off."

Edmund was wearing a white apron that hung beneath his knees and just above his ankles.

"You got a different uniform, then?"

"Two things the army can't do without, my friend – good shots and great bakers. You protect me, and I'll feed you. Pretty good trade, eh?"

"O'Grady, move it. Now."

Sarge pointed to the Lieutenant still standing beside his gentle bay. I trotted over. I don't know why. I must be getting into the habit of movement. I stood and waited but I was conscious of missing my mug and my uniform being out of order. He finished with his aides and took a step toward me. The cold blues eyes looked me up and down.

"You are a disgrace, Private."

"Sir, yes Sir."

"I understand that you killed a man, the enemy creeping around our borders, is that so, Private?"

"Sir, yes Sir."

"I also understand you disobeyed a direct order to do so."

"Sir."

"Don't do that again, clear? Even if I do say not to go against your home-grown instincts."

"Sir, yes sir."

"Dismissed, Private." He saluted me.

"By the way I will mention you in my dispatches and please consider your pay grade to be commensurate with that of Skirmisher.

I had no idea what that meant of course but I saluted and marched back to the twenty-nine that were left in my group. I asked Sarge about the mention.

"Nation needing some heroes, that's all. It'll make your local papers back home." I didn't like the sound of that.

"What's comensurit mean?"

"Where'd you get that word?"

"Lieutenant said pay was commensurate with Skirmisher."

"Shite, kid. You're one of the two and you got a pay hike. Not only are you a bona fide hero, you're gonna be a rich one."

I got out of the way before he patted me on the shoulder again but the others in our small group came to shake my hand.

A grave was being scraped out of the hard forest floor. Corporal Andy showed up from nowhere to take Hugh's dog tags from him. It's how I found out about his last name, I guess. We started to move out again right after a chaplain showed up from the same line of nowhere hiding our Corporal. The army consists of four lines: front, rear, nowhere and enemy, who no doubt have an identical set.

"We'll be there by nightfall, men. Valentine's day, I think they call it. We're supposed to be snuggled up with our gal tonight. I don't think it'll be possible fellas." Sergeant Major sounded like he knew what he was talking about, but in the army way I shrugged and nodded my agreement, making my mind up to find out about a day for a snuggle and a girl.

Chapter 26

*We took our positions, spread out so far from each other,
but only faith allowed me to believe the others were still
with me. The sun was leaving, the cold was coming and
dark crept up on us from behind. Horses were tied up
behind me. I could hear them. They were nervous. How
wise, I thought. All I could see in the dwindling light was
a hill I had to climb, and it was full of tall trees and
brush. We wouldn't be given the order to move until the
morning but in the meantime, I had to crouch or lie here
in the dark and the cold, keeping alert to any movement
ahead. I wondered why anyone would come toward me
out of that wood and down that hill. What was on the
other side of it that made Sarge consider the dark as if he
was looking into the future. I watched him shake his
head as he turned for the rear so there we were, all
twenty-nine of us, stretched out in the silent night, left to
our instincts, to survive until dawn. I settled into some
dead leaves, but they crunched every time I moved.
I wasn't even sure about the smell so much; wet death is
how I would describe it if I was asked.*

*There was nothing I could do except wait. Waiting
for something to happen that most likely wouldn't be
pleasant will keep a body awake. Leaves rustled off to
my left, so I stretched my ears as far as I could. It was a
steady movement. I sensed more than one set of legs.
God. Where had the bastards been hiding. It was so*

cold; the Sharps might fail me when I most needed it. Raising myself on my elbows I gently lifted it into my shoulder, sighted it and scanned the near distance. More rush of leaves, this time further to my left. The intruder was looking for another target. I traced its progress in case it doubled back. It kept going. Then another and another sound of a set of legs followed, making me feel useless because I'd been given nothing to aim at, but this was my job, I'd been told. *Don't shoot until you've got something to say to the rest of us.* There was shifty movement in the woods. Until I could name it I shouldn't say anything, and I couldn't see it or smell it, so I kept shtum. Good thing, as it happens. When dawn arrived, a few shots had been heard down my line so there were a couple of transactions leading to the capture, in one case of a Fed on a prowl for information but when Sarge shook me to move – and that wasn't easy, let me tell you – the sounds I encountered were most likely caused by the movement of deer, if the stoor spoke to the truth. He encouraged me to return to the rear for coffee and maybe some bread if the regular infantry hadn't eaten all of it. Good thing Edwin saved me a bit – with jam, no less.

Gunfire. Heavy gunfire in front of us and from the river. The Lieutenant showed from somewhere to order the infantry forward but not me just yet. We would follow this time. Our job would be to make sure we couldn't be attacked from behind, so I ducked behind the wagon to get out of the way and to finish my breakfast. I was amazed by the amount of men filing past me, left and right. How had they stayed so quiet all night? Surely to God, they couldn't have slept in this cold. They must have huddled near a pit fire or something. My nose and cheeks were burning with the frost, my back starting to melt water. We all were frozen to the bone. I jumped up and down a bit to get the blood flowing in my feet. If I could, I would take off my shoes to look at them. I didn't want any black bits like Buck had last year. I much preferred my feet to stay where the Good Lord meant them to be. No, I didn't want my toe fed to the wolves as Buck's were.

"Stupid thing to say, but it was a cold one last night," Edwin said.

"How're your feet?" I asked.

"Too scared to look, but been told not to bother. If you're froze you're froze. Boots will hold onto your toes, come to that."

"Suppose." He didn't cheer me up any.

Sarge marched past where we were leaning on the wagon.

"Onward and upward, lads. Up a hill and down to the valley below before the real trouble starts."

I should have asked how he knew.

Our outfit was a strange one. None of us spoke much, probably because there was no need. We knew each other by face, height and weight. One guy, Ashton, as it turned out decided he didn't much like the cap the army gave him, so he stuffed it in his bedroll and stuck a feather of some kind into what looked like a weathered top hat. I was marching beside him at the time we met, so it was purely by accident I met him at all. When we did the speed up marching we weren't of a mind to talk.

Sarge Harrison held up his hand to stop us, which we did, right smart. Then he moved his flat hand down, so we obeyed his order. He came to us in a crouch, indicating we should spread out again. This was getting stupid, I thought. Just let us at the buggers. He looked at every second man and pointed up at a tree. I was a first man and mighty grateful for it. He said something to the man on my right and I got the gist of it. The whisper flowed down the line. We would back up the infantry from above because the attack was about to begin. In front of us an extended line of men stood to move forward. The guns started. A roar came from the river. I heard cracks, pops and screams in front of me. A clod of earth caught me on the side of my face. I finally fired my Sharps but I'm not sure at what. I reloaded. I lay on my belly. Something trickled down the side of my face. A movement. A shot. His, not mine. A shot. Mine, not his. I moved forward in a running crouch, strictly against orders, most likely. I had killed because this kid was missing half his jaw. I focused forward. All of us charged forward. None of us knew what we were heading toward or where we were going to but if we kept going no harm could come to us. The air was smoky now and I choked at times on the rancid smell of cordite I think they call it. Forward. There was Ashton from Boston he told me last night. Gone. Feather from his hat stuck in the ground.

The enemy was gunning for us. Forward, upward through the thickets and thorns my head throbbing and thirst growing. It was true. I heard a bullet go past my shoulder. It wasn't the one meant for me, then. We retreated a bit then tried again, retreated a bit, then tried again, this time getting to the top of the hill in full daylight which was a good thing because the Sarge was right – there was a valley as low as the hill was high and on the other side of the valley, the Fort we'd been looking for, surrounded by hundreds of logs with pointed ends like pencils and all pointing at us, piled on top like bricks in a building, each tree filling a gap with the one beside it. I sank to my knees. Behind the pencils were walls of wood and behind the walls of wood were what I recognized as cannons. Behind the cannons, many rooftops. Underneath these rooftops must be the Confederate Army. I sat to take a slug from my canteen, to look for stray turkeys and to see a hole in the wall opposite. There must be one. Just one turkey would make my day worth it. I didn't know Ashton long enough, but he was one of us. I needed a feckin' turkey.

This time I took the trouble to check my rifle before I reloaded. I wasn't going to do any good to me or the Army if it was wet or overloaded. She was fine. I was angry. Me, angry. I was angry like the time Silk held a knife to my throat. Hell, that was only two months back at Christmas in Validation. That was the night I stopped being a kid – the same night I'd been given my first shot of whiskey. I lay down again.

I scanned what was ahead of me.

"Psst. Grady. It's Andy."

"What you doing here, Corporal?"

"Got nowhere better to be. You?"

"Look over there."

"Yeah, I know, Private. We gotta get down and up again."

"Then scramble through the pencil things, somehow."

"It's called an abatis."

"Knowing the name of it is why you're a corporal and I'm only a private."

"It's only a couple of hundred yards, O'Grady." He swallowed out loud.

"C'mon then." He moved forward in a low run but was forced to slow by the thickets. I stayed behind just a bit to see if he would attract any attention. He most certainly did, and we were both glad of it because it turned out we were the furthest forward and the first to discover the enemy had somehow managed to dig in some rifle pits. The bullets were fired from all of them at once, I think, so it was by the grace of God neither of us were hit, but they'd made their presence and location known to the men behind us who were now crashing and tearing through the undergrowth.

Where the hell were the officers? Orders would be a comfort. Some of our men were mown down but others took heart somehow, racing up into ultimate danger and towards the mouths of the cannon. I could see one of the gunners, or at least his shadow, so I aimed at him. Another one stood up, so I killed him as well – four confirmed notches on my gun if that was allowed under army regulations. Yes. Time for me to go. I charged through the brush, easier for me because most of it was trampled, loading and firing as I went as were most of the boys, although I did see one rifle blow up as it was being fired most likely because he'd forgotten to fire it between loads. That was not very pleasant. The soldier's parts were spread amongst his colleagues. The ground was slippery with more blood than had been swept from the decks of the ironclads at Fort Henry. I felt bad I couldn't stop to help any of the men screaming for their mothers or pass them a drink from their own canteen but the job I was hired to do wasn't done yet and all of us charged forward.

Many of us pushed through the abatis, thought we'd won the day and discovered the cunning of the

Confederate Rebels – more rifle pits, or maybe even the same ones, for all I knew, opened fire and fully five regiments turned their guns on us. All of us, thousands of us, it seemed, stopped, but we braced again, not knowing what else to do as there was no obvious officer to give orders since some of us saw an officer on a horse felled by a ball, cutting him in half, his legs stuck in the stirrups. I shot blindly into the thick smoke that had been created. Thinking it sensible, I reversed down the hill to stand near a flag – thank the Lord for a rallying point – and then we charged uphill again, knowing what we were in for but seeing no alternative. We did this three times. The last time the battery above set fire to the leaves on the ground. We could do no more. The flames crept down behind us as we returned to our lines, occasionally showing defiance by sending a shot to the enemy. It did not help our fallen comrades as the fire found its way downhill to burn and smother them. The Confederate Army, for all their loud talk of behaving as a Southern Gentleman and of honor, didn't have any.

That night we weren't allowed to light any fires at all. I lay down in a ditch and behind a log. Others found a bush or even wrapped themselves around a living tree somehow. I'm sure an enemy soldier slept like a babe. He must have been real close. I think lots of them tried to follow us home in the dark. No Union man had so little conscience he was comfortable enough to snore. Leastways, they must have been equally cold.

Dawn came slowly or at least seemed to. The sun didn't share much warmth with me. I could see a bend in the river. It gave me heart to see the butt end of a pair of ironclads. Later, there was busy rifle fire coming

from the Fort which didn't concern me too much
because it wasn't aimed in my direction – I heard the
pinging coming from the iron castings of the steamers.
I'm glad I was no longer aboard because I pictured the
blood and the state of the decks above and below. I
wondered who was busier, the surgeons or the carpenters
but it was only a passing thought, not one to dwell on. I
would have when I was younger. No one was stirring
yet, but I had to simply because of a natural demand.
My uniform was stiff with ice. I was aware of it snapping
at lightly falling to the hard ground where I'd been
resting. None of the men were where they should be.
The pickets fired.

Instantly we filled the woods around us, all looking
for the hive to which we belonged. Then we got busier
than we'd knew we could be. What was I saying about a
hive? Well, let me tell you, our wasps buzzed for at least
two hours and never stopped. Men around fell by the
score, it seemed. The smoke clung to the hedges and
treetops clinging to them like clouds, so preventing me
from seeing my foe and most likely doing the same for
him. Branches of trees fell on those below, the underbrush
flattened, cleared as if by locusts. Word came to us –
and now I was only a man with a Sharps who joined
with the man beside him, whoever he was, whatever
regiment he was in – that we must hold at all costs.
The stranger told me it was only ten o'clock. I took a
choking, dirty breath – the first conscious one since
dawn – just to prove to myself I was still alive. The next
order we heard was to use the ammunition of the dead
and severely wounded. Meanwhile, a bugler blew a weak
retreat. None of us had heard it before but I observed
men walking back to their colors once again. I felt more

than angry this time: I was frustrated, tired and hungry. None of these feelings would leave until I got warm – maybe even in hell, for that matter.

Now, tell me what goes on in the mind of an officer. Rifles were heard on the other side of the fort. The action only lasted for about ten minutes, but I wondered what was going on because it meant there must be men on the opposite side of the Fort. A cloud of gun smoke rose from the woods and the next thing, we were re-supplied with ammunition. Then we were ordered to wait for orders. I sat down on the very log I'd been sleeping behind. One biscuit was all I had. One biscuit was all I needed. Clean snow would clear my throat and wash the powder from my mouth. My teeth would wait. My nose was starting to run. The day must be warming.

From another direction more rifle fire, followed by a severe cannonade. It had nothing to do with us for which I was grateful – mostly Iowa lads, we thought, with General Smith. There was a pause of men and machine but that afternoon and up that very same hill, the regiments formed, and I participated in the last assault on Fort Donelson. My comrades and I lurched through a different abatis this time, loading and firing the whole time and finally watched as the Confederates left their rifle pits. It was getting dark now – maybe about three. Now, this is what I don't understand: why didn't we finish the assault then and there? We were ordered to spend another cold sleepless and fire-free night. We did.

Some of us were appointed to care for the wounded. I don't know how the surgeons operated, but they did, all night I think so even if I'd wanted to sleep I don't think I'd have managed with all the screaming and shouting carrying on.

Dawn is beginning to carve a peculiar place in my heart because that morning, when the battle should have been all over apart from the final charge, two more steamers arrived. Confederate ones. I watched, in the Fort, a full brigade being drawn up. A General, if his uniform was anything to go by, led them quick smart to the steamers where he promptly boarded and left. Another General looking person made his presence felt, troops fell in and he left too. I still find this funny. The wind was fierce that morning and all I could think was something Miss Haggerty told me back home: an ill wind that blows nobody any good. Then, would you believe it? Another General. We had to stay for one more day before we got to go in to finish the job. They surrendered, I was told.

"Should have done that days ago," I said to a loose horse.

Chapter 27

////////////////////////////////////

At least, now that the enemy wasn't there anymore or was under arrest, we could light fires once we found a place to settle. Supplies were jamming us up the rear. Men were being buried as best we could and with as much gravity as we could handle their identification being removed to the authorities that take care of these things. It was the first I realized we had a minister of religion with us. We were to call him Padre for some reason, but the only Reverend I'd met was the one in Validation, Reverend Parker, and there was a rumor he only did the job because we let him and because he owned a Bible. The church gave him somewhere to sleep of course, and all the widows made a terrible fuss of him. I hoped for the sake of those who believed, this Padre was the real thing. The Padre had work to do, though. Many times, he held one service for about twenty of our fallen and when he wasn't busy with that he was in the hospital tents praying for the surgeons or the boys who were making heavy weather of losing an arm or a leg, sometimes one of each. I only heard whispers of these facts because I certainly didn't want to witness it. I thanked the God I knew from home that I was yet unharmed. I wanted to remain so. I cleaned my Sharps, inside and out. I made sure my powder was dry. I took stock of my ammunition so that when the time came for us to be ordered somewhere I could report for my allowance and make sure I had a little extra. Being a bit short of it, having to scrounge from a dead soldier taught me to be more careful with my supplies.

"Want some coffee?" Edwin looked down at me from what appeared to be a skinny height – especially for a cook. He squatted in front of me, mugs in hand, offering me one full of obvious, glorious heat. I rested my rifle across my crossed legs. I was sitting on a rubber blanket I'd found lying in a pile of stuff that had been salvaged from the deceased and injured. Edwin joined me. "Glad we're both still here." We tipped the edges of our mugs together but neither of us smiled, we listened to the noises around us, watched as the herd of fresh beef moved into view, observed our Sergeant becoming upset with a line of horses that had the potential of getting in the way, saw the mules bringing up the end of the line, one of them carrying, of all things, what appeared to be a proper writing desk. We couldn't see the top of it, but the shape as defined by the blanket covering it and one of the good shapely legs dangling between the two nearside legs of the poor mule, made it look like a proper desk.

"That's the end of the line, then," announced Edwin. "The mules belong to the officers in command, they tell me."

"Where are the officers, then?"

"Oh, they're well up in front, making plans for the rest of us poor sods I shouldn't wonder."

One rifle shot broke the cold air. I jumped to my feet.

"There might be another one, Joss. Bet you're glad you're not killing hogs anymore."

"Did the butcher just shoot a hog?" I was disgusted, really. Not only was it a waste of a bullet, it was a waste of good meat.

Edwin pulled me back to the seat. "The shot is only used on the beef. Where do you think your dinner will come from later?"

"Do you like working in the commissary?"

"It turns out I'm not a good shot," Edwin sighed before he swirled his coffee in his mug. "Matter of fact, it has to be said I can't shoot at all, really. I don't seem to have the coordination, they tell me. Could even be something wrong with my eyes. So, I had a choice given to me – honorable discharge and thanks anyway but I'd be a danger to my fellow in the field, or I could volunteer for the wagons."

"I'm sorry to hear that, Edwin, I truly am."

"Don't be," he winked. Don't know why.

"Well, yes, after all the trouble I went through to get here, the least I could do was to make the best of it. Remember Sarge Harrison saying he'd find something for us to do? Well he was true to his word. The only problem is, and believe me when I tell you…"

"… of course, I will. We're chums."

"The cooks eat last."

I was saddened by that. "Is that why you look so skinny?"

"Yeah. The uniform never fitted me but know I'm using belt and braces. See?" He winked again. Was he getting twitchy?

It was the first laugh I shared in many days. The sun was trying to join us, I think but it was getting to the end of February so the wet and cold clung to us enough to keep us in line.

"What are you doing?"

"Just soldiering, that's all."

"You've got one of those special rifles, though."

"Yeah. They ran out of the others." Now I knew Edwin would never get a gun, I didn't want to tell him the real reason.

"Get one for me, Joss and don't try to kid me. I know that gun means you're a crack shot."

"Not as much as it's made out to be," I felt embarrassed.

"Better get back. I'll get some breakfast or lunch or at least food of some kind. If I come across a good piece of beef cheek for us, we can maybe share it later. Come find me."

I watched determination march away from me. Edwin had courage. I found a hardtack box in the loose belongings pile. I would use it, as I'd seen many others do, as a writing desk. Socks would be such a good thing to own. Postage stamps would be useful too. I didn't want to rummage through a dead man's clothes, but still, if I came across some, I wouldn't turn down my luck.

Someone started singing Yankee Doodle. Others joined in. It meant, surely, the worst was over. I was so cold still. I discovered I wasn't keen on the company of many others. It may be because I couldn't hear so well if they just spoke to me, but I could hear music. It was because of all the noise of the past few days but I felt out of place, disjointed, not belonging to the world. It was time to write home. I would ask for socks. I would send it to Ryan. He'd tell everyone else. Miss Shona could knit. I remember she cared for Buck that way when the doc chopped of the poor guy's toe. My stomach growled. When was the last time I ate something? I wanted to see if there was anything to see in the hardtack box I picked up. The hardtack was soggy, as it was with most of us. I stared into it. I remember staring at it, I don't know for how long because the next I know, the dinner bell was sounding. There's one thing'll make a soldier move faster that a shot coming for him and that is, without a doubt, the dinner bell. Dinner also means a chance to start the thing a soldier is best at – especially volunteers like me – griping. Even a Delmonico steak would never be good enough for any of us. The fact that I didn't know what a Delmonico was didn't matter. The fact is, the army was never as good as Ma's stew, cake, pudding or pie. The best pie was a pecan pie, an apple pie or even a blueberry pie, depending on what state you represented. The army just couldn't do it. So, why was there never anything left by the time dinner was over? Why did we all lick our plates –don't tell me to clean 'em – why did most of us fall in a heap afterwards, burping and picking our teeth clean. Some even manage to catch a bit of sleep, but when they woke they'd mention the beef must have walked a great long way to get there, for it was as tough and tasteless as a cooked Christmas turkey in January and most likely just as poisonous.

I watched movement in the fort. Officers were out of their buildings – the ones owned by the Confederates just a couple of days ago – a horse was mounted, but not hurriedly. This officer moved down to the river to have words with another, this time on board the Carondelet, one of the ironclads. I can hear a bugle. It's a good thing, as a soldier, I can hear a bugle. We were to break camp. We would be receiving orders before we kipped down. I wondered how far south we would be going, because all the flat land in Kansas was my land but this land, these gentle rolling hills, the Kentucky Buck said I should aim for was all around me. I was becoming attached to it. It didn't surprise me, having a feeling for the land. I only wondered what it would look like when the mud was all gone. If we headed south I may be here in spring and have the time to find out what Buck was on about. Why had he said it was good horse country, because all our poor horses had pulled cannon up hills and through thickets. They'd become nasty when left tied in the pouring cold snow and rain a couple of days ago.

I turned to look toward Edwin, who rubbed his stomach and grinned at me from the seat of the wagon.

A runner trotted to Lieutenant Wright's tent. Sergeant Major Harrison ordered us to prepare for inspection. Most of us were old hands by now, so pulled down our sleeves, slapped on our hats, straightened our boots, belts and haversacks etc. and moved together as a worm would find a hole in the ground to hide from the onslaught of a wren.

Lieutenant Wright entered the ersatz square, officer's sword glinting in what was left of the sunlight.

He gave us a cursory onceover after our Sergeant reminded us to form up and then finally told us, – I would like to say cheered us on, but no, he just plain told us – that the southern boys were on the run and it was our job to keep them going, all the way back to Atlanta if they didn't surrender first. We tried to cheer but it didn't come out right. Sarge dismissed us and I went to Edwin to see if he knew of any postage stamps anywhere. I could send the letter before we left. It didn't need to be a long one, after all.

Chapter 28

The equipment finally caught up to us just as we began our march to Tennessee.

"Did you know we were in Kentucky this whole time?" I asked Edwin as I kept him company on the wagon. It was good to be in an outfit that only made me account for myself once a day.

"I think I was told." He seemed distracted.

"You making bread?"

"No, coffee for later."

"Glad I opted to carry my own."

"No denying it'll probably taste better."

Noises of tins and mugs, shouts of frustration and anger circled in the air. An army wasn't an easy thing to get moving, it seemed. There was a place for everyone and as I said, the officer's mules took up the rear but still, there wasn't much difference between here and Cairo: noise, smell and a band playing what was supposed to be music. One of the drummer boys didn't look more than eight or nine. His uniform fitted him so well it looked like his Ma had sewn him into it. His eyes were wary of everything and everybody. I remembered feeling that way when I was his age, so I didn't go up to him to make a fuss. If anyone in Validation had done that to me, marked me out to be a near orphan, I'm pretty sure I would have cried. This kid couldn't afford that luxury, so I didn't push it. He hit his drum hard, once with every fourth step, as I remember.

I decided to try to get ahead of things, see if I could find the river. It had settled some as had the air about me. It wasn't running so high or fast. Perhaps Kentucky contained a little of spring warmth. A halt was called for a meal, I hoped. Yes. We were ordered to fall out. I sat where I was because the road was dry. I ruminated about the last couple of weeks. I wasn't bothered about the death and destruction. I was bothered that I didn't care anymore. No. My concerns were food, heat and getting rid of the lice that were coming on with the arrival of warmer weather. Some of the old soldiers must know a trick or two about the little bastards. I ripped off my shirt jacket and picked a few from my collar.

"Take a match and burn their little asses, kid. They sizzle and die that way," Private Collins was from Maine.

"Nah, drown the sons-of-bitches in the nearest puddle," Private Temperance was from Vermont, I think.

"Well, now. Best thing to do is cook your coffee real hot, add them to the mix, skim them off the top and watch 'em add to the flavor. They've had the taste of you, the least you can do is to return the favor." Sergeant Joynes sat beside me. I'm not sure where he's from. He looked no older than maybe Buck, but he had no beard or even the thought of one. It made his mouth stand out because his lips were so thin they didn't look to be present. I couldn't take my eyes from them when he spoke because his letters didn't sound right. When he laughed his top lip never moved – not even to twitch.

"You did well, for a Kansas man."

I didn't rise to the bait: "How many of us do you know, then, Sergeant Harrison?"

"Just the two of you."

I kept picking at my clothes as if I didn't care, which I didn't, really.

"Met a man called Ryan O'Grady once long time past. Any relation you think?"

Now, if he'd told me that when I was green, like for instance on the day I enlisted, I would have probably blushed and got myself in a fluster, but now I was fully grown I shrugged: "Kansas is a big state, Sergeant." I even looked him right in the eye when I said it.

"Knew him to be a heavy drinking man. Chip on his shoulder when he had a whiskey in him."

"Wouldn't know anything about that." I threw my shirt over my shoulders while I started the same job on my jacket. "You take sugar in your coffee?"

Sarge stood to clean the dried mud from his backside but he was considerate enough to turn himself away from my pitiful little fire. "Going to visit your little chick, Edwin. He's always got a hot one and no, don't get carried away with sugar in your coffee, Private. There will be plenty times when you'll miss it if you can't get it."

Private Collins shimmied closer: "Here. You got distracted. Want some coffee? I got lots. We can trade later."

I accepted his kindness but managed to keep my distance. I didn't know too many and after seeing the bodies and wounded at Donelson, I didn't want to be any more affected than I was. I could buddy up, I could even share my half bed with Edwin, but friendship was not to be a consideration. We were here to do a job and only a job. Then, once we won, we could go back home or make a dream come true, whatever it was. The trick to it was to survive and to live uninjured. It shouldn't take any longer than to Independence Day, surely. Yes, I planned on being back in Validation by the time Poppy's babe was born, medals earned, and war done for.

"Hirrup."

Sergeant Major Harrison marched toward us as I cracked a hardtack with my fist. "Boots on, canteens full, three days rations from the wagon, report back and in line by time of next drum."

Now, I know I was supposed to pour my hot coffee onto the ground, but I didn't. I put my boots on though and shook my jacket and shirt one more time. The coffee Private Collins so kindly gave me I poured down my open throat as I rose. Sarge was staring at me.

"Sergeant?" I asked.

"How did you do all that in one piece? Where's your gun?"

I swung it in front of me and slung it across my chest, wondering if I should salute but knowing it wouldn't be appropriate to salute a Sergeant, so I just stood to attention. He eyed me up and down.

"You always look so damned clean, boy." He walked away. I shrugged at Private Collins: "You need anything?"

"No, but you are awful tidy all the time. You're an amazement. Hell, I bet you don't even got blisters."

"Packed my boots with socks, didn't wear 'em. Feet don't slip that way."

"Might try that next time I have a pair."

A drum called us to muster. It was the little fella. Maybe it was the only thing he could play, but he did it well.

Further south it was. We fell in and got going. I trotted alongside for a bit and then up front. The *skirmishers were ahead of even me so if there were some greys lurking in the shrub the main body would be alerted. That's when I found out why Buck told me I belonged in Kentucky. I skipped up a hill, enjoying my freedom, thinking my thoughts of nothing, daydreaming as Buck would have it and as I saw the land below, I lusted for it. Lusted is the only word I can use. My knees grew weak, my breath escaped, I choked back tears, I scanned the horizon, and I imagined horses. Good, strong horses, all colors, proud horses, horses that belonged to themselves and only allowed a man to tame them if they wanted to be tamed. What was wrong with me? I must stand. I must leave the dream behind. I was at war. Men were counting on me. I wiped my eyes to clear the blue color of the grasses from them along with my tears. I continued the ridge south.*

The sun went down, I reported to the Lieutenant that nothing of note was in our way to the south.

"You look like you need a strong stew. The cook tent has surpassed itself tonight. A fresh kill of cattle is available. Dismissed and put your eye back in. The skirmishers came across twenty Confederates and took no prisoners. We did capture two horses. I thought you would have seen more."

"No Sir." I saluted, withdrawing to see Edwin. It's such a convenience to have a cook as a dog tent friend.

"Glad you're here. Been saving this bit of meat for you – so fresh it's still squirming. Want me to grill it, boil it or fry it?"

I looked at it and yes it was still purple and bloody. "I'll find a green stick and burl it over one of the big fires. Want to join me?"

"Not a bad idea. I've had some stew, but I know where I can find a slice of cake. I'll bring you some."

"This cooking thing is making you sound girlie."

"The soldier thing is making you sound like a killer."

We looked at each other for just a second or two both thinking about how much things had changed since our train journey and to be honest, both of us being grateful for it.

"Cairo was boring for drill and this is boring for daily duty but if we ain't bored we're deaf, choking and shitting our pants."

We laughed at each other. I wandered to the nearest fire, fortunately containing Privates Collins and Temperance where I was made as welcome as one of my trade could ever be. We were all feeling comfortable. I asked permission to roast my steak and was introduced to another four men all busy at sewing socks, removing lice, lancing blisters or paring nails. Life in the line was like this – patchy.

Horses were heard entering camp, voices were raised near the officer's tents, rifles were stacked, a harmonica started in the rear somewhere. Edwin joined us as my steak was turning my preferred color of black on the outside and pink on the inside. I reached in my pack for some treasured salt and pepper, held the piece between my bent knees and bit into it. I didn't know how hungry I was until I did it. Edwin passed me a mug of army coffee which as usual was weak and awful, but at least better than nothing.

The boys leaned forward when he opened a box containing a large fruit cake.

"My sister sent it."

I made a mental note to ask him two things: when did he get it and was there anything for me? Meanwhile he cut decent sized slices for all of us and then Private Temperance belched which made all of us grin.

"I gotta go to the trees a minute," I announced.

I wandered nearer the officer's end of the camp. The mules were chomping away at their dinner, so I ducked past them. Shit stinks, I thought. I'll add mine to the pile. A massive black stallion snorted at me as I squeezed past. The brand. Sweet Lord, it was Buchanan.

Chapter 29

////////////////////////////

So, there we were, all settled in nicely. We were marching south and content to do so despite the blisters and the food – good thing I had a friend in the cook tent, though. Weevils are a beast to contend with. Everyone thought the same of them – another thing in the soldier's daily ration of what to grumble about next. Grumbling came with the ammunition and the guns – part of the job as most of us say.

The Lutheran showed up. Even he grumbled, and I was of the opinion he, as a man of God, wouldn't be good at it, but I was wrong. He was maybe the best. He can make a prayer to Jesus of it. Yep, he would ask for relief of blisters, corns, cold feet, overheated feet, rough Sergeants, drunk Lieutenants, and while he acknowledged that lice and weevils were creations of the Lord, we could do with less of them here. We would be happy to share them with our enemies, if they were feeling short or some nightly company.

Once I'd met up with Buchanan and discovered he was just passing through, had been renamed Abraham, was now in the charge of a Captain Grey who was a good rider, I relaxed about his care. The MacLaren would have been proud to see his horse in his cavalry cloth and saddle. Abraham himself was pleased with his lot – he held himself well.

"Hey-up," Sergeant Major Harrison bellowed. "Form-up for orders."

Now, I wondered, what the hell? This hadn't ever happened in the middle of the day. At least it wasn't raining.

"When I call your names, you will fall out."

Mine was called. There weren't all that many of us now. Sick-call had been useful for some, and I know that a private had been deemed to be so sick he was sent home. There was no shame in it. He could come back when he got better if the war was still going on.

Anyway, a few of us got the better end of the deal: we were sent to the Tennessee River and a waiting ship because, and the twenty or so of us were told this privately, that we would disembark at a place called Pittsburg Landing, so we could reconnoiter the lay of the land, south. I was excited, I don't mind saying, until a couple of days later we got there.

I don't like heights. (Have I already said that?) I don't like looking up at them either and that was a tall, tall cliff-face. There wasn't much land at the bottom of it. The Landing didn't look big enough to take much more than supplies, a few wagons and a bale or two of cotton. When we got off it was in the near dark, so we decided to stick together for the night. A decent fire was built just part way from the dock, music tried to be heard – this time not from a band, just a fiddle and a mouthie. Someone joined in with the spoons a bit later, the moon got up a bit and we slept in our dog tents, finding a partner who would suit for the night, feet to the heat.

"Got something for you." A gentle kick woke me. "You got something from home," Private Collins said.

What a parcel. I wrote back as soon as I opened it. The Christian ladies made me six pairs of proper knitted

223

socks and wrote a letter of admonition for leaving as I did. Poppy enclosed a cake in a tin she must have been saving for years because she wondered if it was possible for me to send it back, so she could send me more. I could put my return letter in it. Shona sent stamps – a hint, most like. Ryan sent a letter. I burnt it. I didn't like what it said. Buck was coming to get me out of the army. What right did he have? What 'right' did any of them have to tell me what to do?

"Bad news?" asked Private Eon Collins.

"Sorta."

"Why only sorta? It is, or it isn't."

I told him it was. A guy we call the Mindwalker at home is on his way to rescue me from the army.

"Why's he called the Mindwalker?"

I told him Buck's mind goes for a walk every once and awhile. He's nice enough, but not a full brain. I didn't tell him he walked with a real limp.

"Why'd they send him, then?"

He's the least busy, I said. Everyone else has a job of work.

"He'll need you to protect him from himself, by the sound of it."

And that, I thought to myself, is exactly what worries me.

"Don't know how he'd go about getting you out of the army by now unless you only signed on for the three months." Sergeant Major came to sit with us while the coffee was brewing.

"I'm free to leave on April 12th, Sergeant."

"You want to?"

We heard drums and a band forming up on the slush covered jetty. Yankee Doodle was back, and I was *getting tired of him, you know? Was it the only song they knew? Sarge moved off as I found a place in the cliff to squeeze into for some privacy to write back. I didn't mention looking forward to seeing Buck in case someone could read between the lines and spot my lie.*

A Post Office was my next stop. The things the army could do in a flash of time never ceased to flummox me. They could find a Post Lady, wrapping and a stamp but extra blankets, well, that'll take time and maybe next week. Then you could see piles of them behind a stack of tents along with steel frames and mattress beds, but you couldn't just get one blanket until they were stamped as clear to go. At the minute, I needed something to wrap Poppy's cake tin in, so I stuffed my knapsack with all the clean socks around it as protection and then came across a most odd-looking lady, partially dressed in a cavalry top coat, a white neckerchief and skirts that reminded me of the sailcloth from one of the wooden ships. Her grey hair was pinned up by a knitting needle, I think. She was wearing good boots. She had the right priorities. At any rate, she very kindly helped me once I explained the necessity of returning the tin. The poor woman had one eye forward and the other apparently looking to the right. I presumed the one that worked better was the one she used to watch the scissors as they cut the twine for my parcel and it turned out I was right because the squint eye reciprocated my smile. She had young teeth. I felt at home with her.

Unburdened of my thanks, I slung my rifle across my chest, found my compatriots, all independent thinkers such as myself and made plans for the day. I volunteered to see if there was an alternative to climbing straight up the cliffs. One of the men remarked on the height of them, another remarked on the odd yellow color of some of it and we all agreed we would come back here before dark to report to each other before we reported our findings to the Lieutenant. That way, we would all have the same story.

I trotted off south, rifle in my hand, at my knee, loaded just in case and of course far away from the cliffs. My what a mess of mud, snow, sleet was churned up as the army began to take over an area full of old cotton fields. It was a reasonably flat as far as I could make out – a few farms, a proper painted small church off to the west, a few birds twittering away, and spring must be coming because there were buds on the trees in a couple of small peach orchards. The sun was warmly up, the earth responding to it by inches and I began to forget the coldest night of my life at Fort Donelson. I wandered up through the bramble bushes, now thinking about growing again, pushed my way through the debris left by winter, using the saplings as leverage, scaring the bejesus from a hare or two and finally coming to a clearing in which the artillery was beginning to rest or set up, I wasn't sure which. Big guns and their functioning had no fascination for me although I had cause, already, to be grateful for them, even the ones on board the warships which tried to keep the Donelson one busy for us as we tried to climb into the Fort.

I wandered over to them, not really needing to converse but I could see coffee cooking and hoped they would let me add some of my own to their pot.

"You look young to be here, boy."

Yes, I'd been told that before now, I agreed. One of the cannoneers jabbed the man that said it in his ribs.

"That's a Sharps. Means he can shoot. Can you shoot, boy?"

I told them I could, but I'd be grateful for a coffee. They said they'd let me have a coffee if I shot something for them. I chose to shoot the hare I'd seen but thought the better of coffee with them because I didn't want to share the meat. I would take it back to camp now and start cooking it in time for us all to report to each other. I just walked away, sure in the knowledge they wouldn't argue with me. On the other hand, I was sure I would not have anything more to do with them unless the Lord set me to give them a hand in battle. They did not appear to me to be a generally sociable bunch. I'd heard they considered themselves, in general, a cut above the rest of us. I'll make a judgement of this one day.

By the time the others returned to the fire I was roasting the hare and boiling the coffee. Poppy's cake was lurking in my bag, but I would share it later. Only a half dozen showed because we'd been split into roughly three teams of six. No one told us of course, but this was the army way of it. Privates find out stuff once the stuff is done.

We had a Sibley tent given to us during our dinner. It was suggested to us we erect it at the east end of the formation, so we would be more easily accessible to the General when he arrived in case he felt he needed skirmishers and his crack shots to further investigate the land before we headed off toward Corinth. We looked at each other because it was the first we'd heard of it. I asked if we should look at the other end of the field tomorrow and the answer was no because a rail track was already blown up and the area near the church had been scouted by another group of us.

So, it was confirmed then, erect our tent well beyond that small peach orchard, near that field of old cotton facing the woods across the way a bit, and await orders. So, we did that but honestly, I wondered about the farmer because he hadn't done a respectable job of clearing – some of the cotton plants looked dead even if they were as high as a man's head.

Gonna put my feet up and set a spell before I write more. Smells like rain.

Chapter 30

Buck set a small fire amongst the circle of stones he'd formed. The flames teased the bottom of his kettle-pot, holding the right amount of water for a mug of coffee. The morning was warming as the bright sun began to rise, clearing the mist from the wet fields below. From the prominent position above the river, sheltered from prying eyes by the shell of a burnt-out house, he could take his time to admire the seemingly endless rows of tents and the beginning of movement around them. Men were organizing themselves, stretching suspenders, scratching their buttocks and beards and spitting out what was left of their nighttime saliva while their eyes scanned the horizon in Buck's direction. One or two hovered near a low campfire, coffee mugs still empty. Some shouting was heard, but not much: it was still early in the day. The sun hadn't properly risen. Buck's head took on a powerful itch, most likely the worst he'd ever felt. He threw his old slouch hat down on top of his bedroll. Stretched out and steady, elbows resting on the support he had created, he could take his time to move his spyglass from west to east. He scanned a small white church, more than one farm – some old fields, some new – a fence, of sorts, a wooded area that looked to be a peach orchard with all its pink blooms, a pond. He thought he saw Indian mounds. They looked out of place. A road was right below him, leading near to the landing and he observed a crossroads. Neither were in great shape, probably due to winter weather. No Joss.

His head made him want to dance with the bother it was giving him, so he settled it by humming quietly, as The Raven taught him back home. As the sun began to show itself, he adjusted his position in case the light reflected in the lens of his telescope. He didn't need to attract attention to his whereabouts. In the very far distance was a forest, dressing in spring green. He could see roads, some of which were muddier in appearance than others. On the steamer, he'd overheard the talk that the roads from Corinth were no more than a sludge of mud, perhaps so wet it could be called a tributary of the Tennessee. This blue army had been here for at least a week before he had taken passage going south. There was one thing certain – the army was a busy one. Not a single soldier, apart from a very young looking private, had paid him any mind, which was just as well, really. He acknowledged the young man's salute with a nod, followed by a quick exit.

A distant sound of trumpet reverberated a bit late, it seemed, as the men below were already milling about, looking to their breakfasts or their rifles. Occasionally a head would poke from one of the larger tents, one of the small negro boys hanging around outside, looking for sustenance it appeared, would run to the smaller tents in the back for some reason or fetch a bowl of water from a canteen hanging on the handle of a campfire stove. Some men appeared to be limping, others, apparently fresher to the war, were swaggering up and along what appeared to be a straggling front line. Not all were fully dressed yet. One or two only wore the uniform trousers and suspenders over a loose shirt.

Some bent to struggle with a sock or their boots. Laughter filtered to Buck when one of the men slid sideways into the clay colored mud.

Activity in the woods near the church end caught Buck's eye. Scanning for further information he gasped when he thought he saw horses and an unusual color of uniform lurking in the trees. Steadily, he swept the tree line on the other side of the patches of farmed fields. There were more grey uniforms sliding in and out of the trees, toward the middle of the field, where the old cotton field was – and the wooden fence was pretending to do its job of protecting the property line. On Buck's side of the fence, the Union camp was at its strongest.

The wind picked up a bit: Buck admired the Stars and Stripes as it lifted its head to acknowledge the day. Then, a boom from the woods opposite and a little to his right. Then another. Rifle shots. Men in blue stood from their sitting and shaving positions to listen, their belts and powder adjusted to a practical position on their person, the small noise of it taking up the space in the air between their breaths. No one needed to speak. The smell of incipient killing had begun. It reeked of cloying gunpowder, sulphur, sweat, and fear masquerading as bonhomie.

The monster in the wood let its belly rumble. Men snapped to attention, fell naturally into self-protective and trained groups. The guns, the great grey guns of the Confederacy found their rhythm. Union trumpets trilled, drums gave out the long roll making sure the assembly would be picked up from the landing to the tiny church, most likely two or three miles distant. Men licked their lips, hearts pumping found the surface of their shirts. They danced around a bit and waited for a charge or an order for one. Some stood, others lay down, and Buck began to look in earnest for Joss.

Buck smelled rain in the air, the spring blue and yellow flowers were making their presence known just below where he had camped the night before. They quivered in time to the cannon fire, mother earth reacting to the noise.

He controlled his breathing to begin the search again. Joss was only a skinny little fella when he saw him last in January. Boys at fifteen or sixteen could grow a might if they were well fed, but that was unlikely in any army. He extended his instincts. They led him to a farmer's field near the fence – the exact one the greys were heading to. Joss. He was in uniform. It looked on the small side. His hair was longer. It touched the collar of the blue coat jacket. He had grown – like a good foal: all leg. Buck unfolded himself from the ground, slipped the knife Ryan gave him down his real boot, tossed the strap of his medicine bag over his head to his shoulder and began a deliberate slow progress down the hill and through the scrub and trees toward the camp. He was aware not wearing a uniform may attach the wrong type of attention from either Union or Confederate. He weaved his way down the bluff, following the lie of the land, using the saplings as handholds. He heard ordnance of every kind, but he didn't lose focus on Joss and kept going despite the noise. There occurred a volley of fire. Men ran for their weapons, including Joss, who unknowingly, ran toward Buck, followed by another young private.

Cannon fire whirred and whipped and whistled overhead. Grey suits were seen running from the trees and toward the Union camps. It felt like hundreds, if not thousands of them. The ground twisted and shook. It regurgitated the mud each time a cannonball found its target. Joss and his friend ducked into a ditch. Buck jumped in after them, nearly whacking Joss' head with his crutch. Joss turned his rifle to him. "It's the Mindwalker from Kansas, Edwin. The strange one I told you about."

Edwin was counting and reloading. Buck dragged Joss deeper into the ditch. The brown eyes of the boy who worked so well with horses were now hard and black. Edwin fired. It was the first time Buck had been close to a rifle round. God, the smoke and noise. He gasped in the air stupidly thinking it would be clean, but he could taste the powder. He wondered if he would ever hear again as the Great Spirit intended.

"Been sent to fetch you back." He yelled over the oncoming charge of what appeared to be armed, bedraggled young men charging toward them.

"Tell your buddy to go back to Kansas or start shootin," Edwin bellowed.

"Come on, Joss. Out of this place."

"Later, asshole." Joss fired again.

The two young soldiers ignored him. They kept firing. Buck couldn't see what they were firing at.

"Let's go. Both of you."

"You dickhead. Piss off." Edwin didn't even look at him.

"Look, we want it over and done." Edwin ditched his cooking job when the wagon got blown up.

"Come to give me a hand?" Joss shouted back and seemed to be counting for a bit. He stood up and fired. Edwin sat down to re-load. Back to back, they seemed to have a system of their own the army knew nothing about, but a trumpet sounded, and both took steps to the rear, one covering the other's back at each move.

"Gonna join up, Indian?" Buck was reminded he was still in buckskins. He felt no shame in it and no conscience about remaining neutral in this craziness. Edwin's eyes reminded him of a look in Silk's. He was repulsed by it.

"Ya can come if ya want," Joss stood up, shrugged at his old friend, shouldered his rifle and calmly began a zig-zag away from the noise. He counted again. He turned, he fired, another man down. Joss reloaded as he walked. It seemed to Buck he was tempting death.

An unholy screech accompanied a massive group of butternuts attempting a head-long assault toward the Union line. Someone screamed 'each man for himself' and the mass of sensible soldiers flowed toward them. Buck felt they were all aiming directly at him, so grabbing his cane he began to hobble away from the onslaught as fast as a hawk diving for its lunch. Inadvertently, he tripped up a retreating private, got a devil's glance from him as balance was recovered and lost sight of Joss in what was developing as a proper mess of a skedaddle. Out of the corner of his eye he was sure he saw rifles remaining stacked, campfires lit to cook breakfast, buckets of water with shaving brushes perched on stools, and shoes or boots half polished still lying outside the tent flaps. The oncoming men looked filthy, but they carried a red and blue flag with them so proud looking it appeared to wash away any sin. Jabbing at the sky, taunting at the blues, poking ahead, poking down, Buck had a terrible instant vision of many bodies lying under it – naked. When this day ended not all lives would be accounted for.

A bewhiskered officer on a squat chestnut horse galloped across the retreating lines.

"We have to hold, boys," he screamed as he flashed past, his sword making a whirring sound as he whirled it around his head. "You volunteers, you swore to die for the cause and your country. Now's your chance to do it."

"Freakin' regular. He can just take himself straight to hell," said Edwin.

"I ain't stopping till I find some cover," Joss shouted at Edwin.

Both headed for the wooden fence structure.

"Look, there's a ditch, Joss. Hurry."

This time, Joss grabbed Buck's shoulder, throwing him behind a piece of wood that may have been a tree at dawn. "Stay down, Injun." He fired his rifle again to realize there were far too many enemy – they were early. They had no right to be here. They were supposed to be in Corinth, weren't they? Corinth was further south – a day's march away, surely.

Edwin loaded again. The boys were on a happy. Eyes were gleaming, whoops of joy exploded from them when they had a success with their aiming, and more blue colleagues joined the lucky pair to help them with their work. An officer showed up again, just briefly to call them good lads, but then the trumpet sounded somewhere, and it seemed to echo long ways to the left. There was so much smoke nothing could be seen in front or behind and Joss began to cough like he did when he was four or five and had a caved in chest due to hunger. All the men in the ditch obeyed the call to retreat and as it turned out, in the very right amount of time because the Greys were beginning to enjoy the breakfast and dry underwear left by the retreating Blues. It wasn't the right time to hold the line exactly there. They would have to drop back and see where their defense would be better, but how far?

The guns were making the ground shake, the Stars and Stripes hanging proudly but abandoned in front of the officer's tent, responded to the gusts of air created by cannon fire, by flapping like a captured eagle. Union canon were warming up to something big, now. The bugle sounded again: this time a call to arms. Drums tried sending messages to each unit. Edwin and Joss responded to it like children to a dinner bell. A cluster of officers just behind and to their right expelled a lone rider, rising in his saddle, galloping for the river. He was clipped by a Rebel shooter who, oblivious to his own fate, remained standing as he received a cheer from his fellows. Joss got him, through the neck, blood pumping and continued pumping and the beardless Reb put his hands up to staunch his life force. Joss sneered as his young enemy gasped for air before his knees gave out and he collapsed into the mud of a farmer's field at Shiloh. The union rider kept going. The Reb soldiers stood to see who had taken down one of their own.

"You ready, Edwin?"

Edwin brought down one of the onlookers. Joss took out another.

"We're pushing our luck, Joss."

"Not the cleverest are they, but I guess we better clear back a little." He indicated the direction to Buck.

The boys moved toward the hill. The officers on horseback watched them. One even nodded his head.

"Appreciate that shot, private."

"Yes sir, thank you sir." Joss kept moving. "Suggest you move a bit too, Sir. Rule of Battle, Sir."

Two of the officers laughed at him: "What rule is that then, son?"

"Don't make a show of yourself." Edwin saluted. "Could be used for target practice."

The officers stopped laughing and moved to a different bit of land, around a corner a bit, if you could call the end of a fence that very thing, but not back far enough, their conversation being more important. A cannonball found both. Joss swore as he ducked an intact flying leg. Buck got his first baptism of blood – his buckskin front was already covered in mud and dung, so the blood mixed in well with it. He was now sitting in a mess of wet guck. He felt something hard land on his back.

"Don't move," said Edwin, right into his right ear. "It's the closest you're likely to get to a cavalry hat, but the owner's head is still in it. I'll get him off. Just sit still a minute. Can I borrow your stick?" Edwin wasn't keen to get his gun any dirtier than it already was.

Buck could see Joss, the boy he'd come to rescue. He watched him counting again. Edwin returned Buck's stick to him, now covered in blood. Joss was holding his breath, he fired, and none of them moved.

The bugle sounded. Buck supposed a great, glorious assault toward the Confederate ranks was to occur. He was wrong. Even more soldiers were coming toward them – in battle order, marching shoulder to shoulder and upholding that flag, sun shining well enough to make their bayonets glint like a thousand shards of silver. He couldn't tolerate the thought of what had been lying on his back, so he began to stand. Joss grabbed him.

"We're to retreat. Can't you hear the drums? The bugle is theirs, you idjit," Edwin shouted at Buck. "Move it you squirrel hunting little doggie." He growled at him and Joss was already well away.

The cannons had stopped for a bit, but Buck felt bullets hitting the ground beneath him and heard them buzzing past into the trees ahead and around the pond. Some of the branches were snapping under the weight of lead, making it harder to jump into the sparse group of trees to spy out some cover. He limped quickly to where Joss had taken his stand behind a collapsed fruit tree of some kind and used his stick as a pole to vault over it and land in a pile of fresh horse dung. Joss fired his rifle. Edwin joined them.

"Gotta go again, Buck," Joss shouted to him as he recognized the mess Buck was in, "Maybe get you to the river for a wash, eh?" Both the young men he'd fallen in with were considerably cheered now that Buck was in as much mess if not more, than they were. Joss appeared to be the cleanest, though

"Come quick. Let's move together to the river," Joss was in charge. "Don't want to get caught in with an officer – they attract attention by their finery and make trouble to the rest of us."

"We can always find our boys later." Edwin appeared to be methodical, practical and callous.

"Aw come on." His shoulders slumped. "Look Joss, there's more of the johnnies."

"One more volley each before we go, then," Joss aimed just a little because the enemy was only about a hundred yards away. "Damn. Missed."

"Never mind, kid. You hit his arm. He'll need the surgeon later." A large red-bearded man threw himself down into the ground beside Joss. His tattered blue uniform used to have three chevrons on the arm and Buck noticed his hemmed trousers only came down half way down his massive calf muscle.

"Hey, Sarge. How ya doin?" Joss was pleased to see this man.

Edwin grinned, showing his powder black teeth.

"We're ordered out. What you doin' here?" Sarge was loud and serious.

"Ordered away from that old road over there. See? The one with all the horses and fuss. There's a wooden fence hiding how sunk it is." Joss still had a part of him that was fifteen. He held his bragging rights.

Edwin remembered his job. He brought down another man and watched as the poor bastard screamed as he began to rip his uniform apart, over his stomach, looking for the wound. Edwin reloaded. Once the guy found his guts he began to shake his head and sob. Edwin fired his Minnie ball into the young Reb's head. Buck threw up.

"I just did the kid a mercy is all." Edwin's blackened mouth laughed at Buck's awkwardness.

"Don't waste your bullets. One per customer. Move it laddies."

Buck grabbed his crutch: "Where're you going, gymp?" Sarge shoved him down on his ass.

"Can't be slowed down. Sorry. You shouldn't be here." The look in Edwin's eye concurred with the Sarge's feeling on the matter.

"Edwin, if anything happens to this guy, you can write the letter home."

Edwin was in a semi squat and counting but he nodded in recognition of Joss's words just as Sarge whacked him on the back of his head making him stand up on the double quick. Noises, even more noises were coming their way but this time the symphony was of voices, horses and a clash of steel. The sounds echoed around the hills and trees – not much of it absorbed by the Tennessee mud. The four of them were squatting as best they could, a position not much enamored by the view of what appeared to be an organized rout of an unorganized professional army. The screaming of men, horses and the turning of wheels on carts and gun-carriages competed for attention. All that mattered to the johnnies was to run past the last bivouac, the one the black boys had so diligently taken care of, to the ranks the tents had sheltered, and wonder what breakfast might have been like. Steaming camp kettles were removed from their fires. Buck thought he saw a half pig lying in the dirt. It would be edible to whomever won the ground that day. The confederate cannon fire wasn't adjusting its sights in time to keep up with their infantry, so it looked like they were running into their own canisters and heavy ammunition. A gun-carriage moved forward – a struggle witnessed by all – it's horses straining in panic, to drag it up a road through the mud. It began to slip sideways. A soldier in grey, who was standing to eat some leftover Union breakfast, didn't get out of the way in time and fell backwards screaming as the caissons wheels ran over him. His body gave the horses a little extra traction, but it took manpower to straighten out the heavy weapon, so it could be returned to use. The action bought Joss's small band some time to retreat further.

Joss stood up, shouldered his rifle and calmly began a zigzag away from the noise. He counted again.

He turned, he fired, put another man down. Edwin fired. Joss re-loaded as he walked.

"I thought you couldn't shoot."

"I lied. I shoot when it matters." Edwin winked at his buddy.

* * *

An unholy screech accompanied a massive bunch of butternuts attempting a headlong assault toward what appeared to be the middle of the blue line. Many horses, especially of the blue uniformed variety, and wearing gold embroidered saddle cloths, were caught up in the frenzy. Cavalry swords sliced the sunlight, hoofs reared, bullets cut the cavalry beasts into pieces, but still they held fast, kept their courage, protected their riders until they finally collapsed, drained of intention and bloodless, into the sediment of battle. For a time, the Confederate Army retreated.

"God Almighty. Who is that?" Joss asked.

"Don't know. Prentiss?"

"Well he's not having a good time, whoever he is," Edmund said. "If that is Prentiss, I wouldn't want to be a Reb. That Lieutenant would rather die than quit."

He fired his rifle.

Another young man, perhaps an aide to an officer, galloped past them as they headed toward the river, or at least they hoped they were all going the same way for the same reason. It was all mixed up. No one knew exactly what direction was the right one, it seemed to Buck that the only true way to go was away from the men shooting at them and they were headed, it appeared in their thousands, straight into the campsite that only at dawn, belonged to hundreds and hundreds of men in blue uniforms. There was a word for it, he knew: not ambush, not attack, a raid. Yes, a raid. This time the Confederate army had concluded an audacious raid; a declaration of war without any preamble. They had disturbed the peace of the day. They came to test the Union forces and so far, it appeared to Buck, that the raid had found them wanting. Surely the officers should be conducting this in better form. Didn't they know what they were about?

"Your mind gone for a walk, Buck?"

Buck focused on Joss for a time: "Yes. Sorry."

"We could die here in this orchard. Where the hell is your gun?"

"Don't carry one."

"Here, take this one. Only used once, by the look of it." Edwin shoved a Henry into his hands: "You got something in your head about it not being right to kill folks, because if you do, that's fine, but I'd be glad if you could see your way clear to kill the son-of-a-bitch that's aiming at me. I swear I'll return the favor if it comes to it."

He bellowed his field lecture directly into Buck's face. The cannon started. Right at the men near and around the orchard. Rifle shot spat, cleaning the bark from the trees. Cries of Mama echoed one man to the next who needed water and crawled to the pond.

"If you're not gonna fight, find some powder and shot. Get us some ammunition, Injun," Sarge screeched at Buck who dropped the gun. "From a corpse, from a corpse. Ammunition. Now."

Buck, in shock, rolled this way and that. He had no problem finding a body or a new stock of ball and powder. He tossed the equipment to Joss and rolled back under a tree. He wondered how anyone could survive this. Joss looked so calm, just acting like the automaton he'd seen at the Leavenworth fair. Why was he sliding forward? Why was Edwin moving back? The Sarge stayed put. Joss rolled on his back and fired. Two greycoats fell. Edwin killed one. Joss killed the other. They stayed where they were. Sarge fired a shot that seemed to past right past Buck's nose. He grinned at him and shrugged, "'nother one down."

A reb crashed through the underbrush, straight at Buck. He threw Ryan's killing knife, straight at his heart but missed, sticking him in the gut. The man fell on his face, screaming. Buck slid up to him, retrieved the knife and apologized as he slit his throat. He didn't acknowledge Sarge's, "well done." He did, however rescue the man's canteen. It seemed half full. He took a slug and passed it over. Joss was staring at him, no doubt wondering who'd been educating this farm boy.

The sun was warm now. The land stank as well and the heat didn't help. Thinking was not possible beyond survival. Even Buck could taste gunpowder and he hadn't fired a shot. Breathing fresh air was a dream of last night. Breathing at all was, for some, just wishful thinking. How many damn guns were there? Thousands?

The small group of four were forced to hide and run alternately but they got to a place where, if it was possible, even more disorganization and chaos were taking place. There was a proper landing. Two steamers were tied up. Men were being pushed from behind and trying to board. More ships of the line could be seen offshore, some heading toward them, others weighing anchor. A ships' horn sounded. It pulled away. Some tried to follow it by swimming, others floated out on torn bits of fencing. A belly deep sounding ship's horn sounded from well back. A large yellow dog was seen bouncing back and forth along the shore, yelping for its master. A steamer headed for the opposite shore which, when it could be seen through all the cloud and smoke, looked like a sandy, floating island. Cannon shell screeched into the river. The earth trembled, men braced themselves against the shock waves, the air being blown away from them. A steamer returned, a smaller one, perhaps even the *Black Warrior*, slipping out of the blue smoke permeating the air. It took on as many more survivors as it could without capsizing and turned back to the heaven that must exist on the other side of the Tennessee River.

Another, larger ship bore down on the Landing, but chose to anchor off. The whole effect was one of a square dance with no corners and a dosey doh with no caller. No one knew their partners for sure so were dancing along in slow rhythm until a beat caught up with them as they knew it must.

It was said Grant wasn't here for the first gunshots, but that was definitely the *Tigress*, his headquarters tied to the landing. The hospital ship, *Tyconn* was arriving; it was said.

Everyone said: they were a bit late to attend the concert. The army was running on scuttlebutt as normal.

Well, whichever ships they were, they were tardy. With any luck, maybe the navy would manage to fire off a cannon or two – just to keep the Rebs in check and give the Union something to cheer about for a change.

Sarge and the boys sat on low hills partly enclosed by forest. Light was fading but activity could still be seen and heard. Around the road and fence where Buck had first seen Joss, men were falling back after many bloody attacks. Joss, Sarge and Edmund observed as a Union officer stood to present his sword to a Confederate.

"Oh sweet Jesus." Edmund mouthed. "It's Prentiss." He gripped Joss's forearm. None could watch any further.

* * *

Never was so much cannon fire heard and most of it was coming from the Federals. The air never settled. Men and animals were dropping in shock. Hawks and vultures circled the area where Joss had been sleeping last night.

"Na, na. It can't be," Joss's voice sounded like a cat giving birth to too many kitties at once. "They're at the boys, look. See? Is that a whole regiment down?" The scavengers flitted about on their two legs, looking for juicy pickings from the corpses. "Sweet God in Heaven," he whispered.

A fizz of shot flew past, probably wild, but lethal if it was someone's turn to die.

"Been hearing hornets all day," Edwin said as he tried to cool his gun enough to clean her.

"Why do you count, Edwin?" Buck was curious.

The young man rested his long arms on his knees: "Joss and I figured out a while back at Donelson, that every ten seconds or so the enemy had to stop to breathe. We could see their breath in the cold. Dead giveaway."

"That means there's a second or two of silence if you listen for it," Joss said, "That's when you shoot.

Most folks gotta stand still and think when they're scared, just to take a breath."

"You don't look scared, Joss."

"After Donelson I didn't think I would be, but this... It's why we work well together, even if he is just a cook." Joss elbowed his buddy in jest. Edwin tried to hide an agreeing smile.

"When did you turn into a killer?"

"Donelson was a messier place when we left it, eh Edwin? Did Ryan get the letter?"

"Yes, but, you've turned your back on Validation, then?"

"Lord in Heaven." Joss looked straight at Buck. "Wouldn't you? I got a choice: clean horseshit or practice shooting all legal like. Couldn't even write a word without having to hide it."

"For the time being, anyway," Buck wasn't ready to give up, "The war will come to an end soon, Joss and then what'll you do?"

"Then I'll sit down and have a think. Right now, I'm busy, if you notice."

Edwin fired again: "Tired getting. Starting to waste ammunition – just winged that bastard."

"Who the hell are you, anyway?" Sarge had come back from what was probably a call of nature. He glared at Buck. "For God's sake leave the home talk 'til there's time."

"His mind goes for a walk sometimes. Time flies when a body is busy. Is it getting dark, or is it just gun smoke?"

"Light's definitely leaving for the day." Sarge had purloined a couple of good looking rifles and was loading both, but he'd been in a terrible hurry. "Fit for squirrels, maybe." He fired one and dropped it, feeling it to be unsafe. "Must be as old to have come over with the Pilgrim fathers."

He chose to lie on his back. A tree branch gave up trying to hang on to the tree trunk. He used the second rifle's butt to defend himself. "Lord keep us from any more sneak attacks." He rolled on to his corpulent stomach, forcing him to see what they had been defending.

"Don't drink any water unless it's flowing free and it's not a variation of red." The pond around the orchard was changing color from red to light pink. Pink petals floated amongst the dead who must have been attempting a last sip of water before they left this world for the milk and honey of the next. It may have been a peach orchard – an oasis of peace, maybe even for picnics and passion. Sarge was saddened to see the branches broken, some with a fine spray of blood clinging to them. A fizz of shot flew past but thudded into the root near Buck's good foot. He twitched.

Dusk was coming, and Buck smelled rain not far away. It would replenish canteens, not a terrible thing in the middle of battle. Gunfire was seen now: tremendous flashes at the top of the hill just above them, nearly a half mile away through the trees. The wind was taking most of the noise away from the tiny group, but mass anger from both sides remained palpable, and was carried so heavily in the spring air. Buck thought to himself the smoke might clear, but the fear and rage, never. It would soak into the land with every drop of blood, never to leave it.

"My god – we're finally firing back. Look at the flashes. They're going south, boys. The cannon balls finally be sent the right way." Joss's elation was catching.

"Worse in the dark, and we're underneath it. Run up, men. Hurry. Before our names are taken for the dead lists." Sarge took charge this time. He was the heaviest and oldest – most likely to crash his way through. He took a bayonet he'd found lying around and trusted it would be sharp enough to flail through the underbrush. The others charged up behind him, not looking back, only using their instincts to dodge a flying missile of any or all description. There were a dozen or so tired and dirty men around them, but they were organized into gun batteries and proper regiments. Determination showed through the creases of dirt and their cracked, dry lips.

They found a good space well behind the guns, slipping into the trees in and out of the shadows, knowing they would be unlikely to be spotted. Hundreds of demoralized men cowered under the bluffs below them, all clinging to the hope of a rescuing Union Navy ship.

Joss, foot-sore and hungry, took off his one good boot and threw it away: 'I've got one foot red raw and the other bleeding and blistered.'

He stretched out his legs in front of him and decided his socks, such as was left of them, were of no use either. "Can you fix me up a pair of boots, Buck?" He sneered at him. "If you stayed home you'd be fixing boots long before you fixed people."

"So, you got a name?"

"Buck Ross. Yours?"

"Sarge."

"He's not really a Sergeant though. Just got the right attitude for one. You can tell he's not real - he's ripped off the stripes – a real one would die first so I figure this

Sarge got his jacket from that very man. If you want anything, ask this Sarge. He'll probably do the most amazing deals for things – including women." Edwin sniggered. He'd been in the army too long already.

"I think there's a lot of things that don't appear to be what they are. Did you know that Joss won't be sixteen until next month, I think?"

"Nobody gives a damn about age, as long as you can do good soldiering and I was marked as a good enough shot to be paid as a skirmisher as soon as they set up the unit last month."

Buck took ointment from his healing bag and got to work.

"So, all that practice against squirrels and turkeys has stood you in good stead." He grabbed Joss's ankle and propped his small cold foot on his knee to begin working on the blisters. "I'm going to slice this one open." It was all the warning the farm boy got before Buck's knife flew across his heel.

"Hey," Joss yelped, "That wasn't nice." He glared at his doctor.

Sarge appeared fascinated by the battlefield aid, such as it was. "Do mine, too?"

Buck was inspecting the rest of Joss's foot but came up with no other problems, put an unguent on it and wrapped his heel in the clean muslin some kind soul had put into his medicine bag; probably Poppy.

Sarge sat to remove his boots. There was an audible suction and then a noxious smell. Buck glanced at the problem. "Wash your feet in that puddle over there. I won't be able to tell the difference between a lump of mud and a dirty toenail if you don't. I'll see Joss first and then come to you, if you like, Sarge."

Edwin had his back to everything until Sarge moved in front of him, but he turned to Buck, then: "You a girl or something?"

"Why're you asking?"

"Not in uniform, real concerned about clean and no rifle. Most folks that matter made up their minds which side they on couple years back."

Buck was working on Joss's other foot now.

"Anyway, I can get some light on this, Joss?"

"Not without giving away our position and I'm not doing that after all the time it took us to get here."

Buck shrugged and continued to scrape, gently, the bottom of his patient's foot. He took water from his own canteen and trickled it onto the affected areas.

"How'd you keep it so cold, Buck?"

"Don't hold it close to me I guess."

This time he took muslin to wrap the wounds and then ripped a pocket from his own buckskin to create a sort of slipper for his friend.

"Will you be able to put your boot back on if I slice the stitching a bit for you?" He considered Joss's eyes for the first time since the morning and for a cherished second, recognized the soul that he knew back home.

"Yeah, I can do that, Buck," Joss, the soldier, was back but Buck knew the boy was within reach of rescue and decided to stay with him until he could accomplish it.

"So, nurse, what side are you on?" Edwin had moved closer.

"I'm on your side, Edwin." Buck stood suddenly, like a snake scared out of the bushes. Edwin flinched. "More than anyone you've ever known, I'm on your side. You took care of Joss, I take care of you. If you are true blue, I am true blue." He settled back to the ground as smoke settles in the still air. Edwin followed as if mesmerized: Joss had seen this trick done in Lexington but then the poor woman had burst into tears when she found out she had admitted to various nefarious deeds and been arrested on the spot.

"You came to the Union to escape home."

"How the hell do you know that?'"

"Nothing difficult: you flinched when I got taller than you."

A cannon went off, followed by another, then another. This time much closer. They'd been taking things too much for granted. Sarge threw himself down on the boys.

Flames arrived from nowhere, throwing themselves about, dancing in the wind. Shells burst in air, their peculiar ring proving they'd hit their target. Muskets and rifles twittered in the gloaming, their blue smoke forming a quilt of invisibility, partly because of the color and partly because of the amount reaching the eyes of the soldiers, stinging, insinuating, making the man feel he'd got out of bed for a bad reason. The stench was strong enough to make the throat close. Maybe it was why the Rebs chose to yell the way they did. If the ears popped as they did at first, shouting at something was a massive clever way to clear them.

The experienced ear could hear the music of victory was marching to the river. The bullet unlucky enough not to find its target whispered past as if trying to hide from its failure. Round shot seemed to come all at once and from the left. Cheers were heard from far away. They didn't last, and the boys didn't know who had won a skirmish of some kind: they kept their heads buried within the brotherhood circumstances had created for them. Sarge lifted his head briefly to look at the river.

"There's ships coming. They're ours. They look like gunships."

Edwin moved to stand but was forced back down by the man in charge: "Wait until deep dark. We will be more use then."

Lying as they were, they could feel the earth being pounded by guns, some Sharps, others an ongoing, spreading rumble.

Joss peaked out.

"You're right. Those gunships look like they're shooting at the bayou below. Must be where the enemy are."

"There's men on the other side of the river," Buck remained lying down, but he stretched to see. He didn't want to get involved in the conflict, but he was now. No killing; he would heal where he could, but he couldn't resist looking in admiration. How did all these people know where to be at the same time and do what they were doing? What would happen if ten said they were going home because the crops needed to be planted. These questions flew through his mind possibly faster that one of Joss's bullets, but still...

"Lord in heaven, those damn Rebels are firing into the river, killing any swimming for our boats," Sarge growled. "Men of honor my arse."

Buck slapped him on his shoulder, the way men often do: "Good thing you haven't got your boots on Sarge. Sorry. You'd be right at 'em if you could."

This statement kicked off a seizure of merriment.

Edwin had the loudest laugh. He tried to cover it with his hand, Joss struck it away, the two young men fell into each other's arms laughing until only one of them was crying. Edwin had been shot clean between the eyes; the right side of his face was destroyed. Maybe he'd been hit twice.

"Na," Joss returned his comrade to the battleground, gently, as he would a newborn foal. "He was baking bread to feed your own sweet lambs, Lord. That's all 'til today when he only killed to defend or out of a kindness..." The sound of battle grabbed the words away and flashes of cannon, musket and rifle made the scene look like one of the brown and cream viewfinder machines that Buck had seen when passing through Willow Creek just before that battle, maybe. Things turned slow.

Sarge slid toward Edwin. He only nodded at Joss. Then he shoved his face down into the ditch. "Get down, I don't need to lose two of you at once."

"Edwin's gone. I must do something for him. We promised each other."

"He'll still be here in the morning, lad. There's nothing can be done except say a prayer for his soul once you've got a minute and that minute ain't right now." Sarge was brutal and right in the same course. He tried to find his boots but couldn't, so accepted that he'd have to go barefoot.

"Get down you son of a bitch," He indicated what to do with his hand. Buck did not move except to scratch his head.

"Get down," he screamed.

Buck stood up to move to Joss. Sarge scrutinized him like he'd seen something not of this world, something eerie, something to be more than wary of, something so unreal as to be downright dangerous. He released poor Joss.

Buck crouched beside his friend. "Come with me now, Joss." Sarge heard him quite clearly, through the noise and hell going on around them.

"Come back now, before more of this starts in the dawn of the day." He extended his hand. Sarge was sure he felt more than one person with him and began to back away. "You should come with us, sir. Your mother is needing you." He looked Sarge directly in the eye, through all the smoke, noise and fading light.

Joss released Edwin's haversack, took Buck's hand and stood up, tall as any young man could. He left Edwin's tags where they were, knowing his family would be officially notified and his friend's body would receive a Christian burial, but he left him covered with his dog tent over his face, just to give him a bit of dignity. He weighted it down with two large rocks that he hoped someone would trip over – just so Edwin would get the last laugh. He locked eyes with Buck and a peace passed between them. Sarge didn't understand anything at all, but he knew, deep in his bones, he was meant to follow these two boys from the Great State of Kansas. It wasn't like any of them were really signed up yet – just the ninety-day stint – so a clean send away was very possible.

"We better get rid of these clothes," Joss said, stumbling over a root.

"Let's get down to the river first. Maybe there's washing hanging out," Sarge said. "It's how I got this uniform. Boots would be good."

"Ah, is that why it doesn't fit?" Buck had a feeling Sarge would come in useful on the way back to Validation.

Joss took up the rear, the shock of it all setting in.

Buck threw his arm around his shoulders and grasped his wrist, knowing it would help his walking. The trio were far enough away from Edwin's last resting place for him to start planning an escape from the battle. "Down to the river, then, see what we can find, down-river a bit and then cross to the other one. Should be able to stay away from things if we're careful," Joss said.

"Normally I'd say to travel at dark, but I think there's probably a great many jumpy boys in those trees over there," Buck was right; Sarge, if that was his name, was going to prove very useful. "I'll go down to see what can been seen. You lads stay here."

Buck smiled a bit: "We will stay here until that new steamship locks onto the landing. Then Joss and I will leave. You can follow or be here at that time. It is up to you: always your choice."

"I intend to be back long before that damn ship ties up."

"That is good, Sarge." Buck was Shadow for a time, now.

Cannons were starting again, one boom after another in the organized fashion of a professional artillery brigade and flashes that reminded Buck and Joss of the unexpected fireworks at Christmas last year. Then, the air stank of powder and fire, but this was so much heavier. Sarge loped down the narrow valley in front of them. The worse thing was the noise and smell were becoming normal to them. Their senses were being trained in the daily way of things.

Buck threw his hat down and sat beside it – the ground feeling damp and chilled by the night air.

Joss sat beside him, arms resting on the bent knees cradling his rifle, head bent in exhaustion, Edwin's haversack at his side. There was silence between them. Every time a cannon or gun was fired it seemed the noise was getting closer. Joss jumped with every sound as if he was a dog forced to endure yet another whipping. Buck was digging with his hands into the loose dead leaves provided by last year's autumn crops of spruce and maple. He found, after just a little while, a small toad. Lifting it gently, keeping it within its sleep time nest, he knocked Joss's elbow to force his attention on it. The lad's face was seen to be tear-stained in every flash of the goings on about them.

"He'll sleep a while better if a person can assure him he won't get stepped on or blown apart," Buck said, handing it to his young friend. "Why don't you put him in that packsack for the time being."

"Should I call him Edwin, then?'" Joss sounded surly.

"I don't think Edwin's kin would like that. If you must call him something, call him Lucky, I guess." Buck was feeling surly himself, now. "What did you promise Edwin you would do? Tell his folks what happened?"

"Yup."

"Where do we go before we go home, then?"

"Kansas City, Missouri, believe it or not."

* * *

"That's fine, then. Just fine. It means we can just skip over the border, Tennessee to Missouri then skip over another one into Kansas." Buck shook his head in wonder.

"You didn't have to come for me," Joss said.

"Oh, yeah, I did, I really did." Buck moved his body closer. "One, I'm going west and I'm damned if I'm going to leave a dirty trail behind me. There's enough of that going on. I'm in no way going to be another Silk or anything like him. When I go west, I'm going with a clean name and a clear conscience. Poppy, by the way, wants you there for the birth of her daughter. I don't know why. Must be a woman thinking thing."

Joss hadn't ever heard him speak so vehemently.

"When you go west, can I come, too?"

"You can if you prove yourself on the way home from here."

The conversation was cut off. Joss tucked Lucky into his top pocket.

Sarge had returned, carrying stuff that didn't belong to him.

"Got stuff that don't match at all, so we'll just have to make it work. No girl stuff though. Maybe a bit Indian because there's a funny red hat, probably match a red man."

"That's part of a uniform Sarge. You remember that Officer that looked a loopy and had a whole bunch of other loopys with him on horses? Nah, sorry Sarge. One day I want to own a horse and be able to tell him I would never embarrass him by wearing that one." Joss was shy about refusing things normally, but not this time.

Sarge had already found himself denims that fit him so as Buck was already kitted out in civvies, Joss had a good chance to rummage through what was there. The officer's slouch hat was fine as soon as Buck stripped the fancy gold roping from around the dome. It was just a bit big, but it made Joss look taller. Buck didn't say he looked younger in it, but he did. It suited his healthy red beard. He gasped to stare and recognize what he'd noticed but never actually taken it in. "You're growing a beard, Joss," he exclaimed. Already new dirt was clinging to old worn-in dirt on the face of a kid who was just growing out of an age where he could cry without being expected not to. "Not much choice – not a lot of time for a shave, lately," Joss said in the newly tenor voice that would help to converse with horses and later on, women.

A vest and a boy's jacket of the sort worn to Sunday lunch did honor to Joss's frame and then, as no trousers were available, Sarge had a clever idea and brought wonderful high leather boots. Joss shoved his too long army trousers down into the top of them, tufted them out to make them look like cavalry wear, and sighed with relief as he stood up. Sarge had purloined an old deerskin and a stoker's hat; from just outside a privy. The pair of boots he was now wearing were not army issue. They looked shop made and expensive, polished to a high tan color as they wore no Tennessee mud even on the soles.

"That long piece of wood down there, is called Pittsburg Landing for some reason. Nowhere near the place as far as I know – thought Pittsburgh was north. The big steamer is General Grant's, the *Tigress*. About time he showed up, eh? I think I saw him walking around down there, but I could be wrong." Sarge sounded distracted.

The hat was good on Sarge and he looked like quite the gent in it; maybe his mature red beard gave it added distinction. The buckskin jacket made him look like a frontiersman. He tipped his finger to the rim of the hat.

"You look like a little shit of a thief, kid." Sarge shouted as he pulled Joss down into a sitting position.

"Can't make a target for yourself, you little bastard. Not now. Not ever. Thought you'd have learned." Joss just nodded his acquiescence, staring into the fierce green eyes that had been developing a twitch over the last few hours.

Buck thought it had been a great long time since dawn and it was time to get moving again. His stomach rumbled. After everything he'd been taught by the natives, a stomach rumble or worse, flatulence, was not a subject broached in his lessons and, Buck felt, it should be. If your body let you down while you were, say, trying to hide, all the lessons in the world to teach him to hide in his shadow and not scratch his head when it was itchy, would be no good to him, no good at all if he farted.

"Let's move, then," Sarge moved with the flow of the river.

On the other side, men, as clear as shadows, showed in the skittery covered moon. The steamboats were over there picking up bunches of shiny new blue men and boys, rifles polished, belt buckles glinting in the moonlight. The trio lay above to watch the first of a force of what must be reinforcements crossing the Tennessee River from a small town they thought was called Savannah, for Pittsburg Landing just below them.

What a mess it was: men, veterans of the day, desperate to escape, tried to get on board. Then men, terrified of what was to come judging by the condition of their brothers, and the noise of cannon and screaming of the dying on the edges of the water, felt it urgent to leave the small steamer, heightened by the pressure of those following behind, some slipping into the cold Tennessee River, losing their footing, gliding dead to the Confederate troops upriver.

Cheers were heard all around – they seemed to rise and fall like a wave – whether blue or grey, depended on where you were when you heard them.

No one knew or cared who had won what piece of ground. All that was sure was that the land you were standing on was yours for the time you were standing on it. If you moved away, the best thing to be was getting higher up into the trees and away from the river. A live soldier could get crushed at the river side – his skedaddle sent him the wrong choice: his escape was limited, his destiny most likely in the hands of the Gods. He could get shot, blown apart, or make the effort to survive up top: choice. A live soldier always had choice – hell, he could even disobey orders if he had to, but he could live that way. Survival was everything.

Buck indicated to Sarge that he wanted to move again. He was humming to himself to avoid scratching his head. More men, he reasoned, meant more fighting and he wanted to go downriver, away from it. They crawled past bodies but not many, as they seemed to be further away from the battle below them. Noises could be heard, yes, but fires could be seen in the near distance and apart from each other. Some were small, others were obviously the signs of a burning house and worth avoiding. The small fires were off to the left a bit; it was starting to rain, and Buck stood up, feeling safe enough, judging by the lessening of his itch. Joss stood too.

"Are you two loco?" Sarge was sometimes sounding like a mama.

"You go first, Joss, just a little. We'll be right behind." Buck pushed him gently on his waist. "Don't carry your rifle in front, sling it over your shoulder so you only look like a bad squirrel hunter or some such. You too, Sarge." He had noticed a small fire in the near distance.

As they approached it, expecting it to be a camp stove, no one came to greet them. A group of trees with pretensions to grow into forest gave some cover. Sarge was unsure, so stayed back a bit, expecting trouble.

"Too good to be true," he stated. Joss was expecting food as a young man his age should, so was truly disappointed. It was going to be a cold, wet night he felt, but maybe there was time to put on some coffee. He muddled about in Edwin's packsack and found a tin of beans: brown beans, suitable for sharing if he could get it open. Buck squatted to find what was left of his coffee and Sarge, curiosity aroused, crept closer to see what was on offer. He handed in his canteen. "Fresh from the river," he said.

"I'll boil it first, if it's all the same, Sarge."

"You can be prissy at times, son. Real prissy." He took a swig of it. "Not dead?"

"Not yet, anyway," Buck murmured, not to anyone as he began to build a brace to hold his kettle-pot, but he did accept the canteen.

A click.

"Don't move."

Buck turned his head away from the voice – a young woman's.

"This your fire?"

"Was, just a minute ago." She stepped out from behind a birch tree.

"Not meaning any harm. Just hungry, ma'am."

"Makes four of us." She stepped out, holding rifle in front of her like she'd made it her best friend many moons ago.

"Got beans." Joss's voice suddenly became high pitched, like the young rooster he really was.

Sarge, made a move toward her. Buck flew up and tripped him with his walking stick. "Sorry, ma'am. He must have been bitten in his ass or something."

"Watch your language, Sir." She spoke clearly, like a schoolmarm; not that Buck had met many, but he had heard of them: maybe this one was as scary as he'd heard, maybe not, but either way he wanted a coffee more than he wanted anything else.

"My apologies, ma'am..."

"Miss, if you please." She had the soft accent of a northern girl, the tied up brown hair of a city woman and the clothes of someone with money who was new to being in country. Her leather boots were made for her and she was all of a match. Buck was glad to see she was wearing gloves. She probably had soft hands that needed protection. He also took to her dirty little face, sitting as it did angled on the stock of her rifle, eyes of hard blue staring him down, wisp of brown hair resting on the determined chin. He felt his masculinity stir below his waist and was glad nothing was noticeable in the dark. Coffee was now the second thing on his mind.

"Can I move to help my friend?"

Sarge had learned his lesson and remained face down where Buck had dropped him.

She waved the muzzle of her gun and nodded toward the injured party.

Buck helped him up and dusted him off. "Behave, she's a lady," he whispered in his ear.

"You boys off to enlist, then?" It was a fair question but not an easy one to answer.

"Be grateful if you'd lower your gun, Miss. I can make a good coffee for all of us if you want me to," Buck said as he risked walking around the fire to face her. Joss hadn't moved one little bit, but Buck felt anger rising in the lad. Sarge was comfortable near the fire and the rain was starting to splash instead of spit. Apparently, without thinking, Joss stood up, pulled an overcoat, perhaps the one from Edwin's packsack, over his head and sat down again all in one movement.

"Missed your chance, girlie. I bet you've never even shot a rabbit, let alone a man," he said.

She put her rifle down to keep the powder dry and then let out a shrill whistle. A small roan pony came to get her. She jammed her equipment into the saddle holster, grabbed a poncho and slouch hat from her bedroll, threw them on herself and generally got on with feeding her beast.

The men stoked the fire as best they could in the rising wind, so after using Edwin's and Joss's pack sacks as a frame for a windbreak, Buck opened the tin of beans and placed it firmly into the hot ashes. Then, he finished making the coffee.

"Want some, miss?"

She joined them.

* * *

"I'm Buck, this is Joss and I don't know the name of the man with the beard. We, all of us, just fell across each other."

"Didn't I hear you call him Sarge?"

"That's a byname Joss gave him, I think," Buck said as he stirred the tin of beans a bit.

"Nope, not me – just glad to see another friendly shirt in a fire fight is all."

"What is your real name, Sarge?"

"I'm Adam. Adam Dary."

The group huddled around the campfire looking at him, waiting for more information. "I'm from Illinois."

"Oh. Well that explains everything. You're from the same state as the President, then," said Buck.

"How does that explain that my real name is Adam Dary?"

"I don't really know, either," Joss said mulling it over as he poured some of the hot beans onto a tin plate he'd removed from his pack. "I'd like to keep calling you Sarge if it's all the same. You look more like a Sarge. Have no earthly idea where my real sergeants are – dead by now I guess. They kept leading from the front of things."

There was an inexplicable pause as the girl hauled biscuits from her pack. She handed one to each of the men and kept one back for herself.

"Where'd you get flour from?" Buck wasn't lustful, he was falling in love with a woman who could produce, as if from nowhere, biscuits in a rainstorm.

"Just have to know the right people," she shrugged as if it was obvious. "My name is Shony, by the way. I've come to nurse our soldiers."

"Stupid bitch, then, aren't you?" Joss growled, "What you gonna do, gag 'em while they're screaming?"

"Quiet, Joss."

"She doesn't know a damn thing, Buck and for that matter neither do you so keep your own trap shut," Joss lay down where he was sitting, hat over his face, overcoat along part of his legs. Buck let him be, mouthing a sorry to the young woman who had the grace to look shocked but the fortitude to stay still.

Food was shared and distributed, Buck poured the first small amount of coffee into Shony's apparently, porcelain mug, and then into everyone else's, finishing with himself. It was selfish, he knew. He got the best of it, but heck as like: it was his coffee and he didn't absolutely have to say he had it, let alone share it out.

Sarge finally broke the silence: "You're not fit for that, miss. Stay away. You'll get yourself ruined."

"Don't go miss. You're too pretty," Joss spoke from behind his hat, but finally sitting to accept the coffee Buck made for him.

"If I can get myself here all the way from Missouri, I'm sure I can take care of myself near a war."

Buck spoke: "They're still shooting Union people in Missouri. Big battle at Wilson's Creek, remember? I've come all the way from Kansas. I have seen what goes on near this river. Don't go." He was serious.

"From what I hear there are no medical facilities set up anywhere. I'm going," Shony pulled her wet hair back behind her ears. It didn't seem her hat and poncho were standing up to much.

"You got training, then?"

"My Papa is a doctor. After Ma died I helped him so yes, I got training."

"Buck got training, don't you, Buck?" Joss was impressed that Buck had spent some learning time with the doc.

"Does your papa know you're here?" It was a good thing the night was a dark one, but Buck was sure he saw her tears reflected in the firelight and said no more.

Thunder arrived to cheer up the night as did strong flashes of lighting, one after another like bedded-in cannon spouting out their ordinance, wrapped in flames, sputtering out with hisses as it connected with the soaking earth. A large rock was struck and split in two, enforcing a will to survive on the four young people. The roan, not being tethered, had bolted into the trees.

"C'mon then, nowhere else to go: follow the horse."

Another slam of thunder, this time only a second before the rip of lighting.

"We're right in the middle of it, now," Buck shouted.

"Joss, move it." He was standing at the split rock, calm as you please.

"You go. Lighting won't come back once it's been," he said. "I'll stay put, Buck. See you later."

"Dear God, the boy's in shock of some kind." Shony came behind Buck, grabbed his arm and led him in the woods, and started out into the middle of the clearing. "I'll get him."

"I'll go," said Buck, "he's my responsibility."

"No sir, I'll go. He's not expecting a girl. I may be able to jolt him out of it before you can even get him to stand still."

"Oh, for God's sake," Sarge blasted past their discussion, stomped through the mud, threw Joss over his shoulder, and continued with him until he caught up with the escaped horse. Buck and the girl followed quietly, both feeling overeducated for the situation. The thunder was receding, the lightning was fading, and the rain was heavier than ever, but Joss was safe – indignant, but safe.

"Shite, I wish I had a whiskey," the big man said. "I'm not going to say sorry for swearing, not now and not until I actually get a drink of something other than coffee that tastes like heaven and warms all of me to the soles of my feet." He slid down the slim trunk of a fir tree and into the prickly bits on the ground, but he didn't complain; he was grateful for the end of his day.

Shony shook water from her hat and poncho and gave Joss a blanket from her bedroll which Buck wrapped around the lad's shoulders.

"Won't keep you dry for long but it's better than nothing." Buck was concerned.

No one should see what this 15-year-old had seen, especially not the shooting dead of a friend who was probably about the same age. At least he was nearly eighteen when he saw the destruction of the Pecan Farm and the desecration of his Aunt Jenny's body. It hadn't been easy, but he'd known what to do and that helped him cope along with the help of dear friends. Joss was helpless within his grief – totally unguided and alone. He would have a talk with him much later but in the meantime the only things that could be done were physical. He got him to lie down on a patch of dry leaves again. This time he used no distraction technique: he didn't even mention Lucky, the sleepy little toad now peeping out of Joss's pocket.

He sat quietly and waited for him to sleep before he rose to thank Sarge and to continue his conversation with Shony. It was odd that he felt comfortable in his leadership role again. His head wasn't itching. Now it was time to begin a plan to get home.

"You are a healer, then." Shony remained hidden under her hat and in her poncho so her voice was muffled.

"I had just started my training before the townsfolk sent me to get Joss back. We think he's only fifteen and the owner of the livery yard, Ryan was mithering after him because he has a true gift with horses." Buck tried to meet her eyes: "The town also thinks Joss is his son, but no one really knows or cares."

She sensed his movement, looked up at him, saw the affectionate twinkle in his eyes and said: "Oh well, then. Kin's, kin, isn't it. How about his mother?"

"Lives above woodyard, or at least in back of it. Town thinks she's a waste of space and drunk 'cos she shakes all the time and her breath stinks, but I'm not so sure it's true. Never seen her falling about."

"Joss probably thinks Ryan would have hired someone else by now, which he may have to do if I don't get him back soon. Don't let on, please."

"He asleep. Best leave him that way."

"We've been up since before dawn."

"You better sleep too, then. Tell me, was it so bad that the three of you decided to desert at the same time?"

Buck laughed at her: "I don't think Sarge signed up and Joss is only signed until the 12th of April – the three-month thing – so we can't be accused of that at least. The only uniform I wear is one fit for living with the natives or doing business with strangers. No, I'm going back to finish my education and Joss is going to finish his apprenticeship before he goes to work with the horses on the fields of bluegrass in Kentucky after the war unless he goes west with me – at least that's what I hope he decides to do. Matter of fact I have to retrieve my city clothes from the ruined house I left them in before we can get to moving on so I'm going to slope off now, in the dark. Let Joss know I'll be back soon if he wakes up before I get back, will you?"

"What about Sarge?"

"I think he'll have to shave first and then go back to I don't know, maybe Cairo, Illinois after the war? It's a busy place now but someone will have to clean up afterward and I think Sarge, or Adam Dary if you prefer, may be just the man for the job." Buck leaned back on an elbow. The thunder was returning. "He scavenged the clothes they're wearing from the outside of a privy he told us."

"Lord Almighty."

"I'm sure the owner of the items said a great deal worse than that when he discovered their loss." Buck was grinning. He knew he shouldn't be, but there hadn't been much to smile about that day and he took his amusement where it lay – much like a native would.

"You are awfully sure of yourself, sir." He was trying to stir life into the fire.

"Yes, miss and so are you. Do you have an idea where you are going?" Shony crept a little closer.

"Down to the hospital ship on the river."

"You want to nurse the boys on board."

"Exactly." She brushed her hands down her denim skirts, recognizing she was covered in mud.

"Miss, from what I saw yesterday, you will be able to do a great deal more good if you roll your sleeves up before you get to the landing. The ground is slick with blood, bits of men and horses, crying and dying souls and not nearly enough care of them to go around. No, Shony, if you're going to help, give unseen, unnoticed help. Don't wait for it to be assigned by a doctor."

'Just stay out of my way.' She abruptly lay down, curling herself into a kitten shape, knees tucked into her chest, hands over her face.

Buck had intended to shock her, and it seemed to have worked. He stayed on guard. It was the first time he'd been alone to think since he'd looked into Joss's dead blank eyes all those hours ago. He hadn't had a chance to look over his stick. His armpit and hand were bruised and blistered, so he doctored himself as best as he could in the intermittent moon. He found the fancy rope he'd cut from the officer's hat Sarge stole, wrapped it around the stick's hand hold, splitting the end and making a knot of it around the back. He had felt it giving out while he was racing up the hill in the late afternoon so now it may hold until he could find more hickory. When ready, he told Shony he would be back very shortly and left for the ruined house, hoping the chimney he had stashed his gear in was still standing.

He sent his instincts well ahead and was pleased to see that the house was just above the jetty and a bit behind where his friends were encamped. The journey took very little time and Silks' coat that he had wrapped the rest of his clothes in was easy to find even in the dark. He put it on, shoving his city clothes into his small carry case, the socks and underwear into the cap of his bowler hat which looked so out of place he laughed at it until he remembered the gravity of Ian's giving. He returned to the campfire to find Joss still asleep, Shony stretched out and the Sarge snoring lightly.

A flash of lighting, but only a spit of noise: the same spit as a roast pork would give over a fire alerted him to company arriving.

Mark made his presence felt. Another flash. Raven arrived. Mark was standing over Joss, then Shony, then Adam.

He nodded his approval and made a sign that he and Shony would go together into the melee tomorrow.

Buck stood in the rain but shrugged it off. He spoke to Raven without saying anything aloud.

"How did you leave this life, friend?"

"I just slept away." Raven looked sad.

"You must have done everything the spirits required you to do."

"I still have something to finish, and then I can go back home I hope." He was fading into the mist forming on the ground. Daylight was beginning to show. It was odd, feeling the cold coming from the beginning of a day.

Shony sat up suddenly: "Who are you?"

"It's Buck. Sorry. This is my old coat. Didn't mean to scare you."

"When did it get so cold?"

Her teeth chattered: "Why are you standing in the rain?"

"Thought I heard something in the bushes."

"What bushes?" She looked around for them.

Buck sat down again.

"It's not raining so much as spitting, now." Buck looked over at Joss, just briefly, wondering how he would cope after yesterday's horrors. He wasn't all that sure he would be able to sleep again without a bad dream. Buck didn't believe Raven was dead. His statement that he'd slept his life away didn't ring true. Shony juddered as a person does if someone, as they say, walked over her grave, but she wasn't cold anymore.

"I've got a sparker in my kit, if you can find leaves and wood." She stood up to stretch. "We'll have to move toward that river to see if I can help."

Buck headed to the little forest, shaking his head and knowing she would have no choice but to turn away from the cause she had set herself. The professionals were there, in the back and on the ship. She would only be in the way. He admired her for her willingness to work and no doubt she would not falter at the first, but once the enormity of it landed in her head and heart she would take an honest grip of her shortcomings.

When he returned with as much dried wood as he could find, Joss was up and building a circle of stones for Shony's fire. It was a relief to see him functioning. Sarge had been performing his ablutions a few trees back. He returned to the group carrying wood as well. There's nothing like a young lady to pull out the best in a decent young group of men. If it didn't turn into a competition, things would be fine, said Buck to himself. He suddenly felt like the old man of the bunch. He couldn't be, of course. Sarge looked at least twenty-two.

Shony struck her flint as the sun began to rise but even so, it was still raining.

"It's gonna be real muddy on the river edge." Joss spoke quietly as he encouraged the fire. "Don't go down there, miss."

"Don't you worry about me, sweetie." She pulled her dark hair back so hard it lifted her forehead. "I'm a whole lot tougher than I look." She smiled at him. One tooth was chipped.

"No, you're not." Joss blew on the flames and then added a stick of wood. Sarge and Buck kept their own counsel. "You have a dream."

"We should all have ambitions, don't you think?"

"First of all, I'm not your sweetie." Joss' black eyes fixed her frozen in her place. "Sometimes your hopes and dreams don't come to be and then you gotta start again, but with the edge off."

"When did you get so grown up?" Buck spoke from behind him as he slowly sank into a sitting position. Joss turned to face him.

"Fort Henry. Saw a rocking chair float past me and heard cannon. Until then I just wanted to join up. I arrived at Cairo just fine, got spotted for not being old enough even to shave, so given the heave ho. Back to Mama, they said. War will be over long before my balls dropped they said." He paused to remember the shame, probably. "It would be a noble thing to do, just to follow on and find bits of uniform as I went. I could skulk in the rear, I thought, probably like Sarge did I guess, though I don't know why. There were thousands of us they told me, but Edwin and I passed the health checks. Then they found out I could shoot."

Shony handed Buck some fresh water and holy of holies, coffee grounds she'd hoarded. She nodded to him to make use of the fire.

"It was pretty well done in by the big naval guns, they told me. Lost track of Edwin of course. We weren't needed, anyway because the rebs surrendered, but the General wanted us to go to the other one on the other river; Fort Donelson, so we did. Twelve miles we heard. Dropped blankets and jackets on the way, weather so warm and fine. It's where I met Edwin again. We were so cold. Neither of us had a blanket or an overcoat. We huddled together both of us looking for the glory in our troubles. Lots of men froze to death by the second night."

"Was that thunder?" The ground shook.

"No, miss that's cannon fire. May be coming from the river, though." These were Sarge's first words of the day. He was standing to look south-east.

"I met Edwin at Donelson," said Sarge, "but before the first foray, and then lost track of him 'til I caught up with you in that bloody awful field. Named after the farmer that owned it I heard. Well poor farmer Duncan will have a job ploughing into straight lines this year. At first, I thought Edwin might have been sent to guard all the prisoners the rebs left behind, but then he was supposed to be a cook, so I wasn't sure. Now that was a sight – all those thousands of cocksure rebels. A few were led astray to Nashville I heard, but still, there were lots left behind."

"See? That's why you shouldn't go. Saw a man hit by a cannonball. There was nothing left. It blew him into bits. There's nothing you can do with bits, Miss," Joss told her.

"He's right Shony. It sounds like the battle has started again which is a good thing I think. Maybe those boys coming off the ships were reinforcements. Maybe the Union will win this time. The Lord knows we haven't been doing spectacular so far. The only thing is there will be more death, blood and bodies to saw."

"Oh, for heaven's sake I've seen an amputation in my time." She poured a bit of coffee into Joss's mug.

"Not while he was screaming for his mother, though."

"Our boys will be given ether, don't be so silly." Shony was pale though. Joss's words appeared to hit home.

"I've had one," said Buck.

"Where?"

"In Validation. The doc did it in the bank. He didn't take enough so the natives finished his job. No ether."

"I can see there's something wrong with your foot. What part did you lose?" Sarge was more than just curious.

"Want to see it?"

"Have a coffee first," Shony said. Her reaction to events was as a woman serving a morning snack. She poured the rest of it for everyone. "Where did you go from the Fort, then Joss? The papers were full of it of course. Blame it on this one, blame it on the other. Grant took his time. No, he didn't. Grant's a genius. What a nonsense."

She was beginning to irritate Joss and Sarge, for that matter. There was serious activity below.

"Edwin and I followed down to the field Buck found us in. That's where I saw the man get blown apart. It was at dawn. Edwin got killed near sunset. Don't go down there, miss. Please. I couldn't stand the thought of you looking at all the bodies lying in the mud and listening to the crying of the men and then screaming for water, their mothers, their wives or even Jesus or Allah. No doubt they had to give up their dreams too. If you go, there your own dreams will be ripped away from your very innards. Don't go."

"Look down there, Sarge, in the ravine. Is that cavalry?"

"Get down, Buck. Just look at that man. He's almost too big for his horse." Joss was horrified – for the horse's sake.

"What bird has a feather that big?" Shony noticed. The man looked to have a feather in his hat that was purpose built to attract attention.

"I think they're facing up to charge but lordy it's not even a good set daylight yet." Sarge stated the obvious. "I don't like the idea of being caught here looking like skulkers, especially by that man and you little miss would be taken as a camp follower; not a clever idea at all."

"I'll wait 'til the clearing is empty and then go in."

Joss groaned. "Nobody will think you less if you go down and think the better of it if you have the sense to stay away and wash bandages at home." He stared at her. "My pride very near got me killed. Lord in Heaven woman, swallow yours."

Buck was astounded by the age of the young boy. Joss would have trouble fitting in back in Validation. He'd be welcome until he was found to be out with Ryan's control. Then, compromises would have to be made.

Silence sat on the four until the troop rode away from them. Shony was the first to stand. She found her pony and wiped him a bit cleaner with Joss's help.

"He's a funny size and shaped pony. Tough, short little legs, though." Joss was in love – with the horse.

"Papa sent to Scotland for him for my last birthday. They breed them there because the land is so hilly and wet. Thoroughbreds like ours aren't tough enough, on these Tennessee hills, they say."

She fed him a bag of oats.

"Seems a rock-solid temperament."

"Stuart can be more stubborn than me, believe it or not."

"Is that what you call him, Stuart?"

"When I'm talking about him, yes, but not when I'm talking to him." Her eyes sparked of humor which relaxed Joss just enough to take a curry comb to the horse's mane.

"You're good with him."

"Joss is good with all animals, Shony. He hasn't even woken the toad in his pocket."

"What toad?" Shony jumped back. "I don't like slithery things." She stepped back further.

The men looked at each other, thinking of taking a chance on teasing her to screaming stage and they would have, probably, but serious things were happening below, and they didn't want to attract attention to themselves.

Joss walked behind a tree, bent down and let the toad go into the undergrowth. Dawn was just really arriving now or maybe it was hunger, but he stumbled on his way back, giving them all a startle.

Shony mounted her horse. "You can follow if you like. I thank you for your mannerliness, gentlemen and I wish you all the best in the future once this silly war is over." She set her hat on her head, adjusted herself in her saddle, flicked her small riding crop on Stuart's withers and walked him down the path that had been made by the Union Army.

"Will we go after her, then?" Buck was not amused.

"Better had." Sarge agreed reluctantly.

"I'll keep an eye on Stuart."

"Don't take anything with you that will clink like an army bit of tin and you'd better leave the pack sacks behind, Joss; don't want to be accused of anything if we come up against it."

"Can I put Edwin's letter to his mother in your medicine bag, then?"

"I wondered if the coffee was the only reason you took his haversack. Now I know you'll have the right address when we get there."

Buck was saddened, but at least Edwin wasn't sending Joss's letter to Ryan. "That's a good thing to do, Joss. Was he going to do the same for you?"

"Yup. We both wrote letters of no return I guess you'd call them." He returned to the tiny, now defunct campfire, to retrieve his errand and then vanished into the trees again, patting his top pocket on his return. "Not gonna leave my lucky toad behind, am I? Not for any girl, that's for sure."

The trio felt lighter as they followed Shony at a safe distance. Doing something right and active brought out the hero in them.

Chapter 31

"God that woman is stubborn." Buck shook his head, slapping his hat against his thigh. He watched the small horse as it appeared to waddle up and down the hill, but he was impressed by the good grip the beast had of Tennessee and wondered if its ancestors had just a tight grip of the hills of Scotland – the ones Jenny had so lovingly described.

"We better just go before someone takes a shot at us." Sarge looked disappointed. "Look at the lad. He's gone up the hill without us.'"

The scene below would only make sense as an afterthought: blood, too much blood. Historians would explain why but just now the causes didn't matter a good God damn. Blood appeared to congeal in an overly large puddle most likely created by cannon fire, just below what was left of a peach orchard, most of it smashed into sticks by yesterday's disagreement. One branch hung from another. Small blossoms clung to it as did a spray of a delicate red that could only be blood. A drop of thicker stuff fell into the pond as Buck watched. It had never been much of an orchard, just single trees trying to put down roots, but some hadn't completely given up, any more than the men in grey who were still trying to finish the job they'd started. Eagles and hawks circled and hovered. Buck could have sent his soul to be with them, but he knew he wouldn't like what he would see, and his mission was not to let his mind walk before he took Joss back to Validation.

"There's a great many orchards around here, I think." Joss said once they'd caught up to him. "That's a fair-sized pond, though."

Men dying of thirst had crawled there, died and were beginning to bloat in the mud. There were so many corpses at Grant's steamship now tied at Pittsburg landing, it would prove difficult to get back to the field of battle without offending some mother's son. Surely one or two would be retaining gases. One poor soul was lying beside his leg, an arm wrapped around it for comfort, maybe.

The place stank – blood smelled of iron filings, the smell of burning bone could be mistaken for nothing else, cannon flash smelled hot and continued that way even when the roar stopped. Gun smoke smelled of rotten eggs, wet, the stink gagged people and made them blind and sick.

Sarge had tears in his eyes as he scanned the miles in front and to the right of him. "Let's get out of here."

"I'm not sure where here is," said Buck.

A horse bore down on them from above the field and along the river.

"Which side are you on, boys?" The fiery cavalry officer, the one they'd spotted earlier, dark haired, bearded, and wild looking, still wearing the massive plume in his wide-brimmed hat, held his horse well, as it pranced and danced in place. Joss felt sorry for it.

"Looking to join up with the Union, sir," Joss knew the routine well. He saluted. As did Sarge.

"Good timing, boys. Go down to the tent near the privy. He'll take you on, will Lieutenant Lyle. Yep.

If he's calmed down from losing his britches last night, he'll do you the honor of taking you on."

"Thank you, Sir." Joss saluted again, as the soldier headed further down what was probably an enforced branch of the Savannah road. "Being I'm wearing Lieutenant Lyle's trousers, I better not be seen by him."

"Can you see Shony?" Sarge asked, ignoring the remark.

"She's standing past the puddle, off her pony."

The noise of war kicked in again. Buck felt himself angered by it, especially by the sound of cannon. It seemed to him to be the big bass drum of the thing – keeping the tempo, insisting on completion of the music. At least there were no little bands trying to build false hope and courage. He saw the men with bagpipes. They appeared to be more than a little crazy. They'd march through the lines looking like their lunacy would prevent them from being shot, and nine times out of ten, the caterwauling worked.

"Let's go then, further down, will only take a minute." Buck took the lead. "She looks like she's going to be sick." His crutch propelled him forward.

Underfoot felt like moving in suctioning swamps and bits of wood and trees came alive, snapping at ankles, knees and backs of a man's legs. Buck had the easy bit, he supposed, because he used his stick to test what he was coming toward, and the others followed him, native style. The ground shook as the temperature of battle rose in time to the heat of the sun blinking through the morning clouds. Men were maneuvering toward each other from every direction now. The men in blue had eyes despairing of comfort and sustenance, the men in grey had eyes and jaws keen to kill. Buck tried to run to

Shony, right in the middle of all this swarming mass, but Joss and Sarge leapt past him. Sarge didn't ask the lady's permission, he just flew at her waist to bring her to her knees as her pony flinched and charged down into an open field of sorts; at least where the only men were lying down. They loaded lying on their backs, rolled and fired flat on the stomachs. Buck saw a Reb bullet draw a stripe lengthways down the back of one soldier as he was lying there, just after he'd fired. The soldier looked like he'd fainted. At any rate, he didn't move again but Buck saw him breathing and sent a mental message to stay where he was for a bit. The lad was seeping blood from the wound.

Union cannon fired; from the boats on the river perhaps, but who was to know except those on either end of the gun; a weak cheer sang through the trees on top of the surrounding hills. Grey uniforms were leaving. Musketry, the likes of which had never been heard before was coming from a field somewhere downhill and to Buck's right. He finally sat down beside Sarge to watch the greys charge, then the blues chase them back repeatedly. The noise attacked every bone and muscle in his body. Sarge refused to let Shony look. He took full advantage of his red beard and flashing eyes, using them as a warning as he pulled her dark bonnet into his chest.

"Where's your little chick?" He shouted into Buck's ear.

Buck indicated into the field below where the pony had thought to take refuge. They were lying down together, Stuart the valiant little beast, lying on his side, Joss leaning over its belly and spine, gun primed and ready to use by the look of it. There was nothing for it but to get closer to him. Buck used a hand signal to inform Sarge of his plan and then began to slither and slide down until he'd accidentally built up a dyke of mud in front, forcing him to stand just briefly enough to be stung by a bee. Shony had bolted from Sarge, and was picking her way down from behind screaming, her hands over her mouth, apparently stuck where she was standing. Sarge flung himself at her to bring her down. Buck had been shot. It may have been the first time she'd seen the event in real time. There was little doubt now she should go home, surely.

"I'm getting good at this." Sarge expostulated as he snatched at her. Joss fired his rifle and was heard reloading.

"What's the fuss?" Buck brushed the top of his thigh as he collapsed into the mud, Sarge released the woman so he could get to him. Damn. Did he have to get hit in his bad leg – again?

"Keep your head down, girl." He snarled at her before he abandoned her.

"I'm bleeding." Buck only made a factual statement.

"That's a good sign, kid. It means you're alive. At least you haven't sprung a gusher. Let's look." Sarge was quite rough about it: he tore away the hole created in the buckskin and poked his muddy forefinger underneath. He had experience of this. Buck had a flash of him at an earlier time in his life. Yes, he learned the guts of war in another theatre. He would be a good companion later. Buck tried to look into Sarge's eyes. There was pain floating in them.

Joss let another round go. "Running out of ammunition, anyone got any?" He gazed toward Sarge. His black, dead eyes had returned. His toad peeked from his top pocket. Buck watched it taste the air with its tongue and swallow before it returned to safety. The war was having no effect on it at all. The activity surrounding the Mindwalker slowed to a clip of one scene at a time, one noise, one smell and even one thought.

Cannon fire shook the ground again, making the few trees sway about, especially those whose trunks had been so badly maimed by bullets they looked like Aunt Jenny's flour sieves. One especially stood out in Buck's mind because it was so destroyed it looked like the top branches were a hickory switch.

"Looks more like a deep cut than anything else. You got anything you can cover it with?" Sarge's voice brought Buck back into focus.

Buck's head was in more than one place. Joss looked at him, briefly.

"I said: have you got anything to cover it with? In that fancy carpet bag of yours?" Sarge shouted right into his face.

Buck looked blank.

Joss, just a few yards away, was counting and when the inevitable split-second pause happened he shouted to Sarge: 'Leave him. He's just taken his mind on a walk...' The guns started again. This time another cheer reached them and the sound of a drum calling a retreat. The sun was showing a mid-morning struggle to reach them. It might have been imagination, but the small group were beginning to hear cries for help and the shrieking of the injured. It meant, as far as Joss had experienced, that the sound of guns had lessened enough that the sounds of battle could be overheard. He hadn't needed to fire in quite a while, so risked lifting his head up. Nothing and no one was in sight, but he did see, in the field below, a group of horses without their riders. Joss, being Joss, couldn't stand still.

"I'm going down there." He pointed and began to jump from hillock to stone, over a corpse or two, his rifle over his shoulder and hanging on to his loose and nearly empty ammunition pouch only nominally attached to his belt. "Take care of your horse, Shony. He's fine."

Someone fired at him before he got where he wanted to go but he didn't stop to look or care. It could have been a soldier from either side. He looked like a civilian with a rifle who was running to the Rebel side or a civilian with a rifle who was chasing them away; he was fair game, he supposed.

When he reached it, the slimy field held enough dead body parts to have been blown up twice. There were six wounded horses, their heads drooping and eyes waiting for death. Joss removed a booted foot from a stirrup still attached to what was left of the saddle sitting aslant on the back of a dark bay gelding. The horse gave up on life immediately once relieved of his last burden, folding down on his own weight with a grateful release of breath. Joss stroked his ears in case there was any vestige of feeling, but began to move amongst the herd, one at a time when he watched the eyes cloud over. They managed to come closer to him, recognizing they would be safer, somehow. Their world was silent amidst the noise.

The cannons were still firing but not as insistently so no longer as loud. Shony arrived to see to her own mount and Buck guided Sarge away from Joss before he could put the beasts out of their misery, as he was sure he was thinking. Sarge pronounced Buck to be lucky: a through and through, he'd said, before he helped him back to his feet, throwing the lad's arm around his broad shoulders.

"What a waste of horseflesh. We could shoot it and eat it I suppose. I am more than a bit hungry." Sarge came close to drooling. "Could build a pit in that crater over there, carve a slice from a rump and bury it in coals."

Buck shook his head. "Don't let Joss hear you say that." He'd come back to the present.

"Get down." Sarge screamed at Joss, who ignored him, but Shony, just encouraging Stuart to stand, fell on her grimy knees as she hung onto the reins. The pony skittered away, dragging her with him further down the hill. Buck groaned in frustration. If he had both intact feet he knew he be after her to stop her slide. A bullet flew over his head. Sarge must have seen danger in the trees ahead because coming toward them were blue and grey uniforms, some with white cloths tied around their blue caps.

"That's what the Rebs did up the road near the Capital." Sarge appeared to be much better informed than he should be for an undecided. "It's the only way they can tell each other apart, because they don't have enough uniforms to go 'round."

"I am going to get Joss out of here." Buck stood up and marched to Joss as best he could, once again grateful for his stick because it stopped him sliding down. The bullets were still buzzing and one of the wounded horses caught another one which knocked off the tip of its ear. Joss had moved to the animal immediately to put pressure on it, attempting to stop the blood oozing from the delicate area and the beautiful, but filthy pinto stood for him. "Bring them with you. We're leaving for home."

"Good. We'll have to make sure they can walk."

Sarge slid into them, looking like a rabbit that had been flushed from its hole.

"Can't you see what's happening?"

"Can't you, Sarge? We can do nothing. We can't defend ourselves. We can leave. All of us can leave and that's what Joss and I are going to do. You can join us if you like or stay here to fight and die. Shony can do what she needs to do, once she wins her battle against her pony."

Joss had checked the feet of the remaining horses. "We can take four." He had tears in his eyes. "If you want your dinner, Sarge, shoot the one with the bloody mane. It's not his blood, but he doesn't want to live. Look at him shake and shiver."

"Sorry, kid. Didn't think you'd heard me talking about food." It was an odd thing, seeing a man with a red beard blush. It made Buck smile, though.

"Let us get up into that forested bit first before you do it."

Joss gathered his adopted herd together and walked them back up the hill, Buck taking up the rear, now remembering the sting he'd received only a few minutes before. He'd look at it once he got to a brighter place.

A shot was fired followed by two more which sounded less intent, less clear. Joss hoped that Sarge had made the first one.

The boys from Validation, Kansas didn't turn to check, back home and out of all this was what concerned them.

* * *

The sun was rising and the rain only an afterthought. The trio found an old Indian mound, where winter houses and such had been built before the natives were forced to move into the west by the Federal Government years and years ago, even before Buck was born. The small group decided to rest to observe the disorganization and disaster below. The air still stank of cannon smoke, fires were smoldering a bit in places, especially where the Rebs were now leaving it with a bit of dignity but the attitude of a cursed stray dog. Some shooting was continuing far to the right.

"That General seems to have his dander up." Sarge was chewing on a blade of grass. "Look at him go; all the way to Dixie if he's not careful." He was enjoying the sight of a few hundred men chasing down to what was probably the Corinth Road they'd heard gossip about. "Never seen him but maybe that's actually Sherman."

Joss stood with the horses, speaking to them, trying to calm them, wishing he had some oats, running his hands down their flanks to check for any wounds that he may have missed.

"Wonder where that silly do-gooder got to?" Buck asked. He would love a suck on his pipe but in the meantime poked at the hole Sarge made in his leggings to see what the sting was about.

"Last I saw, she was with her horse and heading for the river I think, but stuff was confusing so I'm not right sure. How's your leg?"

"Should be fine. I'll stitch it, wash it and plug it, maybe use some moss as a draw." He pulled his kit from the medicine bag. Sarge's eyes widened. "You're right. I'm lucky it was a through and through. Two holes for the price of one but at least I can get at both."

"You got learning to do that?"

"Not hard. You can watch if you want."

A fine porcupine needle with even finer leather thread were already attached to each other, so Buck did exactly what he said except that he began to hum in time with his heartbeat. Four stitches later, a chunk of moss removed from a tree after permission was asked, and a bandage applied just as Buck said, Sarge looked amazed.

Joss joined them, bringing firewood with him.

"Great idea little buddy, but how you going to spark it?"

"Buck will have something in that bag of his, won't you Buck?" He grinned at the two of them. Once again, Buck was reminded of Silk: the incongruity of a mouthful of teeth, gleaming at him from under two blank eyes. Joss would take time to recover, if ever, but he was only just fifteen, so perhaps he would be granted a long healthy life.

"Got a chance to mention about that coat you're wearing, Buck. Suits you fine. Silk's?"

"Don't know how your ma got it, but she said you might see me better if I wore it."

Joss dug a shallow pit before he surrounded it with stones.

"She's good, then."

"Good. Not great."

"But you didn't wear it until after you locked onto me."

"Nah. Had to scramble through the brush and things."

Buck brought out his flints.

"Why did you let the girl use hers?" Sarge was learning things about life he didn't know he needed to be educated about.

"It made her feel useful, Sarge and why should I bother to risk mine getting wet." Buck was always practical. "Have we got anything to eat?"

"Yup, we do: one squirrel each." Joss was pleased with his find. "They look fresh enough. Found them at the bottom of what used to be a tree until a cannonball got it. Must have been killed by the sound because they're all of a piece." He pulled them out of a saddlebag he'd scavenged from one of the horses.

Buck took them and in the Cheyenne language, blessed them to a better purpose. Now Sarge was shocked.

"You don't look like a native." He rattled his rifle as he began to turn it toward the young man.

Joss prevented him by using two fingers to push away the barrel.

"The Cheyenne at home saved Buck's life when he was frostbitten. Put that gun away you idiot. There's been enough of that today and you're picking a fight that's getting old." Joss growled at his friend. "And don't let your ire show, using the red hair as a reason – that's getting old too. You only fought at the end of the Indian Wars so stop letting on you did it all be yourself."

"How'd you know?"

"Army ranks don't keep secrets, not like Generals."

This time Buck was saddened: all these men trying to make a fire to cook squirrels, the boy he'd come to rescue had just rescued him, and still they managed to disagree about something. He shrugged it off as he began to skin and clean the little beasts.

Nothing was said for a while. Joss recovered a glorious thing – a small iron frypan – from the other saddlebag and even more wonderful, green coffee beans. The men stoked the fire a bit to roast the beans until they were black and oily, Buck used his small grinder to do one cup at a time. While the squirrels didn't fully satisfy, they did help a bit and the coffee made them feel of a one mind again. They were relaxing like kings, or perhaps even generals because it looked like the battle was over and the sun was starting to think about leaving the field to men with torches to find the wounded or the dead.

Joss's troop of horses weren't tethered but needed a drink all the same. Grass had done them fine for the day, such as it was, but now the night was coming they needed more care, so Joss began to lead them to a bit of running water that wasn't the broad river or tainted with the days' leavings.

"Even if we had a map, we wouldn't know what to call this bit of water, but it'll do for them if you'll give a hand. I think it's making its way from the northeast to feed the Tennessee. Not all that big, but full up maybe from last night's rains."

"When did you find it?" Buck was curious.

"I came across it while I was scouting. When I saw it the last time I couldn't tell the difference between sludge and slime."

Sarge was feeling grumpy. "I hope to hell it's clear enough to fill our canteens."

It was the first-time Buck heard him walking. No cannon fire interfered, nor did clogged up hearing. Sarge clunked. He had all sorts attached to his belt apart from the nearly empty powder box. He should have been more observant. A man's tackle, his trinkets and junk, said a great deal about him. Sarge saved souvenirs. In Buck's experience, it meant he hoarded and hid things, including his opinions and past. Was that a scalp dangling from his belt? The top half of an eagle feather would have been better suited to wear in his hat. A pair of tin cups were tied by shoelaces to the other side of his belt, just beneath where he carried his rifle. Somehow, remembering that Sarge was the lead scavenger made Buck wary.

"When did you take that scalp?" Buck walked beside him, step by step his stick between them.

"Found it." Sarge was boasting. "When I relieved Lieutenant Lyle of his possessions, remember? I guess the cludgie is the best place to be in a battle but it's a good way to lose what's important." Sarge walked with his head down, smiling at the ground.

Joss stopped. He indicated with his hand to get down and then braced his gun on his shoulder as he bent his knees. He released his horse, quietly, without fuss. He crept up behind Joss, Indian style and looked where Joss was pointing his rifle. After a slight pause, Buck threw his knife. The small pig dropped like he was a willing guest at his own dinner party.

"You're real good, aren't you?" Sarge was stating the obvious.

"Just tired of being hungry." Buck shuffled toward his kill.

"He'll be a bit of time Sarge. He'll thank the spirits and stuff. Give me a hand with the horses, will you?" It felt good not to shout. Joss replaced his rifle and started to walk down to the little stream. "Good thing there's no noise – the animals have had enough, just like me."

"Strange sort, your friend." Sarge moved his hand in the murky water, seeing if it was clean enough to refill his canteen. "Known him long?"

"Buck is what the town called a Mindwalker. He takes his mind somewhere and then comes back with the answer to a question that nobody thinks to ask. There's a girl at home, Mary. He was sweet on her for a bit but then his mind went for a walk. When he came back from it he wasn't hurt or bothered that she'd taken on with someone else. She never truly took to him, anyway. He told Poppy Diamond, our saloon owner, he was glad she was happy and shook his head, real sad like, but he never looked back once before he left for Indian country after the Christmas snows. Course, he is rich. He owns the farm Mary lives on with her husband."

Sarge found a clear bit just below the horses. He filled every canteen he could see.

"So, is his mind going for a walk right now?"

"No, I think he's listening to something." Joss swung his rifle in front of him, taking up a guard position.

"Is that footfalls?" Sarge whispered, bringing his rifle in front.

"Oh, yeah. Sounds like Mama Pig." Joss raised his rifle and cocked the trigger.

Buck took a step toward the sound of feet sludging in mud. He spoke to the noise coming toward them. Mama pig came out of hiding, sniffed her baby, snorted twice and returned to the forest.

"See? Neither of us wondered where Mama was but Buck just knew. He must have sent his mind ahead to scout. Matter of fact, probably how he found me out of all the thousands."

"Kid's spooky, then."

"He's good to have around, though."

Buck picked up their dinner in his arms and brought it to them. "We can eat well now and maybe even smoke a bit for later if it's safe to start a good fire. I had my instincts and a spyglass don't forget – I'm not all that spooky." He turned directly to Sarge. "I have God blessed hearing and eyesight too." He winked.

Sarge, slightly startled, said he'd be willing to go back a bit to see if the battle was well and truly over so Buck began to clean the pig, starting with chopping off its ears. Joss was a little shocked at the hacking because after all, he was the trained expert, but Buck was going to use every last bit of the animal. It would be an education to see what would happen to the ears, though. 'Start a decent fire, will you, while I get the wood to make a spit? There's a few small fires showing down below. See?'

Joss did as asked, hoping theirs wouldn't be the only one situated on the top of the mound.

Another rustle was heard, this time from behind him. Rifle in hand, Joss squatted this time, feeling the noise came from lower down in the brush. Buck laughed at him as he returned to the campsite.

"What's so funny?" Joss whispered.

"Remember that yellow dog that was running back and forth on the shore of the river and barking at the big paddle steamer? He's followed us. He's been ducking in and out of the trees and scrub land for the last couple of miles." Buck tossed one of the ears in the direction of the noise. The dog scrambled out of his cover and then back in just as fast. "I thought he'd like that. Relax, Josh." Buck sat down cross-legged. Without turning to look at him he asked how his leg was.

"Which one?" The young men looked at each other for the first time since Buck had found him on the edge of the farmer's field.

"Sorry Buck, but it wasn't me that invited you to the party."

"My new wound will be fine in a couple of days, my missing half leg, not so good. You are my deepest wound, Joss. You should be in Kentucky like I told you."

"That's not as easy as it should be right now. There's a war on."

"Don't shout, Joss. You don't need to. It's just you, me the dog and four horses." Buck leaned on his knees and reached for his knife. He hacked off some twigs and began to erect a strong spit. "Give the fire a poke, will you?"

"What do you mean you have a half leg?"

"I was lucky. Foot turned to gangrene, native medicine man, White Raven, took it off high enough up to make sure the blood would flow right."

"How'd you get here?" Joss couldn't take it in. He'd had his problems with blisters just like everyone, but his feeling was he should stop the complaining.

"Want to see it?"

"God, no. Seen enough for one day."

"Good looking fake. Red with silver trim." Buck lifted his pant leg which didn't turn out to be a good idea. It was the first he'd seen the blood seeping into the padding.

"Put it away, man."

"Yup. I'll deal with it after dinner."

"Wonder what happened to the girl?" Joss changed the subject.

"If she's got any sense she's on her way back to Missouri, but I doubt it: she's just as headstrong as you."

"So where are you going next, Buck?"

"We are going back to Validation, just as I promised. You can do what you like after that but in the meantime, you're going home with me, so I can fulfill another promise, this time to Poppy. I said we would be there for the coming of her babe."

Buck's eyes showed Joss his mind would be vacant for a time, so the lad began to fix their dinner. He'd seen so much carnage over the last few months, pig gut had no effect on his sensibilities. He could hear the dog snuffling about and wondered if he'd like another ear but decided to go down to the horses instead because he knew they would understand him best. Everything was normal now. The birds began a short trill, a lament for the day and a welcome to the evening. No sound of guns came from below although there was an occasional scream and the screeching noises of steel on steel which may have come from the ships in dock or even the re-location of cannon but Joss felt Buck was right. It would be better to go home now. The war would be over soon. It had been proved at Fort Donelson and now, after this yet unnamed battle, Joss knew the North was about to win so, comforting himself with the foregone conclusion he decided there was no more he could ask of himself. He could leave with honor, but he would have to return to the army just long enough to get the piece of paper that said he had fulfilled his term of service. Once he got back home, he could think about coming back to Kentucky as Buck said, and if he could nurse these four horses back to strength, maybe he could start his own bloodline, just like Bully Carlson had planned to do with Silk's newborn stallion, Thunder. Now, with the sun setting, they looked content enough.

A raindrop fell, but from one of the trees he was standing under. The river was high but not flowing quickly. One of the horses flicked what was left of his tail over its torn-up rump before the flies could bother the wound any more. Joss bent to find moss to place over the injury and spoke to him gently but not with words. Basically, he snorted and whistled along with his patient, trying to show empathy. Even an animal he'd never met before had more in common with him than Buck ever would. Buck knew stuff, but Joss was the one that would have to get Buck home in one piece. He leaned his head against the horse's neck and it nearly fell asleep now it had the comfort of the moss in place. The tail stopped moving and the animal shivered in relief, bending to find a tender bit of grass. Joss saw the jaw was still intact, if bloody from being jerked at by its rider now missing, probably one of the many bodies lying in the brush of the blackberry bushes. He could see down to the landing and the two steamships. There was movement everywhere. He stroked the mane of this horse, noticing it was nearly black under all the mud and scaring and then did a quick check of the other three before returning to Buck.

Sarge had returned. "There's thousands of dead down there." He poked at the fire with a short stick. "The burial details are out; for the horses anyway. I overheard that Lyle fella say there may be as many men gone as twenty-thousand." The tears in his eyes must have been caused by the smoke in his eyes.

Another raindrop fell, and another and another. "Aw, come on, please; not more of being wet." Sarge stood to stare up at the sky, clouds now rapidly filling in the spaces between the stars and obscuring them one by one in a chase to the finish.

"Are the Rebs leaving yet?" asked Joss.

"Most of them down the road they came from what I could make out."

"What a waste of time the last two days were, and I don't understand what we must have done right to win the day. I mean, we must have done something to scare them off." Joss pulled a jacket over his head. "I guess we've proved to Johnnie Reb that the Union can put up a proper good fight."

"How's the piggy doin'?" Sarge asked.

Buck stirred the embers. "I'm going to chop it up some. With all this wet we won't eat it until the end of next week and look at that dog, he knows a good thing when he smells it." Buck found a large flat enough stone, took out his Bowie knife, plopped the poor pig on the level and sliced off its head followed by the legs end then did a fine job of butchering the rest of the body which he then laid onto the frypan one bit at a time. He laid the ribs on the searing hot stones.

"Oh my, I have the hunger on me." Sarge spoke in a rumble to match that of his stomach. Joss moved closer to the fire, pulling his jacket a bit over his head while the sparks flew up to meet the splodges of rain crashing down through the oak trees. Buck faced the forest behind Joss's back and the flames of the fire gave an occasional idea of what was in the offing. The yellow dog let greed overcome distrust and sneaked up to Buck's left, nudging his elbow. Buck fell in love with the dog's brown eyes and greying muzzle. Yellow Dog fell in love with someone who might feed him without giving him a kick to remember him by.

"You've got a lot of buddies tonight."

Joss was shocked into attention; a proper soldier stance. Sarge stayed where he was, Yellow Dog scarpered for the bushes and Buck turned slowly, dropping his knife to the ground.

"MacLaren. Good to see you."

"Aye, well, there's a war on, don't you know?"

The two men grasped hands right up to the elbow and then grabbed each other's shoulders.

"He found you, Joss. Or did you find him?"

A horse fell in behind the big man who Joss thought had gained weight – must be married to Shona. If possible, his smile was broader too, and his voice loud enough to scare the stars from the Rebel flag now that it had made its official appearance.

Buck made a fuss of the edgy stallion. It wasn't Buchanan but was still a fine specimen.

"Joss has changed a mite." Buck stepped out of the light of the fire, so the young man could be better seen. "Red beard, don't you know?"

"Oh, sweet Jesus, kid." Benjamin MacLaren whispered. "Not even the O'Grady will recognize you."

Joss took a step forward. The big man reached for him. Joss finally broke down. He collapsed at the feet of the MacLaren who held him while Buck gently pointed out Sarge, who nodded at the big man before slinking nearer the fire.

Yellow Dog belly-crawled back into the fold and Buck finished cooking all the pork. Ben threw his pack over to him, Buck gratefully rooted around in it to find a canteen of fresh water and holy of holies a tin of beans followed by a small, a very small, flask of whiskey – in case of medical emergency, Shona had said.

All was silent. Joss was asleep and it was decided to leave him like that for a bit. The horses he rescued came closer to the people, Ben gave them a small bag of oats each, contentment spread despite the rain which was getting heavier, but the Spanish Moss acted like a tent to the worst of it. Buck thanked the Great Spirit for the pig and the pig for sacrificing its life.

"How'd you find us?"

"Silk's coat. Good thing Joss' mother gave it to you. When I got to the muster station near Brown's landing, Lieutenant Lyle responded to my description." MacLaren paused to pull a blanket closer around Joss' feet. "Known the man for years. You were difficult to ignore, Buck – long black coat to match his skinny height, slouch hat, maybe a bowler, long dark blond hair tied back by rawhide strip, walks with a limp. Union thought you were some kind of engineer, Confederates thought you were some kind of writer on their side, like Ambrose Bierce is on ours so both sides didn't take aim."

"Silk's finally done some good." He didn't ask if the good Lieutenant was missing anything.

"What's the plan, now, Buck?"

"Time to go back to Kansas. Joss has to keep a promise in Kansas City Missouri first before he goes home – military promise."

"What about you, sir? You got a home to go to?" Ben's eyes narrowed when he watched Sarge's movements and Buck knew this to be a sign of mistrust but so far, Sarge hadn't earned it – from any of them.

"I'd like to see Kansas for real, 'specially now the Rebs are beat."

"Is the war over Buck?" asked The MacLaren.

"No, not for a long shock but I don't see much point staying here in the way. I'm not likely to shoot anyone, no matter what color the uniform. Dead is dead and the dead gotta be buried and venerated as somebody's kin and that's all. No, Ben. I made a promise to Poppy and I intend to keep it. What about you though?"

"Shona said she'd be in Validation by the time I got back. We plan on going further west, but it's not settled for sure." Yellow Dog sneaked up to him so he ruffled the stray's ears. "Hope this damn dog doesn't snore. I'm turning in." The big man eased to his feet to bed down the horse and vanish into the trees for as long as he needed to do his ablutions. A scatter of feet a squeal of fright, a roar of surprise:

"Bloody hell, woman. Where did you come from, you stupid little bitch?" Ben came skirling from the trees holding on to the waist of his trousers with one hand and the reins of a small pony with the other.

She was back. Shony was not in good order. She carried what was obviously a purloined Hadfield rifle across her chest and then, tears running down her face, tripped over Joss's legs, waking him. He was on his feet, scrambling for his Sharps, the dog yelped, fleeing the scene and Sarge bellowed a shirr up. Dear Lord, Buck thought, more trouble and before all of them left, Joss still had to face Lieutenant Lyle to take his legal leave.

* * *

I haven't had time to jot things and it's been wet. Edwin died, but Buck probably said it already. I don't know exactly where he is now (Edwin, I mean). I've got his letter for his kinfolk. His sister, at least, I hope his sister, will be there, in Kansas City, when we get there. I'm glad the MacLaren is here. He just knows not to mither the details. He was in a war before, I think. Anyway, he's coming with me to see Lieutenant Lyle. If Buck came, or even Sarge, Ben thinks I could be talked into signing up again and I could, at that, but he says I've done my bit and more than most, by the sound of it, so I can leave the army with clear thoughts. He also said I probably won't be able to sleep for a bit once I start for home – the quiet will get to me, he thinks.

So, after a time spend drying off and staying out of the way, Ben rode down to the landing and I walked beside him because I wasn't willing to let any of my horses be taken back to the hell. I didn't take my rifle. It would come out of my pay, because I lost it, but that was fine by me. A rifle cost what a rifle cost. We would need a good weapon on our journey back home because Missouri was still, according to Ben, in a rough condition, bunch of Bushwhackers that they were. There were bandits about, he said – whole families of them, he said. Women, children, sons, uncles, aunts and daughters were out for Kansas Union blood. I took my packsack and all else though – I wasn't that rich. I left Edwin's stuff for Sarge to keep safe. Froggie stayed with Buck. I didn't want him showing his head while handing in my gear. Most soldiers are superstitious. Froggie wasn't regulation and if they kept me for an extra day or two, I didn't want my time to be spent doing paperwork or burying horses.

When we got to the landing it turned out that concerning soldiers leaving the army I didn't matter except for the fact that I was a Skirmisher – an asset to any regiment, but what happened to my rifle? This was asked of me twice before we found Lieutenant Lyle.

Please remember that I had never seen him before, but I was wearing his made to measure boots. He was, indeed a tall man. His boots came up above my knees where they were most likely thigh boots for him and were now covered in mud and shite from the horses. He didn't recognize them, the poor sod. I would have been in civvies, but Ben stripped a shirt from a guy that wouldn't be needing it any longer. I felt comfortable. The lice made themselves a warm home so when I saluted the Lieutenant I looked the part. I passed my warrant card to him and handed it over.

Lieutenant Lyle cared, damn him. I thought he would, with all the other things a serving officer would have to do the day after a battle, rubber stamp it, ask for my dog tags and tell me to piss off but Ben was right: he did try to get me to re-up.

"Army's been good to you, lad."

"Sir, yes Sir." He was shorter than me. I must have grown, just like they said. I looked at the tent wall, into the face of our commander in chief, Abraham Lincoln. He had tired eyes.

"Your rifle?"

"It's elsewhere, Sir." I noticed the bald circle forming in the middle of his hair. Was that why Ian Grant, at home always wore his hat in the shop?

"Elsewhere is exactly where now?"

"I had it with me just under the bluffs, near the landing, Sir."

"Your last pay will be docked $5.00. You know that."

I gulped at that, I admit, but recalling we would need it to get back home…

"Sir, yes Sir."

He asked me my unit number next. Now, please remember there was much noise and wailing going on outside and I became aware the heat of the tent was stifling. I'd stopped noticing the lice, but they were settling in for a long time, I felt. I could hear what I thought were graves being dug. I wanted to leave, so I shouted out my rank and number. Sir.

He was having the same trouble making himself heard, but he leaned forward to reach his desk just as a cannon ball rolled inside under the tent flaps. There was no fire. It just arrived as if looking for a new home or a new use. Both of us stepped away.

"Looks like one of ours, Sir."

"Damn. It's rolling the wrong way, then."

Indeed, it continued to roll out towards our ranks, and having witnessed a trooper try to stop one with his foot at Donelson, and pay for it by donating his ankle to the process, I saluted the Lieutenant, asked his permission and lifted the tent flap so it could exit. The ball kept rolling, now picking up steam, so horses and men stepped out of the way until it finally came to rest in a dip in the nearly destroyed cotton field, now named as Duncan's Field. I saw the newly painted sign. Duncan was a name that seemed to be out to get us, first in Validation and now, here.

The military historians had started their analysis of events – most likely to teach West Pointers what not to do or even what they must do instead. I'd just tell 'em not to be worried about learning to duck. If you're normal your body'll do it for you. If you're not, you're a danger to all your buddies.

Without thinking I asked out loud, I wonder what the hell field we're in right now.

"Sarah Jane's apparently." Lieutenant Lyle was equally bemused. "Come in and I'll finish your paperwork."

It turned out I still had another day to serve in my three months but the exhausted looking man, hiding the strain of his red smoke burnt eyes with frequent dabs of a dirty neckerchief, told me to report tomorrow morning, and then be on my way. In the meantime, this paper gave me my honorable discharge. He flicked his hand to shoo me out, no longer saluting.

"I will deduct your pay, though. You can count on it, son."

I was now re-defined as a civilian and it felt odd not being the member of as fine a group of men as I am sure would ever be gathered together again in one place.

Ben hadn't moved from the landing. He looked anxious, but not for me.

"This is bad, Joss." He dismounted. "Can you go?"

"Technically not until after roll-call in the morning, but yes. I've got my discharge."

He grabbed at me, bringing me close for the least embarrassing amount of time.

"So proud, Joss. Even more now that I know we'll be safer for your company on the way home. We sent Buck after you and now, you poor not so little bastard, you are going to save him on the way home, if you haven't already done it. It's a privilege to have your back, Mr. O'Grady."

I told him I'd salute but there may be a few sharp-eyed Confederates still about and they'd take him for an officer – he'd be fair game especially with that fancy hat of his. I smiled, just a bit, hoping he'd take me as he found me.

"By the way, the army dropped the O. I'm now Joss Grady."

"Well, yeah. I suppose you are now your own man, that is for sure." He mounted, and he encouraged the horse forward, making sure he didn't step on any freshly turned dirt in case there was someone lying under it.

I looked back at the spot I thought I left Edwin. He was gone. Someone must have cared, I like to think. Otherwise he would have been in the way.

Next Morning:

Fell in. Most men still wearing just bits of uniform, but not all. Bunch of guys that came across the river to rescue us not so bad. Private Collins made it as did, of all people, Thomas Van Der Horn – the one saved by his Bible. His 'taches were bedraggled, but his face was skinny now. I still heard him coming and my heart lifted because of it. Sargent Harrison showed up; grumpy old bugger. He'd had his ear clipped by a bullet. Eon Collins was staying. Thomas hadn't decided. Sargent Harrison was in for life, of course. We shook hands, waited to be dismissed and left on our own separate paths – something we were good at. The drummer boy played the right beat. I'll never know how kids that age could remember all eighteen of them. I was supposed to know them well enough to know what to do if I heard one, but reveille, taps, dinner and charge was all that ever really concerned me… I re-joined my new family-sized platoon up top.

Chapter 32

We've decided to go directly west from here and then down to the Tennessee, Missouri border. That means across hills and rivers but it's spring. The dog is keeping up. Buck has a real thing for it. If he thinks it's getting tired of walking, he'll put it across the front of his saddle to give him a rest and he's always checking his paws to make sure they're not bleeding. It makes all of us smile at his soft-heartedness.

The MacLaren says it shouldn't be too bad. I'm taking all the horses and as they get stronger we can use them. Shony and her pony, Stuart are joining in. She's likely to get home faster and safer with our company. You'd think Buck would like her well, because she wanted to help with the healing, but he doesn't show her favors. He keeps his own wounds to himself, as I do. Sarge plods on. I don't think he can scavenge as well as Edwin thought he could. Buck puts his mind into things. We always have enough meat in the pot, exactly when we need it. He is so quiet these days. His thoughts are well away from us.

I can't write all the time. We had to cross a river yesterday. The horses didn't like it much and one of them panicked itself into a broken leg. Ben shot it. I still have two mares and a stallion. Buck said I should go to Kentucky and I must admit the hills of the place, even at the end of winter made me want to cry with the blue beauty of them but, I heard stories there were wild horses out west. I like that idea best. Seems to me the minute you get caught up with the east and their factories that make guns and bullets you get caught up with rules. I don't do rules. I've had enough of rules to last me a while – look at Buck, all in his finery at times. He belongs in buckskin, not in cloth. He wants to go to the other coast. He says to meet Chinamen 'cos they use needles to fix people. They'll be ships there and that means rules and regulations with men behind desks folding money. I can't bite paper – never know it's real.

We're going down the Tennessee border now. Should be near Missouri in a couple more days. Haven't seen uniforms of any kind. Buck says we're being trailed by a couple of Shoshone. There will be more of them. If we don't look like we're going to stay, we will be fine. Buck always does his thing of circling the campsite with smoke before we unpack and start a fire. Maybe the natives feel safer with him doing that little thing. It's spooky feeling though, feeling so peaceful and calm after he does it. Beats the hell out of being so scared at Shiloh though. I don't think I'll ever be so scared again.

The MacLaren is silent. Sarge looks dirty on the inside and out. I know how he feels: unfinished business, maybe. Buck finally took a knife to his buckskins. They needed a scrape down of all the blood, mud and sweat of himself and the horses. Shony vanished near a less turbulent river and came back looking scrubbed. She's pale though. And tired. Weather's warmer now. Silk's coat lies across Buck's saddle horn along with his medicine bag.

ANOTHER DAY – Feels like a Sunday.

It could still be April though. We came across a bunch of people. The Natives left us to it but this bunch of white folk were pointing guns at us. They were lined up in front of a squat wooden house attached to a porch. If either collapsed, the rest would go with it. The ground in front was flat, stretched to what looked like an acre or two and appeared to be a farmstead. They asked The MacLaren what side he was on and he said Union.

"Not caring about that no account thing, we're caring about whether you are one of us or one of them."

The man had the bushiest mottled grey beard I'd ever seen, and it hung all the way down to his waist. Two younger men with shorter beards stood behind him and behind them was a shorn woman what was left of her hair straggling down her back but holding a shiny clean Hadfield close to her apron strap. So, that meant four guns pointed at us. Buck slid from his horse.

"We're just passing through," he said.

"That's just fine then, but you gotta pay the toll," said one of the young 'uns.

"What's the toll, then?" asked The MacLaren as he slowly drew his pistol from his coat. He rested it on his pommel. Sarge and I took our time to ride up beside him.

I may have signed away my papers, but I didn't admit to hanging on to my Sharps. (I told Lieutenant Lyle it had blown up and I had to leave it behind. I don't think he believed me, but he was too busy making lists of the dead and injured. Of course, he had to dock my pay for my obvious carelessness, implying I'd gone off half-cocked or worse, forgotten to fire after I loaded. I showed him Edwin's tags and said I'd be happy to go to tell his people in Kansas City as it was on my way

*home and he said it would be a civil thing to do,
stamped the pre-signed discharge papers and told me to
piss off).*

*So, there we were, staring at each other. The owners
of the abode and the refugees of the war.*

*A musket shot sliced through the hand of one of the
boys just as he went to cock his gun. He screamed, the
rest of us flattened, I looked for the shooter, found him
lurking in a pine tree and brought him down, double-
quick. There was crashing of branches and most likely,
the cracking of bones before the thud of the corpse
hitting the ground.*

*"You got him, kid. You got a real live McMurtry,"
whooped the old man. The kid with the bad hand was
being seen to by his ma.*

*"Now we know what side you're on, you're welcome
to stay a while."*

*"As I said, we're just passing through, but thanks for
the invite." Buck began to walk away from the scene.
The guns were lowered as he passed. Buck always
managed to lower bad feelings just by staying calm. We
followed him, one after another. Then the McMurtry
family attacked the family that had planned to get us.
They came out of the trees and along from one of the
hills that permeate the ground of Tennessee. I'm tired of
the lie of this land and long for the flats of Kansas where
I can see a man coming from further than I can shoot.
We got caught up in it only in as far as if one aimed at
us from either bunch, we fired back but in general we
ran for it. None of us got hurt and none of us knew
what the strife was about.*

*We talked about it after. Sarge thought this kind of
thing happened in the mountains all the time and it was*

usually about a piece of land or a stolen cow that wasn't really thieved but, had just wandered off to the neighbors and then the blame of theft stuck. Chances were, he said, that the cow belonged to a great grandpappy, but whose great grandpappy was anyone's guess...

ANOTHER DAY

Missouri is full of Johnny Reb. We ducked and dived along the roads that were getting busy with the odd pieces of humanity. Money could be made in anything during a war. No one was looking hard at their own actions, feeling the other man was doing worse. Buck and Shony made out they were engaged to make sure she didn't get bothered. Neither of them liked the subterfuge. The MacLaren developed a bad habit of getting a sweaty upper lip when in a tense situation. If he'd been playing poker at the time it would have been taken as a tell but he'd been booking us passage on a steamer and the man was charging double the amount just for taking the booking. If Buck hadn't stepped in with this thumb pinch thing he does (he said he would show me one day) I'm pretty sure a fist fight would have occurred. In the event we got on to the steamer to go down the river for a half day and at a reasonable price once Buck was through with him. This mind meld thing is spectacular as well.

Sarge was spotted as one who was fit to be serving in the Army but told a partial truth when he said he was on his way to Kansas City to sign up.

I'm glad the land is getting flatter. The spring hills of Tennessee, when they were full of birds and song, not shot and cannon, were something to behold, something to inhale deep and drink my fill of the pure running stream water. God must be proud of this creation alone. I wonder how he feels about the flat lands of Kansas, though. Is that why we've got the prettiest weeds? The sunflowers? I mean, the soil is dry and hard but did the good Lord try to make it up to us to give us the will to grow things, yellow things, because we could see that plants were growing in it. Is this why we grow corn and wheat? I just realized I'm proud of being a Jaywalker.

Buck came along side of me today. We haven't spoken much on this journey. There were a pair of eagles in the air. I stopped to stare.

"Walk with me," he said.

My horse, the pinto, wouldn't mind the rest so I got alongside him before I dismounted.

We stood to look up. One bird swooped around above us, getting closer and closer. I began to feel threatened, accidentally moving my rifle in front. I would never shoot this creature – the winged emblem of all that is good in my country.

"It's good to know you can still feel defensive, Joss."

Buck put his arm out. The eagle landed. "Lean toward me, Joss. I might lose my balance." I didn't feel fear as I might have, I just felt my place in the scheme of things.

I leaned into him on his weak side. It meant I could see the eye of the huge bird of prey staring right at me. I took a deep, slow breath and felt I shared a part of me with him. Buck lifted his arm and the eagle injected himself back into the pure sky, back to his mate.

"You are the only person I have shared my senses with. How are you?"

"Humble," I whispered, looking him in the eye. Buck was so much more than he knew. I'm certain of it.

It's not every day a man has a conversation with an eagle.

The others were off their mounts and I swear to you they were so still like a prayer, that they glowed in a gentle white light.

ANOTHER DAY

Kansas City is a horrible place. I thought Cairo was noisy and smelly, but at least it has an obvious purpose. We found Edwin's house. It was three stories high, big curved windows, large garden and bushes and The MacLaren knocked on the large black door using the brass lion's head handle. A maid came to answer. She closed it. Ben waited. A woman in a striped blue silk dress arrived. Shony caught her breath. "My, she's a rich one."

The MacLaren came to ask me to go to the servant's entrance round the back. I left to do that.

I didn't see the woman. I saw Edwin's father. I told him he'd died fighting at Shiloh, in the area called the Peach Orchard. It was a famous battle now. He had every right to be proud. I had, I admit, tears in my eyes. I gave him what little I had left of Edwin's things, out of a kit bag that Sarge scrounged for me somewhere. He dropped them all, even his private's badge, in the wastebasket.

"Better to know. I'll tell his mother." What a cold fish. I left.

I came around the corner to leave. The maid stopped me. "His mother wants to know if he suffered."

"He had no chance to call for her, it was over quick. Right between his eyes. He was brave. Tell her that. Tell her he was a great baker of bread. Tell her I miss him." I said what I thought she would like to hear. I hope she heard my sincerity.

Then I joined with everyone again.

"Ya done good, Joss," said Sarge.

Validation next stop.

IT'S MAY *(near the end of it, I think)*

We got here. There's nothing to see. The stables are gone and here I am with three horses and a pony. The skeleton of the saloon is still standing but it's been put to the fire. Ian's general store is empty, even of coffins in the back. The windows are shattered. The church and the graveyard are destroyed. Why is the woodyard still standing? I didn't know I'd asked this out loud.

"Because the Rebs knew we were Union but the woodyard was kept so they could cut wood. Don't ask me what for." Pete, skinny and grey looking, came from somewhere behind us making all but Buck jump. He was busy scratching his head.

"Poppy?" Buck asked

The MacLaren grabbed hold of Pete. "Shona? She was meant to be back by now." He couldn't see the bank. It was flattened.

"They blew up the safe because she wouldn't unlock it. We got her though. She's at the McNemeny farm with Poppy. I'm here on guard, in case they come back. Then Ryan takes over."

"It didn't happen long ago." Joss said. "I can still smell it."

"Dear Lord in heaven, Joss, is that you? Are you home to us?" Pete wasn't used to looking up at me any more than I was used to looking down at him.

"I'm back 'til I don't need to be."

"I've got coffee in the back of the laundry house. Come. We can decide after you've cleaned up and had some food."

We probably had more than he did, truth be told. He was glad to meet Shony, not so glad about Sarge. Pete always was mistrustful of other men. Shona didn't open the safe because there were too many Union dollars in it, including some of Joss's pay and the Rebs didn't manage to blow it probably because they didn't know how. She had been slapped around though. Ben was ready to enlist on the spot, but it was pointed out he'd better see her before he left. Poppy was fine with Mrs McMenemy, who really should know about everything, seeing as she had ten of her own babies now.

Buck asked for Mary and Tom. Pete snorted at that one and asked Buck how he thought she would be. "She'll sell to both sides, that one. She's done the decent thing and taken in her father, but I know for a fact he'd rather be in the town."

"Your Indian friends came to say they were heading inland, as they call it."

"The Raven?"

"Oh, there's a rumor he is dead. Don't know why. Saw him just last week."

Buck, for the first time since he'd gone to find Joss, laughed out loud.

"While the eagles dance in these skies, the White Raven will stand guard."

Well, I tell you. That's a bit deep for me.

We stayed outside to eat. The horses could at least find water and food so the mood, as the sun began to go down was relaxed. Pete dug his old Jew's harp out of his rear pocket and we began a version of Old Susanna that no one could remember all the words to, and Pete, being Pete, found a half bottle of decent whiskey. It was a little like old time except I took a swig of it and not a word was said about whether I was allowed.

A gun clicked.

You know, I'm getting tired of that lonely threatening sound. One day, I'm gonna turn and shoot and if I kill a buddy, well he shouldn't have snuck up on me like that.

"It's Joss, Ryan."

I stood to face him.

"Your ma's dead."

"Was she sober at the time?"

He lifted his hand. He swore at me from the dirt I punched him into. As I expected, it only took one jolt to the jaw. His head hit the dirt. Eventually, when he yielded I let him get up again. We were eyeball to eyeball.

"You're not the same," Ryan said.

"It's understandable," I said. "You are, and that's not forgivable. Glad your arm's better." Buck had told me on the journey here. I squeezed it, knowing it would make him wince.

"That's enough." Ben said.

We sat down, and I introduced Sarge and Shony as survivors of Shiloh.

"We intend a western trail from here," I said.

A spark from the fire felt quite normal. Buck whistled on the dog. We finally decided to call him Shiloh, the Bible name for peace. Tomorrow we would start rebuilding our small town, invite the stragglers home when there was somewhere safe to live and sleep, and next summer maybe, we could head for Independence Rock and the Oregon Trail. If the Great Spirit allows.

END